Mission Cerex

The Complete Pentalogy

David Colello

For my north star, Meghan, and the little constellation we've made together.

Other Works

<u>Mission Cerex Series</u>
Trillion Dollar Sky
Diamond Disaster
Occator Unleashed
Rebel Uprising
Blue Moon
<u>Skypunk Princess Series</u>
Episode 1 (Mermaid Alliance)
Episode 2 (Paris Underground)
For a complete list, go to www.davidcolello.com[1].

---

1. http://www.davidcolello.com

Part 1
Trillion Dollar Sky

Prologue

Near the source of the Orinoco, far up in the Brazilian jungle, the last Free People lived in harmony with nature, and when the Corporations came for them, humanity succeeded in gnawing off its connection to the world that birthed it.

Soft sunlight shone through the tent, making shadow leaves dance across the canvas, when Pia heard the pounding steps of her father skidding to a stop outside. The flap flew open, and she saw a look of fear that got her up and moving faster than any alarm.

Her little tent was pitched on the edge of a natural clearing, and in the low light she could see her mother running to get her.

"Pia, head to the river!

Her father hesitated, looking frantically between his family and the village where they had lived and worked for nearly a decade, since when Fleur was pregnant with Pia.

"Go now, I'll catch up! I have to warn them!"

And though it tore his soul in half, he turned and bolted into a narrow pathway through the jungle.

"Pierre! Dad!" Both Lamotte women reached out instinctively and grasped at air, then gathered themselves when a squadron of scout drones buzzed briefly and loudly overhead.

Pia held tight to her mother's side as they set off down the hillside trail that led to the Orinoco. Thorns grabbed at their clothes, like the trees were fighting to escape the soil and come with them. When they emerged suddenly at the treeline, their hearts sank once again as several men barked orders in the distance.

Fleur grabbed hold of both Pia's shoulders and stared hard into her emerald eyes. The little girl was trying her best not to burst into tears, the adrenaline and morning chill combining to make her begin shivering uncontrollably in her nightgown.

"Pia!" She hissed desperately, shaking her daughter's shoulders, then forced a deep breath as she tried to focus. She removed her olive green field jacket and draped it around Pia, then got down on her knees to look at her face to face.

"Princess," she began, "we need to reach the river or we'll be captured in minutes." She sighed, then bit her lower lip hard before continuing.

"I'll distract this group, but I need you to be ready to run. Do not wait for me. Do not hesitate. Float downstream if you can. Stay low until you're clear of the jungle. We have friends in Guayana City that will help us escape."

Then she kissed Pia's forehead, hugged her tightly, and was gone.

Her mother crossed a small clearing and snuck through a thick stand of araguaney trees, so when she emerged it was on the far side of the group. The men all turned away from Pia, and she saw large guns slung across many of their backs.

The men rushed Fleur at first, then appeared to hesitate when seeing a white woman in a tank top instead of a local villager. From a distance, Pia watched numbly as the scene unfolded in silhouette. Arms waving in one direction, then another. Angry yells. Her mother being thrown into the dirt. Her getting right back up and into their faces.

Something changed, and everyone calmed down, letting Fleur take a few strides away towards Pia. When her mother raised her arms in front of her, Pia already began to sob, recognizing the sign language they had learned while tracking animals.

"Pia, I love you...Pia."

Her little hands signed back in reflex, knowing her mother couldn't see her. *"I love you, Mom. Don't."*

"Run."

"I can't."

"Run." Fleur hugged herself tightly, just for a moment, then ran for the far treeline. Her shadow streaked into the forest a split second before the gunfire began, or at least that's how she remembered it.

Pia had burst out pumping her bare feet faster than she thought possible. She was down the path in seconds, not looking back once, and was moving so fast that at the riverbank she had to pancake herself back against the ground and grasp wildly at the totora reeds to slow herself. Her momentum came to a halt with no room to spare, saving herself from making a splash that might have been heard even with the gunfire.

As silently as possible given her adrenaline, she slipped into the water and paddled as fast as she could without causing a wake. Despite her mother's plea, Pia found a well hidden perch on some mangrove trees a half kilometer downstream and waited.

She heard the gunfire stop, then a number of explosions in the direction of the village made her finally get back down into the river. In a few minutes there was nothing but silence, and her tears were washed away by the river.

A few hours later and the jungle was replaced by open expanses of clay past every riverbank. She was finally able to get out of the water and walk, but only dared to move at night so that drones wouldn't spot her.

She walked and she ran, she crawled and she cried, across a thousand kilometers of ravaged landscapes, and when she reached Guayana City the battered field jacket fit her much better.

Chapter 1

Pia Lamotte strode into the boardroom leaving tiny puffs of dust in her wake, jetlagged from the eight hour flight to France, and desperate for a decent espresso. She'd been contracted by another Multinational, likely to fix whatever was holding up their latest billion dollar project to replicate and replace plant life.

The room was bright but cold, and three identically dressed business men waited at a plain glass table as she was ushered inside. All eyes scanned Pia, and she could feel them judging whether they had made the right choice. She was a curious mix of natural feminine grace and hardened exterior; slim khakis tucked into field boots, weathered green jacket covering a tight knit sweater, and though her face looked carved out of granite, her feet seemed to barely touch the ground. A black velvet choker completed the outfit, with her hair held up in a messy blond bun using a pen she stole from the plane.

"Mademoiselle Lamotte, thank you so very much for coming to speak with us. We understand this is unorthodox, but discretion demands it."

"Well you've got my attention," smirked Pia with cracked lips, her French accent worn down to a barely noticeable word or two per sentence. She had soft features despite the rough treatment they endured, but her usually disarming smile met a stony wall this time.

"Yes, and while we have it, we also need you to sign this NDA before we proceed," said the man on the right, opening his leather briefcase with a crisp snap before sliding a paper across the table.

"And if I don't?" asked Pia amusedly.

While the others were clearly frustrated at her unprofessionalism, the center suit merely shrugged. "Then we apologize sincerely for wasting your time, and of course will reimburse you for the inconvenience. Our jet will return you to Utah immediately." He was young for an executive type, barely older than Pia, with shrewd eyes that were always calculating his surroundings.

Pia reached up and slid the pen from her bun, signing the NDA with a playful flourish as her hair tumbled down past her shoulders.

"Just having a bit of fun with you, gentlemen. Now that my lips are legally sealed tight, what's the big secret?"

"Pia, if I may call you that," began the lead suit.

"You may," she quipped, enjoying the rare taste of civility.

"My name is Jared Miller, President of the Natocorps Commodities & Acquisitions Division. We're rather excited to have you come in. You have a unique area of expertise, but one that happens to coincide with our present goal." He sounded vaguely German, but grinded down into a sharp edge of controlled power.

Pia despised the rise of the Multinats and doubted she would ever have a goal that coincided with these amoral gluttons. Most likely they wanted a new formula for their food structure base. All food had long since been replaced by 3-D printed substitutes, and it was a struggle to maintain a healthy enough mixture when so few natural ingredients were left to use as a base for the printing process.

"Are you at all familiar with Ceres?" he asked, snapping her out of her thoughts while he and his associates quietly watched her reaction for signs that she may be hiding information.

"Ceres...as in the God of something or other?" she guessed.

"Agriculture and grain I believe, but no, not the Goddess. The dwarf planet."

Pia was genuinely nonplussed at this point. What began as mild curiosity and a free trip home to Paris was becoming increasingly bizarre by the minute. "Mr. Miller, what exactly do you think I can help you with?"

"Ceres resides in the Asteroid Belt. Reconnaissance missions have found evidence of significant water ice deposits in the soil, but more importantly, abundant precious metals and rare earth elements."

"So...you're going to mine this little rock and bring back all its treasures?" Pia offered, still merely playing along with the odd conversation.

"That 'little rock' is over nine hundred kilometers wide, and is as ancient as the solar system. It wasn't big enough for tectonics to churn away at the crust and sink most heavy elements down to the core, as has happened here on Earth. Simply put, there could be trillions of dollars of resources just waiting to be scooped right up off the surface."

"Fantastic, go rip apart another planet. I really don't see why I'm here, Mr. Miller."

"We're going there next month," he said determinedly. "And we need you to come with us." He paused for a response from Pia but, getting nothing except a blank stare, continued with his pitch.

"As one of the few biologists left in the world with prolonged field experience, and by far the best I might add, we need you to oversee plant life for our mission."

Her eyebrows rose for a moment, then furrowed down in confrontation. "No. No chance in hell," she blurted out, not believing for a second that refusing them would be so simple.

"But what will you do instead? Going back to your pristine wastelands might prove more difficult than you imagine." Miller's tone now matched his eyes, with razor sharp edges tracing every word that left his mouth.

Pia felt the panic rising through her chest, like an animal who senses it's trapped before feeling the metal teeth. Somehow she managed to ask, "And why is that?"

"We finalized the purchase of much of eastern Utah last week, and your permits now go across my desk for approval."

She stood up so quickly her chair scraped backwards a few feet. "This is blackmail!"

"Technically it's coercion, perhaps not strictly legal and above board, but...we're kind of splitting hairs at this point, aren't we? Actually, we were hoping it becomes something closer to bribery. Sign on for the mission, and upon successful establishment of our base on Ceres, you will be on the first rocket back to Earth, free to play in the dirt for as long as you wish with our blessing. If all goes as planned, no more than two years from start to finish."

The color drained out of Pia's cheeks. This was more human interaction than she had experienced in months, and now every sentence was a roller coaster of emotions. '*Pando forest*', she thought. "*I could save it from extinction. But two years, and most likely more, not to mention the high probability that she would get killed? Then again, if they really did buy Utah, then refusing didn't really seem like an option.*'

Sensing the kill was within reach, Miller added, "Our survey team is already hard at work identifying where to begin strip mining our new purchase. Nothing great there, some silver maybe, plenty of interesting salts, but enough to recoup our expenses if we dig deep enough I'm sure..."

Pia ran her rough hands back and forth over her crossed forearms, wishing this was all just a nightmare. "You're a real bastard, you know that?"

At this Miller broke out into a genuine sounding laugh. "Oh, now don't be like that Pia. Think of it as a grand adventure, an opportunity to help both of us tremendously. I just know we'll get along once we spend a bit of time together. After all, it will be a long couple of years if we can't play nice."

"You're going too?" This she most definitely did not expect. Even next to his fellow corporate cronies, Miller's manicured beard and slicked back hair displayed a pampered lifestyle that didn't seem a match for a difficult and dangerous assignment such as this.

"Of course," he stated simply. "This is the beginning of a whole new era for humanity, and I will be Commander of the mission that makes it all happen."

'Ego, there's the reason', she thought. "Can I think about it?" she stalled, as her mind desperately tried to keep up with her emotions.

"Alright, we're reasonable people. Someone will escort you to your room where dinner will be made available. When I call at eight o'clock, I expect your answer. Agreed?"

"Agreed," she stammered, glad to be able to flee that room as quickly as possible so she could attempt to gather her wits.

Rocked by the meeting, she shuffled her boots through a maze of corridors, just managing to keep up with the brisk pace of her guide. Upon reaching her room a key card was politely offered, and she was finally left alone. For a few minutes she stood quietly in the empty hall, pacing back and forth.

Suddenly a door opening nearby startled her out of her thoughts. A thinly built man with black jeans and ancient looking flat sneakers with stars on them appeared, eating a designer apple in the shape of a doughnut. He blew a tangle of dark brown hair out of his face and stared at a schematic projection emitted from his necklace, a state of the art holocomp allowing him to manipulate the projection with his hands. After turning towards Pia, he tapped the necklace to turn off the display.

"Whoa, hey," he said. "No chip?" Then as he recovered his composure, he walked up and shook her hand. "Xander McKinnon, but everyone calls me Zee."

"Pia Lamotte, just Pia is fine."

"You here for *you know what?*" He winked playfully and gave her a knowing glance.

"Maybe, I don't know. Besides, I can't talk about it, it's complicated." Pia crammed her hands into her khakis and shrank her shoulders inwards.

"Complicated like this?" Zee countered, pointing to a patch on his t-shirt emblazoned with *CEREX*. "There's only a couple dozen people staying in this whole damn building, and they're all part of the Ceres Express."

"They've asked me to join," Pia finally admitted, "and I have until after dinner to decide."

"Well you have to, I imagine."

"Have to what?"

"Join. Natocorps doesn't ask nicely. If they need you, they're gonna do whatever it takes to get you."

"I'm beginning to realize that." She slumped her back against the door and slid down to the floor. Then after a few moments, she turned her face back up towards Zee. "I could use someone to help me work through all this. Done eating already?"

"Yeah, but I'll keep you company."

She fumbled her keycard through the door lock a few times, refusing help from Zee. When she pushed the heavy wooden door open, what met her eyes was as shocking as it was familiar. It was as if she was stepping into her house out in the Utah forest, down to the smallest detail. The simple furnishings, many hand carved from the very trees she was studying, all in their usual layout.

"Nice room, rather rustic, but a welcome change from the plastic wasteland in most of this place," Zee noted.

"It's...how did they...?" Pia started then stopped as she absorbed the view. She walked over to the table, *her* dining room table, and ran her hand along the edges.

"Holographic copy," Zee explained patiently, "simple enough process, they just copied your place after picking you up. Then they uploaded the design into the building's computer and printed out the pieces here. I guess it's supposed to be comforting, but I always found it a bit sketchy."

"It's creepy as hell, that's what it is," she decided. Everything was wrong, not by much, but by the only parts that mattered. Each object had been replicated nearly to perfection, but still; the rug had no smell of clay walked into it, the table was too smooth to be from any real tree, and the floor was stubbornly free of the creaking that sang to her when the winds picked up strength.

The pair of unlikely companions sat down on faux furniture and waited in awkward silence for a moment. Zee looked around curiously, breaking into a grin now and again. "So who are you, Jane of the Jungle or something?"

"Sorry, I don't entertain much," she laughed gently, grateful for the break from her thoughts.

"I don't mean to pick on you. Just surprised, you one of those tree worshippers?"

"I study them, how some are managing to survive the massacre of what our environment has become."

"I've never seen one in person before, are they big?"

"Seen what before?"

"A tree."

Pia had to check herself before responding. She knew that most people lived in completely urban isolation, but that it might be possible to go one's whole life without seeing a tree drove home the true scale of the devastation she was fighting against.

"For the last three years, my main focus has been Pando forest in Utah. It's far away from human settlement, and utterly unique. Pando is a forest, but also a single colossal organism. There are forty thousand exact genetic clones, and the whole forest is hundreds of thousands of years old."

"How can it grow so old?" Zee asked.

"Individually, none of the trees could. It's their interconnectedness that sustains them. Every square mile contains massive amounts of fungus underground. Entire ecosystems are existing just out of sight, where different species share nutrients to help sustain the forest as a whole."

"Sounds alien," Zee grinned. His arms gestured awkwardly whenever he spoke, but his eyes were calm and kind.

"I don't know why I'm still here," Pia shook her head despondently. "Natocorps is going to get what they want and destroy my work whether I help them or not."

He got up and shrugged himself into a walk around her room. "Well listen, for what it's worth, they don't seem immoral so much as amoral. They act in their self interest, no matter what. Pretty common trait, I find."

"Being common doesn't make something right." Her body tensed as she felt growing disgust with her situation, but Zee went on as if he hadn't heard her.

"You have something they need, and it sounds like they have something you need, too. Talk business to them, it's the only language they understand."

"Is that what you did?" she asked, while ordering up some tomato soup and a grilled cheese sandwich at the wall console.

"Well, I worked for Natocorps already, New York office, but hell yes. Everyone who's being asked to go on this mission is the best at what they do. If they want us, they better pay. Sign up to go, and you'll have the best equipment, the best technology, the best everything. They have 3-D printers I never even knew existed yet, and I'll have a factory full of them when we get back."

Pia said nothing as the soup ingredients were squirted out in sequence, and the sandwich was built layer by layer, then heated until a crispy outer crust signaled it was finished.

Zee took offense at her silence. "You think I'm a dirtbag for working with a Multinat?" His gaunt face tightened, then quickly washed away any sign of stress.

Pia watched him closely, then resumed taking her meal to her phony work desk.

"Not everyone has the luxury of being able to complete their research in the middle of nowhere," Zee continued. "The rest of us suckers need equipment, and every last piece is owned, operated and laser tagged by one of the, what's left now, seven Multinats?"

Pia wiped her lips with the imitation rag she always kept hanging off her cot. She relaxed back into her chair, feeling more comfortable in the familiar surroundings despite her initial repulsion. She swept her arms widely around herself and smiled, a pleasant easy smile that took the sting out of Zee's words.

"So you like my luxurious lifestyle, huh?" Pia teased. At that, both of them laughed. "The truth? I'm more than a little terrified of being shot halfway across the damn Solar System."

"You and me both," Zee admitted. "Try not to think about it, and finish your soup. I'll leave you to think it over, I've got to go work."

Pia put her spoon down and rose to shake Zee's hand. "Good luck, and thanks for the advice."

"I hope I see you again, Pia." With that he tapped his necklace and was off to walk the halls while numerous screens flashed before his eyes. He seemed genuine, oblivious, and eager to help. *'Americans'*, she thought dismissively, but then found herself staring at him as he receded down the corridor. *'Cute though.'*

The room was dim, made to look like candles were burning instead of the LED panels which were lining most of the walls.

Everything she saw gave the impression of meticulous planning, and she wondered if her brief conversation with Zee was no accident either. She sat near the comm console on her table, the sole addition the room had made to her usual decor, and tapped the center.

Nothing happened. She let out a sigh, then heard a voice behind her, "Over here, Lamotte."

A hologram of Jared Miller in an attempt at a casual stance made her turn abruptly in her chair.

"Well, what shall it be? Can we count on you?"

"I imagine you're aware of the sheer magnitude of the challenge facing you, the preparations that will have to be made. This will take longer than the month time frame you discussed earlier."

"Yes, fortunately we began such work nearly six years ago, Pia. Our spacecraft, including life support systems and organics lab, was carefully designed by the best minds available."

"There are only three or four other scientists in the world that would be up to that task, and I know all of them. They were willing to help you get set up, and yet here I am getting the hard sell. My guess is that you threatened their careers, but they all have families and wouldn't agree to get shot into space, so they bargained with you and did the extensive groundwork. Am I close so far?" Pia's face hardened into a ceramic mask, with green eyes boring into her holographic guest.

"Yes, more or less. But no such bargaining for you, eh? No family, no significant other, nothing preventing you from coming with us." Her fingernails dug into the soft plastic chair at the mention of family, but she kept her voice from trembling when she responded.

"I suppose...or, I'm the best, the only person who can modulate a dozen different strains of plant for maximum growth, O2 output, and adaptability, both in microG and low G on Ceres."

"So you'll do it?"

"I have conditions," she growled, hating that he wasn't really present in the room and feeling at a disadvantage somehow.

"I'd have been vastly disappointed in you if you didn't."

"The land in Utah, Pando forest? You can forget your permits. I want it, the full extent of the forest plus a kilometer from the edge in all directions, deeded over to me."

Miller paused a brief moment, then shrugged. "Done. I must say, you were much more direct th—"

"I'm not finished," Pia continued defiantly. "You must have a seed bank, a master repository of some kind that you use when you build your nutrient supplements. I want a complete collection, a few seeds from every plant, bush, and tree left on Earth. That must not be as tall an order as it once was, I imagine. The seeds will be accessible to me and only me at a replica of whatever storage facility that you currently use. And I want all this done and in writing before we leave."

"Well I'll be damned!" Miller smiled rakishly and rubbed his hand on one cheek as he sized up his options. "I'm not gonna lie, you caught me by surprise, but I like that." A few more seconds of silence was broken by Miller.

"The forest you can have, but the seed bank will take time. We can have a contract drawn up stating these terms immediately, but only if you come this week up to the spaceship so that you can make any final changes before launch."

"Up to the spaceship? Am I missing something?"

"Yes, you are, along with the rest of the world. Enough for tonight though. Sleep. The next few weeks will be extremely busy."

"Goodnight then, Commander." The title sounded silly, but no more so than the countless others men have dreamt up. At first Pia did not think sleep would be an option, but her racing thoughts fell away quickly once her jet lag combined with her fake field bed.

Chapter 2

The following morning she was startled awake by room lights and two women marching towards her in snug Natocorps uniforms. One held a small metal briefcase which she placed on the bedside table, while the other carried a neat stack of gray clothes. Pia instinctively clutched the sheets up around herself, but relaxed and sat up after coming to her senses.

The assistants looked like twin librarians, each wearing their hair up in a tight high ponytail with no jewelry, or personality, on display. One had red hair and the other brown, or else Pia couldn't tell them apart.

The brunette spoke first, in a voice both calming and determined. "We're here to assist you in your preparations for launch. There is a great deal to do, so if you would, please get dressed and ready for the morning briefing."

Pia swung her strong bare legs off the bed and stood up, stretching her tall frame all the way to the fingertips. She was confident in her movements, a trait developed from years of living on her own, along with scratches and bruises covering her body.

She picked up the gray heap of baggy clothes and blew out hard through pursed lips in disapproval. The pants got tossed to the floor as Pia opted instead to rummage through her pack for a pair of vintage jeans. As she wiggled her way into them, the twins traded looks of concern.

"We were instructed to give you your uniform, miss," they said, and Pia could tell they wouldn't give this one up without a fight.

"Fine, here, calm down girls." Pia stripped off her worn tank top and stretched into a long sleeve shirt with the company logo across the chest. Then as soon as the twins relaxed a bit, she picked up her dusty green jacket and threw it on.

The redhead softly asked, "Are you really unplugged?"

"Is it that rare?" She was dreading the net implant, but knew it would be required for the job.

"Everyone I know got theirs when they entered kindergarten," the brunette smirked.

"Well I was homeschooled, my parents travelled a lot for work." *'Why am I talking about my parents just to defend myself against these two drones?'*

"Even more reason, I can't imagine being out in the woods with no net."

"Can you just get on with it?" Pia asked.

Both assistants must have sensed they had touched a nerve and regained their professional tone. "The implantation itself is fairly simple, but the transition will be rough, especially for an adult." Pia could hear pity in their explanations now, like they were teaching a beggar how to eat at a dinner party.

The twins continued, "The chip learns your individual brain patterns and will improve dramatically over time. For the first few days it may require you actually saying your instructions so it can use jaw vibration translation, but that will pass quickly. Next you will simply concentrate on thinking your commands, and eventually it will understand your requests without you even having to ask."

"That sounds awfully energy draining. Do they still need to be charged, or have batteries swapped or something?"

"No, not since five years ago," the redhead piped in. "The chip attaches itself to your temporal artery and sifts oxygen molecules from your blood through nanotears it makes in the artery wall. With that and your body heat, it can survive indefinitely."

"It's a symbiote," Pia suggested. "Or a parasite actually."

"It's a work of art is what it is, shame to be given to a novice, no offense...ma'am." The pair were clearly stepping out of line, but Pia let their words flow right past her, unwilling to engage. She suddenly kept having to fight back thoughts of her parents.

Wrong place, wrong time. That's what everyone had tried telling her as a child. The authorities claimed that bandits had killed her parents, but she knew the truth. Their journals showed they were studying in highly contested lands. Eliminating witnesses was just another faceless crime by a faceless organization.

The twins were still busy outfitting her with various security badges when Pia suddenly panicked. "Wait, can this thing read my thoughts?"

"It's a bridge, between the rest of the world and your mind," started one. "Imagine every comp, holo, vid, bot, and comm all connected together like pathways in front of you," finished the other.

"Jesus, can I turn it off?" asked Pia in genuine concern.

With that comment, the assistants were done trying to convert the savage in front of them and began simply answering Pia's questions as if a toddler was asking.

"Yes, I suppose. You can tap three times over the implant site and think, or say, the words *'standby mode'* and that will continue until you similarly tell it *'resume normal operation.'*"

"When will I get this over with?"

"Just lay back down, it's no worse than getting an ear pierced."

"I wouldn't know." Pia took a deep breath and lay down on her bed, where the twins had put down a clean grey towel. One held her head still while the other put the cold metal tip of a hollow syringe at an angle up against her temple. Numbing agents preceded the actual injection, but she still felt its ice cold touch as the implant entered her skin and began turning slightly, its programming orienting it into position flush against the artery.

Then she *heard* it. '*Beginning install protocol,*' the words came through distant and sterile, but at the same time distinctly from her own mind, as if she was the one thinking them. '*Scanning process complete, initiating safety limits...complete.*'

Pia finally opened her eyes and relaxed her body which had contorted itself in fear on the bed. The twins were looking down on her, their lips curled up in amused grins.

"My brain just asked me how it might help me today," Pia said in a daze.

"Come, Miss. The morning briefing will begin soon and you still haven't eaten."

"I'm not hungry, maybe just some grapes?" Suddenly the wall printer sprang into action and in under a minute a plate full of grapes appeared.

"How did it...? Pia stammered. "Did I do that?"

"Of course," said the redhead. "You thought it, you said it, then your chip put a request in with the printer. Actually I'm impressed, your mind is catching on quickly, even if you aren't."

"We'll be late if we don't leave now," chirped the brunette.

Pia finished getting ready and grabbed a handful of grapes before accompanying them across the building. The implant was intruding on her every thought, making it difficult to concentrate. As she walked by rooms she could feel the presence of the various computer systems inside, and the carpet beneath her boots hummed from the cables running between the floors. What was until an hour ago a silent world of concrete and steel was rapidly coming to life around her.

She had to focus. There were only a few days to get up to speed on a possibly trillion dollar mission, and she was listening to the floor purr. They arrived at two enormous marble doors, and as servants opened them up the twins quietly took their leave and retreated down a side hall.

'These are the rooms where the history of the world gets decided', Pia thought as she entered the conference room. The vaulted steel and glass domed ceiling towered above a luxurious round table made to look like redwood, but which was as artificial as the holo coming up out of its center.

The room was awash with noise and imagery as Pia stood stunned at the entrance trying to make sense of it all. Electricity sparked through her mind carrying spaceship component specs and timetables and asteroid field maps and dinner plans and...

"Lamotte?" It was Commander Miller's voice coming from the far side of the table. Everyone turned and looked at her. *'Standby mode,'* she thought furiously, but nothing happened.

"Standby mode," she whispered desperately, her anxiety building by the second. An elbow nudged her ribs, and she darted her eyes sideways in time to see Zee gently tapping his temple in a knowing way. She finally caught on amid more than a little laughter and performed the necessary three taps to trigger her chip. "Yes, sir?" she finally stammered.

"Take a seat, please, Pia." She marched quickly over to a seat farthest from Miller, and let her hair cover her embarrassment as best she could.

"I must ask for your patience everyone," Miller said as the rest of the group found their seats. "Lamotte has only just been chipped this morning. She's the newest and final crew member of Cerex. After the unfortunate illness of our previous biologist, Lamotte has agreed to take over on short notice."

"Yeah, who knew he had a bullet allergy?" whispered a tall man off to the left, causing Pia to sit up in shock.

Miller continued, "Now those of you involved with our lunar colonies know the inevitable Corps War has already begun. Drone raids are a weekly fact of life, and many think a full attack by one of the Multinats is coming soon. Due to this accelerated time frame, we'll be forced to do final assembly of Cerex right out in open space. Too risky to stay at the Lunar Construction Site any longer.

"So it's to be a zero G launch?" asked a young Scottish woman. She turned and began hurriedly talking with a short bull of a man by her side.

"Yes. What Miss Barton and Colonel Vineland are currently discussing is that our new launch plan comes with some other changes as well. The good news is that the extra fuel we'll have by not launching inside the Moon's gravity well will help shorten our trip by..."

"Damn, nearly a month!" exclaimed Ms. Barton.

"Actually 34 days by our models," continued Miller, "but the bad news is that no one has ever launched from zero G before, so logistics will have to be reexamined both thoroughly and quickly."

Pia was worried about the change, but everyone else seemed to be taking it in stride. She decided the only way to calm her nerves was to ignore them and jump in headfirst.

"Commander Miller, I need to be hands on with the Cerex biomass immediately."

For the second time in the brief meeting, all heads pivoted towards Pia, but this time with more deference.

"I admire your enthusiasm Pia, but the crew won't be joining Cerex until next week, once final preparations are made. Security dictates we separate the crew and hold for..."

"You don't understand...sir. Whether the bio lab is lunar based or in orbit already, adjustments need to be made, and it will need special attention when undergoing the G-force of an orbital launch. I need to be on site now. Is there any way to get me there?"

There was a long silence, during which the room stared at Miller to gauge how he'd deal with this demand. It was clear this was a man unaccustomed to interruptions. His face froze for just an instant, then melted back into his smooth corporate veneer of forced calm and confidence.

"Teams of three will separate. Santos, Hixley, and Koeniger will lead the final loading and equipment inventory in Florida. Colonel Vineland, Barton, and Coburn will stay here for now to do zero-g launch sims and to coordinate mission communications. I will accompany McKinnon and Lamotte to the orbital station tomorrow to personally oversee the final assembly. I assume this will be satisfactory, Pia?"

Pia nodded vigorously, and for the first time since Utah she felt up to speed on things. Everyone left the conference room through different doors. Pia chose the one where she entered, but in the hallway she was both relieved and dismayed to find no sign of the twins.

Reluctantly she tapped her temple and tried thinking 'resume normal operation'. Again the building came alive with data, her mind stretching away as far as she was able to focus. She shivered at the thought of what true experts with this equipment were capable of enacting.

With very little guesswork Pia's mental requests pulled up schematics for the building, and she quickly found her way back to her room. Her belongings were mostly still stored in her sturdy field backpack, so she sat at her desk and began practicing control over her implant.

The whole hallway was empty except for herself and Zee according to the building registry. She wondered how he felt about being paired with her to head into orbit early.

Before she could go find out, she felt Miller's comm signal in the hallway with her mind, saw the doors unlock through override, and finally the Commander himself appeared.

Pia stood and began, "I was able to pull up the launch info for tomorrow, and it looks as if..."

"You've done enough talking. You ever pull something like that again and I'll make you regret it." Miller was pacing back and forth and fuming.

"I...what?" Pia stammered.

"You have a problem with the mission? With the schedule? You come to me in private. I don't know what you're trying to pull with this '*I'm so innocent*' act, but it ends now. I was fully aware that a zero G launch will affect the biomass, and your show back there only served to embarrass me. Consider yourself warned."

Miller glared at Pia, then headed for the door. "And I suggest you partner with McKinnon next door to go over orbital prep. Launch is at nine tomorrow morning."

With that he was gone, and Pia was left alone again wondering what the hell she'd gotten herself into.

Chapter 3

The launch went smoothly, with the corporate rocket lifting them quickly out of Earth's grip, turning early morning back into blackness. If all went to plan, that would be the last time Pia saw blue sky for quite some time, and she missed it already. As the Earth receded behind them, the electric web in her mind fell away as well, leaving only the ship's computer filling the void.

Pia had been in orbit a handful of times before on consultation cases. Bumpy rides up, a few days to tweak a malfunctioning life support system, then back down to the dirt. She hadn't been up in nearly four years, and this was no ordinary orbit jumper. Natocorps was a superpower, and its fleet of launch vehicles performed accordingly. Max G nets, aerogel padding, full nanocarbon skin, the ship was downright sexy.

Enormous two stage rockets lifted their small crew vehicle easily into orbit in a massive display of wasteful luxury, first class tickets to space if there ever was such a thing. Pia wasn't sure what she expected to see in orbit, but what lay in front of the viewport most certainly was not it.

They appeared to be approaching an old station from the early days of spaceflight, a clunky monstrosity nearly 200 meters long and 50 meters wide with simple solar arrays stretching out like branches from both sides.

"Are we refueling here?" asked Pia.

Miller smiled and began maneuvering to dock with the clunky station while Zee talked with its computer through his pendant holo.

Then she felt a pulse of electricity buzz at her senses and realized what was happening. Multispectrum and intense, the information that flooded her mind was not a product of the rudimentary station, but rather that of what was hiding inside.

Their transport locked onto the station and Miller led the three of them in unharnessing from their G-nets. Pia may not have spent a great deal of time in space, but moved like she was born there. As Miller and Zee grasped around for handholds, she pushed off her netting and performed what looked like a pike dive as she flipped in one smooth motion and landed lightly against the airlock door.

"Well aren't we the little acrobat," Miller quipped as he and Zee joined her, "out of the way now, Pia." He typed in a secure code and the airlocks hissed in compliance.

Once the room pressurized, they could hear periodic clanking from the far hatch. Voices on the other side got louder for a moment, then ceased as the hatch swung open wide. A giant young man with dark hair and kind blue eyes held the hatch with one arm while his partner jumped through the door. A stocky little man in glasses and a black Cerex jumpsuit, he was sweating slightly after rushing to greet them and then struggling with the ancient outer hull airlock doors.

"Adam!" Pia gasped, and in her excitement forgot about the low gravity. She meant to rush forward, but ended up jumping towards him instead. When they collided, her belly smashed into his face and they both almost went spinning backwards. Fortunately, the gentle giant caught them both and set them back down carefully.

"Trexler," Miller barked, "I see you know Lamotte."

Trexler fixed his glasses and smiled awkwardly. "She is the finest biologist I have ever met, Commander. Back in Argentina, she singlehandedly prevented a famine that was decimating the-"

"Time is money. Give me a full status report." The Commander could easily access the information himself, Pia was managing that exact feat as he spoke, but he needed to flex his power.

"Yes, sir. Fulton and myself are in good health, as is the garden. We've managed to increase the volume by almost ten percent. Power has been kept to a minimum, with only one solar array deployed. We've only picked up an occasional passive laser ping before today, but since your ship's approach we've been lit up like a Christmas tree. Seven separate scans are now watching us, sir."

"Let them watch," Miller snarled through a grin. "Fulton, come help McKinnon start unloading while Lamotte gets a quick tour. I want you and Trexler headed for Luna within the hour. If all goes to plan, this should look like nothing but a routine gas and go."

"Yes, Commander!" Fulton even saluted.

Trexler gestured for Pia to follow as he turned and flung himself down the narrow conduit until he reached what appeared to be another airlock. Sure enough, the far door was clearly that of another ship. A small window in the conduit wall finally laid bare the secret Pia had already guessed.

A Cerex spaceship was being constructed inside the hollowed out shell of an old Natocorps fuel depot. The ship was truly massive, bigger than anything Pia had ever thought possible, and this was little more than the central greenhouse and wiring strapped to a jetpack. The rest of Cerex was to be assembled before launch.

Once they passed through the Cerex airlock, Trexler turned and grinned, "welcome to Eden." Rows of plants were growing in every direction, with shelves of greenery inset into the walls themselves.

"The plants are surrounded, that's great for monitoring and distribution of oxygen, but how do you...?" Pia puzzled out loud.

"Get them enough light without frying the poor darlings?" Trexler answered proudly. "Infrared holography. These tubes run through most of the hab modules, and every straight stretch is controlled by an advanced holographic projector that gets diffused by the mist. Sensors along the way monitor the temp, gases, all that jazz. A gentle recirculation collects the O2 and water, then sends back the needed CO_2. Easy, right? Took me nearly 6 months to come up with the idea though. And another 6 months to build it."

"It's...elegant," Pia admired, "and Fulton, did he help?"

"Fulton is a sweetheart, really, but he helps me best with a wrench in his hand." Trexler raised an eyebrow and leaned in conspiratorially. "Well maybe not *best*."

"And maybe not with a wrench?" Pia offered playfully, thoroughly enjoying her tour.

"Thank God you're here, Pia. I don't know what I'd do if I had to leave my babies with some dull corporate gardener. But come, these tubes are mainly just for the grasses. We still need to see the good stuff, then I'm off to finish packing."

They floated down the passageway, flanked on each side by grass tubes and in front by a ladder. By pulling themselves along by the rungs, they arrived at a wide hatch.

"During flight, Cerex will rev up for rotation and give some gravity to these spokes. There's a dozen of them altogether, four sets of three along the central hub, then the habs, labs, and cockpit will come and get attached to this framework. But the Spine is truly the gem of the ship, if I do say so."

They scurried into an airlock and waited as it pressurized. It was big enough for two people, or one with some equipment, but required them to brace against the walls to keep from floating into one another. A slight shake and long hiss marked a successful equilibrium being reached with the core.

Trexler opened the hatch door lock and swung aside with it to let Pia enter first. She immediately apologized in her head for any doubts she had over whether Cerex people could engineer a proper bio system. After all, she was a part of Cerex now too.

To say this was a cutting edge setup would be selling it short. This was more than that; it was downright futuristic. The Spine housed all the main electrical and mechanical hardware, and it was encased in high strength sheathing at the center of a ten meter wide corridor running over a hundred fifty meters along the length of Cerex.

Rows of multispectrum LED lights blanketed the Spine, delivering precise ratios of light to every segment of the ship. As Pia climbed up out of the hatch, it looked as if she were coming up from underground in the middle of a forest. Ferns and flowers of numerous types stretched out around her, all reaching towards the spinelight.

"Wait, there's gravity? But when did...?" Pia asked confusedly, looking back at the still attached airlock.

Trexler grinned and sputtered out some laughter as he enjoyed his little surprise. "I thought you'd like it better if you experienced it yourself first. The core is circled by tracks at multiple points with airlocks attached to them. They match the velocity of the entry side, the stationary dock entry corridor in our present case, and lock in place. Then they switch and gradually match the inner spin rate and lock onto a new airlock site.

When the other labs and module arms arrive, they'll connect at these circle tracks and get spun up to their particular G requirements. No more single spin rate for the whole ship."

"So what G is the central corridor kept at?" she asked, although she guessed the answer immediately.

"Ceres standard, 0.0275G."

"It's absolutely beautiful."

"Well thank you, but really I had nothing to do with planning that. I'm strictly the gardener, or was. That title is now yours. There's never been living things out as far as Ceres, so you be sure to take good care of them, and yourself. Come, one last surprise then I promise I'll hand over the keys."

They glided in the low gravity along pathways that meandered through the vegetation, stopping occasionally for tips on certain plants or irrigation techniques. Every ten meters or so they passed out of the garden and into various utility areas. Storage racks, water pump machinery, and lab stations filled in the gaps of the clearings.

It was extremely disorienting to see both sunlight and more forest above her as the central Spine could equally be treated as up from every direction. It was hard to keep from bouncing right off the ground with each step, and she felt as if with a proper leap she could make it clear across the corridor. For now, she held onto the makeshift cable handrails along the path and tried to keep up with her nimble little guide.

"Behold your assistants," Trexler announced after coming to a halt in front of a dozen large crates. Pia had her now all too common look of befuddlement as she approached the plain boxes, then froze in place when she heard it. She shot a glance at Trexler, who was betraying nothing of his final surprise, then brushed her hair away from an ear and listened closer. There was an unmistakable hum coming from the boxes. But surely it couldn't be, not here.

"Bees!" Pia exclaimed at last. "Bees? You're telling me we have space bees? Oh my god, I love it! I wondered how you managed to pollinate such a large greenhouse by yourself."

"The hives get released on a set schedule, once a day each. They have been trained to return to their hive when the lights are dimmed to mimic sunset. Some UV strobe lights on the hives help any stragglers get with the program."

Pia drew a big breath and held it behind a smile. Perhaps she had been a bit arrogant in demanding to come see the setup early, but now she was glad to have a bit of extra time to get acclimated before launch. As if he could read her mind, Miller's deep voice came through the ship's comm, "Time's up, ladies. Trexler, get your things and report to the docks."

Pia watched as a tiny bee hovered in low gravity nearby, moving in long graceful hops between flowers, then flew off in search of more.

Chapter 4

Over the next few days, modules began getting rapidly assembled inside the old depot shell. Some came from Earth, others from the Lunar colonies, and each took its turn being swallowed up by the derelict camouflage. Drones grabbed and directed them carefully into place around the core.

In addition to twelve pairs of arms that could swing around the belt tracks, there were massive water and nutrient tanks, a twenty meter command module that sat on top of the entire ship, and several tanks of fuel that would be mixed and injected into the engines at the time of launch.

Along with the modules, the rest of the crew came onboard and began setting up their respective stations. They all eventually found their way along the pathways of her little forest to introduce themselves to the odd young woman sweaty from digging or wearing a beekeeper's helmet tucked into her Cerex uniform.

Besides Miller and McKinnon, there were engineers, techs, and the pilots. Theo Koenig was the first to come by, a hulking teddy bear of a man who tiptoed in a few meters before calling out, "Hello Lamotte! Come on out so I don't squash all your pretty friends." When Pia came out to meet him, he stood there with his feet tight together and his arms down by his sides. He waved one huge paw up by his head and flashed the widest grin she'd ever seen.

Theo was an expert drilling engineer from Norway, but he described his work as mostly just playing in the dirt. Shortly after arriving, he was off helping the final assembly of the ship with Lara

Hixley, the solar engineer. She had come on the same shuttle as Theo, but the two clearly weren't close.

Lara hadn't bothered to come visit Pia, and they only finally bumped into one another at dinner on the third night. "So there you are," she simply said in a haughty British accent. "Well I can see why Theo ran off to find you, but I haven't the time for such niceties. Neither has he, mind you, and yet..."

"I'm sorry? I don't mean to hide or anything, but my work has to be rather kept apart. You know, bees and whatnot. Plenty of time to become BFFs during the trip, I'm sure." Pia's mouth tilted sideways in a playful shrug of a grin, and both women wordlessly agreed to drop their guards.

"Bees...good lord," Lara muttered as she went off to order her food. She was older than Pia by a decade, but was still a statuesque woman, with a strong jawline that stuck out when she talked and a long graceful gait. If Lara had been getting a feel for her new colleague, she appeared to come away satisfied. Pia had always been well liked, despite her aversion to most social situations.

The ship was coming together quickly, with new parts arriving almost hourly. Theo and Lara oversaw the meticulously designed construction, along with a small crew of workers. Zee was also playing a vital role in assembly, Pia was surprised to hear. His nano tech and drones were capable of an astounding variety of tasks, from mundane parts transport to advanced plasma welding in spaces much too small for humans to reach.

Zee kept his comp holo pendant ready at all times, and upon getting some unseen signal or update, would tap out quick instructions on his holo display while eating a grilled cheese sandwich with one hand. Pia recognized a kindred isolation in him, even if it was in the form of total chip immersion that seemed utterly alien to her. It was in these moments that she was able to reflect on how living in a deserted forest for three years must seem equally bizarre to others, and most likely even more so.

When the common areas got a bit crowded, she took her meals back to the forest core and worked hard at memorizing the layout and system timings. Trexler had provided her with a masterpiece, and she was determined to be a worthy successor for him.

The flight team of Colonel Charles Vineland and Sara Barton flew in separately as a precaution; Vineland shuttled in Goeff Coburn, a top notch satellite and communication specialist. Last to arrive was Barton along with the Brazilian robotics whiz Gabriel Santos. That rounded out their nine person crew, though nearly twenty other workers were also scrambling around the Cerex hull, securing hardware for launch and cutting away the carbon fiber trusses holding Cerex to the empty station shell.

Pia would be quietly installing netting around some plants when she would get distracted by endless information updates from humans and computers alike. She could watch the ship's progress in real time as a 3D projection in her head. Most adults had long ago gotten used to the sea of information surrounding them, so much so that it became hard to tell the individual's thoughts apart from the outside data. The Cerex info became so frequent that Pia got in the habit of turning off her chip to cut out all the chatter.

She had just finished her netting work when she noticed the lights slowly pulsing and figured it must be a test of the power systems. She walked lithely along the narrow pathways back to a storage shed carrying her trowel and spare parts, then went to find a rabbit hole to climb out of her area. She finally realized that something was wrong when instead of being spun up to a higher speed to match the dining area, she began floating in zero G.

When the airlock opened, panicked support crew rocketed past her carrying emergency oxygen tanks. Pia finally turned her chip back on and was nearly overwhelmed by the noise. Immediately a voice cut through it all and filled her skull, "Nice of you to join us, Lamotte! We're under attack, get your ass to the flight nets immediately. We launch as soon as you get here. Move!"

Now it was Pia's turn to panic. *'Under attack? By whom? Shouldn't there be explosions or something? Is it even safe to launch? Who the hell fights in space?!'*

Pia used her renewed connection to ask the ship for the fastest route to the command module. Normally she would take the rail transports along the outside of her central corridor, but they all appeared to be locked down. She pushed off a table and somersaulted backwards to the airlock she had just left. Once back up into her forest, she spotted her target at the end of the Spine, dug her feet into the soil and dove forward.

Pia flew through the forest and let the leaves slap at her face, not wanting to start any spins by changing her pose to swat away the greenery. She rose until her back felt the extra warmth of the Spinelight, then slowly began sinking back into the plants. Right before she landed, only a few meters short of the end of the corridor, a strong vibration shook the ship. The leaves rustled against each other and sounded like a strong breeze had blown through.

"What was that, were we hit?" Pia commed, but didn't hear any new outbursts or see any damage being reported.

"Outer hull is being compromised by nanoshells," Vineland explained. "We just opened her up and untethered. Depot is gonna be our shield until launch, so get a move on."

"Only two modules away, I'll be..."

"We can see where you are, just keep going." This time it was the copilot Barton. Pia kept forgetting that everyone on board could be watching her progress, and redoubled her speed.

Waiting for each hatch to unlock was torture, but eventually she was in the command module. She had only seen it once before, and it was equally imposing then as well. It was a cylindrical space nearly twenty meters in length and width, with the Spine running through the center.

At the top were the pilot pods, essentially acceleration netting enclosed in spheres with holo displays and a hardline connection between the pilot's chip and the ship. Pilots were easily identified by the small double port on their temples. They got them put in when they earned their wings, and each organization used a signature style of port. Vineland's was shaped like a U.S. Marine logo, an eagle sitting on a globe with an anchor through it. Barton's was a crop duster plane with spray lines streaking downwards.

The room had desks and stations bolted all around, each one dedicated to a different ship system, but they were merely wall decorations during launch. Between the walls and the Spine was an eerie sight, one that had earned it the nickname Spider's Lair by some of the crew. There were seven large white pods being suspended by a thick mesh of black netting. Each extended from several rings encircling the Spine and then out to anchor points on the walls. Pia quickly propelled up the central ladder to the only empty pod and strapped herself into place.

"So sorry!"

"Save it," Miller snapped, "are we good for launch, Colonel?"

"We don't have much choice," Vineland responded flatly, his hands reaching out rapidly to the various holo displays around him. "Outer station hull is nearly breached. Suggest we fire immediately Commander."

"Agreed, let's get out of here."

Barton was working furiously when she suddenly stopped and yelled out, "wait!"

Vineland turned to his copilot for an explanation, then his eyes glazed as he began reading some digital report. "Damn! We've got more incoming, Commander, this time from Luna. A swarm of attack drones are heading for an intercept point. They must know we're headed for Ceres and are planning on blockading our path."

Pia was terrified listening to all of this in her cocoon, with nothing to do but wait. She had anticipated plenty of danger on this trip, but not before they had even left. As she desperately tried using her chip to access some of the information that they were discussing, Zee shouted up to them from the pod next to hers.

"Launch now, but only with enough of a burst to get us to the intercept in, say, fifteen minutes or so. I can clear the road by then."

To Pia's amazement, Miller barely batted an eye. "You heard him, let's go."

"Locking in," Vineland said, and the pods began contracting around their occupants.

Pia was startled as the viewplates closed toward her face. "My suit! I don't have my suit on," she blurted out, trying to turn her head around enough to check the other pods, but no one else was visible.

"No need for an EVA. Pods will act as life support in a pinch." Hixley spoke quickly, but politely, wanting to refocus attention where it needed to be.

Zee was working even harder than the pilots, until with twenty seconds to spare he ordered his own launch. "Road warriors away, and the rest will be programmed in time for intercept."

"Good job McKinnon," Miller cut in, "let's get moving."

"T-minus ten seconds, nine...FULL BREACH! Bots are through the shield!" Barton exclaimed, then skipped the countdown and launched.

A tremendous vibration shook the ship as the engines began a short burn. All of the crew pods sank in their netting to absorb the acceleration. Pia felt the slightest jolt, and barely knew the launch had begun.

"We're away clean, hostiles falling far behind," Vineland reported after the engines stopped, "sensors tracking over two thousand drones fanning out at intercept. This is a full alliance strike."

Miller grunted haughtily. "They all had Ceres missions too. If they spent less time plotting coups, maybe they would've been further along. McKinnon," he turned his wandering attention back to the approaching battle, "you better have a damn good plan."

"Stages, sir. Yes, sir." Zee's fingers were a blur in his pod, reading long range reconnaissance reports on the upcoming drones and choosing matching countermeasures. He and the flight team were rapidly coordinating the needed maneuvers. "I didn't think they would have so many, but their tech just isn't good enough."

Pia had been happy to stay in the dark about all the corporate drama, but now that her future might be less than ten minutes long, she used the time poring over cyber data on Natocorps' rivals. If she was going to be killed, she for damn sure wanted to know who was doing the killing.

A decade ago, advanced scouting CubeSats had brought news of the massive potential for profit on Ceres. All the remaining Multinats were planning similar Ceres ventures as their populations were crashing from malnutrition. Earth itself simply had nothing left to give.

Untold fortunes and vast amounts of scarce resources were put into these missions, because losing this race meant bankruptcy and hostile takeover. Even for Natocorps, failure would spell a complete reversal of their good fortune. The other Multinats would regain superiority and carve up Natocorps' vast empire. There could be only one survivor, and then a Globalcorp would finally be born. All that was left was figuring out whose CEO would end up on top.

To a biologist like Pia, it seemed like simple natural selection. Whose corporate structure was the most efficient? Who had the most talented staff? And in the end, whose corporate bylaws would get passed down to the next generation? There were no grand causes at play, no moral code. There was just kill or be killed, and right now Pia was a gazelle being surrounded by a pack of hyenas.

Her internal searching was interrupted by Zee suddenly saying out loud, "turn us around!"

Miller erupted immediately, "we are NOT going back, not now. You said you could handle this!"

Zee was just finishing a string of rapid fire instructions and bristled at having to explain himself when time was short "No sir, not back. Flip the ship around, then fire the engines at ten or twenty percent power. It'll be weak enough not to slow us down much, but then we'll have a blowtorch to punch a hole through the drone net."

Vineland didn't wait for a response from Miller. "Beginning manual rotation now. We'll be seeing hostiles in under three minutes."

"Agreed," Miller said pointlessly. Thirty seconds later the maneuver was complete and Zee began issuing fresh commands into his holocomp.

"Nanobot chains are fully deployed, ten in all are spiraling out from Cerex. Colonel, please spin us at ten RPM, but no faster or else the chains may not be able to withstand impacts."

By now the signals from the drones were strong enough that all of the crew could make out their sizes and locations. Most were the size of small dogs, but there was a truly wide assortment, coming as they did from multiple sources. The smallest ones were the size of mice, most likely hull acid or nano, while the largest were satellite killers. Those shot out tiny metal pellets at high velocity, and Cerex would be in range of them any second.

"Ok, let's see what you can do little fireflies. Activating countermeasures now."

All eyes braced for some sort of blinding laser array, but nothing happened. Pia checked the drone blockade and they all seemed to be in the same formation as before. But then, the blockade slowly changed shape. The satellite killers drifted away from their former positions, along with several dozen other medium sized targets. The rest of the armada was converged on their path in an attempt to intercept and latch on to Cerex.

"Shock troops were effective, start the burn please Colonel."

"Ok kid, firing engines, ten percent power."

"Shock troops?" Miller interrupted. "I still count the same number of drones out there."

Zee didn't say a word, merely highlighted a series of reports streaming through their Datanet.

Pia was starting to like the skinny tech more and more. He had some serious skills, and knew how to leverage them to his advantage with Miller.

The reports showed a schematic of the shock troops, a name that turned out to be more than just macho war talk. The miniscule warriors were less than ten centimeters long, but there were hundreds of them working together. They targeted the largest enemy drones, then burrowed towards vital circuitry and fried them with intense EM pulses. Useless against a hulled ship, but drones weren't built for defense. Those satellite killers were all floating space junk now.

The engine began throwing a plasma jet stretching a hundred meters in front of them, and any drones with propellant left were scrambling to adjust their intercept arcs. Cerex began plowing through hundreds of helpless victims while barely slowing down from the weak reverse thrust.

The whipchains held together as they sliced right through the remainder of what was quickly becoming an unimpressive defense. The nanochains ate their way like razorwire through drone after drone, and by the time Zee asked for the ship to be swung back around, no more than a dozen small bots had made it all the way to their hull. A few strategically placed deck guns swatted these last survivors away.

"Alright, let's not stick around for round two. Prepping main mission burn, Commander," Vineland said.

"Make it happen, Colonel. And McKinnon, you're getting a damn raise."

Pia exhaled for what felt like the first time since hearing the emergency sirens. The full power of Cerex's engines was immense, and for two minutes the whole ship shook despite the best dampening systems available. When it finally stopped, there was a brief period of true zero G before the ship began spinning up its various sections. It would be nearly six months before they reached Ceres, and so the crew split up into their respective sections to hunker down.

Part 2
Diamond Disaster

Chapter 5

'*It was all just business,*' Pia thought, shaking her head.

Her life meant nothing to the Multinats, merely a nuisance to be eliminated like Pia's parents were years ago. It made a rage build up inside her, and she felt like she could breathe fire. What came out instead were hot tears down her flushed cheeks.

No one saw her trembling lip, or the blood stained hands where her nails dug deepest. During the battle to escape Earth orbit, Pia Lamotte watched the heroics through her chip implant. It let her feel protected, as if it were just a movie. Once the all clear was signaled, she had rushed back to the privacy of the forest hab and turned off her neural net.

The crew split into management and worker factions. Miller, Coburn, and Vineland formed the Management group, smaller but holding all the power. Miller enjoyed the extra authority that Vineland's presence commanded, along with the war stories the Colonel told.

Back when Earth had reached its tipping point and environmental systems cascaded into failure, smaller nations fought in the devastating Water Wars. Veteran warriors like Vineland were in high demand for their skills.

But as the world burned, traditional superpowers tried to stay out of conflicts, hesitant to use nuclear force on an already decimated planet. Piece by piece, country by country, corporations with vast amounts of capital and no physical location quietly swept up the rubble into their portfolios. In the end, world peace had been purchased with a pen stroke at the Beijing Accords of 2042.

The rest of the crew, who were mostly scientists and engineers, called themselves the STEMs, and grew closer while helping each other on projects in the labs. Sara was the lone exception, as she could have easily stayed with Vineland and the Management group, but had much more in common with the STEMs.

She was twenty years younger than Vineland, and despite constant recruitment by militaries around the world, had managed to stay independent. Sara became one of the foremost smugglers alive, and every corporation left standing had used her skills at some point.

Most armies had been disbanded years ago to conserve materials, and the only warfare came from skirmishes with the Free Earth network. Factories could be ground to a halt, food storehouses raided, and supply drones redirected; a clever mind halfway around the world could hack just about anything. This shadow group opposed all the Multinats equally, and focused on stealing resources.

But even the Free Earth attacks had subsided in the weeks since Cerex launched. Everyone was watching and waiting to see if the mission was successful or not. If it was, then the best business move might be accepting a merger. If not, then a Multicorp Alliance would carve up Natocorps at its weakest.

Ceres had now grown larger in the sky than a full moon back on Earth and final approach was upon them. Theo knocked on Pia's hatch half an hour before the crew was set to gather in the emergency module.

"Time to go," Theo announced.

"Some date, no flowers?"

"Nah, someone's hoarding them. C'mon, let's go find a crater for me to pulverize."

"Theo, he's got you babysitting me?" Pia chided as she buzzed him through the airlock.

"Just following orders." He grinned and offered her his arm. "You *were* late to the launch."

Pia ordered Theo to turn around as she quickly got changed into her launch suit, a pair of skin tight Kevlar nanomesh pants and matching long sleeve top. *'I look like a damn superhero,'* she thought, then doubled back for a chunky knit sweater to throw over top. She smiled thinking of Miller's head exploding when he saw her wardrobe addition.

As she entered the airlock, Pia noticed Theo's suit had a much looser fit than hers. He shrugged, "you wouldn't want to see me in a leotard like that, trust me."

She reached up and lightly yanked on his scruffy beard. "True, you'd bust the seams," Pia teased. "And for the record, I wasn't late. The launch was early."

They arrived as the last of the STEMs filed in, and climbed into the assigned landing pods.

"Telementry shows us near optimal trajectory, Commander." Coburn confirmed a solid connection with CereSat, the Natocorps satellite which had been orbiting the dwarf planet for two years already.

Everything was secured for the descent, but Pia still worried about her tiny forest. Her face betrayed nothing as she sat strapped tightly in her deceleration net. Only her shoes moved as her toes wiggled, longing for soil to dig into. It was deeply unsettling for Pia to be so far from Earth. No matter how many plants she grew, nothing let her forget that she would be living indoors for the next few years.

Vineland was in his element, deftly spinning to perform last minute checks on the flight systems. "Any obstructions showing on final scan of the glide path?"

"None, sir," responded Barton crisply.

"Commander Miller, we're coming up on T-minus five minutes," Vineland reported.

Miller narrowed his eyes as if focused on a finish line that was rapidly approaching. Ceres now took up much of the screen on the forward holos. There were no windows in the traditional sense onboard, however most walls could be used as projection screens by the crew. Miller saw trillions of dollars and the future of Natocorps waiting for him on the utterly alien landscape.

"All crew secure and engines prepped for final descent burn," Vineland barked out, but just then Barton began working furiously and pivoting in her harness like an acrobat.

"Lost contact with engine three, short circuit possibly. Subsystems are working to reestablish communication but we're running out of time."

"What the hell is going on, Colonel? snapped Miller.

"Four minutes til burn, ideas anyone?" Charles asked as he searched through the back channel engine checks.

For a second the frenzy ceased as everyone thought, and in the pause came Pia's voice. "Can't we manually override and fire it?"

"You climbing outside? Miller asked mockingly.

"Not out, in," Pia said.

"The Spine," Zee uttered as he suddenly understood.

"Where can we reach wiring for engine three?" Vineland asked.

"Access panel eight," Zee responded after querying schematics. "Pia, it's right next to you. Hold on, I'll come help." He began undoing his restraints when Pia stopped him.

"There's no time. You won't make it back to your pod. Just talk me through it."

Pia felt her stomach tighten as she climbed out of the pod. She was done being a bystander in her own life. If this was the end for her, she was determined to have it happen on her own terms. "Can you pop panel eight, Colonel?"

"Done. Barton, can we make it with only three?"

"What the hell is going on, Captain?!" Miller demanded anxiously.

"They're trying to hotwire her," laughed Theo.

Pia wrapped her legs around the Spine to hold on in zero G. Inside there was a mass of electronics which her chip displayed as humming with a symphony of different tones. She could see the signals and code passing effortlessly through the hardware, but understood none of it.

"Sure this is a good idea?" Pia muttered mainly to herself.

Then she felt Zee, or rather his thoughts, as he linked into her chip directly. Suddenly it was like having two people in the same brain. He saw with her eyes, and for several seconds he seemed to be the one moving her hands for her. Wires were unbundled and spread apart to reveal thicker cables underneath.

"One minute until the Burn Wall," Vineland announced. "We need to fire, whether it's with three or with four, or else we're going to skip off Ceres like a stone. We'd be drifting through space for the next billion years. What's going on down there Pia?"

"She's almost there, Colonel," Zee answered for her.

"Pia, you're going to have to strap yourself to the Spine, immediately," Barton warned.

"With what?" She looked around in a panic, then froze. "Shit, ok, hold on. Sarah, could you pop Access Panel...seven?"

"Can do," Barton worked at a holo display for a moment, "there you are, we're a go whenever you're set."

She wriggled out of her flight suit pants and tied the end of each pant leg together after threading them through the access panel frames. Once it felt secure she slid up through the loop she had made and hooked her arms around it.

"Hold off a second," Zee demanded, and fished around his pockets quickly before leaning out of his pod. He craned his head around until he spotted Pia dangling half naked from the exposed panels of the Spine. "Jesus, Pia…ok, get ready, you'll need this soldering pen to make a spark.

"Not a word," Pia smirked nervously, "throw it." The pen spun slowly in weightless flight, and bounced off her hand before she finally grabbed hold of it.

"We're good," Pia yelled up to the pilots.

Immediately the ship shook from the powerful plasma jets erupting between them and the rapidly enlarging Ceresian landscape. Pia lost her breath as she was slammed against metal panels, scraping and cutting her newly bared legs. The displays showed a nauseating spin caused by the missing engine blast, but most of the crew only felt the heavy compression of their bodies into the pliant straps of their pods.

Pia groaned as her back and arms struggled to hold onto the improvised harness. Zee entered her mind again, hacking her implant to guide her hands to the correct engine wiring. She scraped it against the nearby casing until the center fibers showed.

Vineland may have been the veteran pilot, but his combat days were long past him. Barton took the lead, and she too struggled to maintain a proper heading. The ship listed to one side, forcing her to let their course drift or risk the ship flipping. "I need that engine NOW!" she shouted at them.

The soldering iron was for working on circuit boards, and while it had electric current powering it, only heat was produced externally. Pia didn't need Zee's help figuring out what was necessary. She began smashing the tool against a nearby strut, again and again until it cracked open and the wires sparked in protest. She touched the damaged soldering iron to the engine wiring, but nothing happened. Then she brought the tip to her finger and saw an arc form before swinging her hand away in pain.

Somehow she held on, her lips curled into a growl. "Alright, damn it, here goes nothing." She wiped sweat off her face then placed the wet hand behind the wiring before touching the iron to it again. As soon as the arc formed, the last engine came roaring back to life, bringing cheers from the crew.

Barton, however, was not cheering. She wrestled with the controls, keeping Cerex stable mostly through instinct and sheer force of will. But now more problems cropped up and the room grew quieter.

"Engines one, two, and four have nearly finished their burns, but three has just fired up. We need to slow down more, we're showing some heat build up."

"Heat? It's a rocket, of course it's hot." interrupted Miller.

Vineland explained, "It's the atmosphere, Commander. Thin as it may be, the water vapor and volatiles are enough to cause plenty of friction at our speed. We'll need to jettison the rockets soon or they'll break up."

"Don't you mean *blow* up, Colonel?" Theo chimed in, keeping a smile on his face despite his nerves.

"That too, yes," deadpanned the Colonel.

"Charles, we need a new target before we lose the rockets." Hixly had been watching the holos intensely and saw no sign of Occator crater, their planned landing site.

"Shit, she's right," Barton said. "The partial burn threw us off course."

"How far off?" asked Charles.

She did the calculations using her chip. "We're looking at a possible dark side landing."

"No, gotta keep it daylit." Charles responded. "Heatshield temp is increasing, but manageable."

"For now," Barton sighed.

Santos chimed in, "what if we jettison just the three engines? Cut our weight and increase the effectiveness of the last one?"

"Yeah, because this wasn't hard enough already," Barton cursed to herself, but Vineland cut her off.

"Do it, now. Only way we're gonna slow in time to stay daylit during landing."

"Engines away. Hold onto your asses." Sara said. Cerex groaned as uneven stresses tried to pull it apart. For a few seconds there was nothing but the overwhelming sound of screeching metal. "Anyone have a new target for me yet?"

"Theo, Gabe, you worked the topography maps, give us options." Vineland demanded. "Keep in mind we have under two minutes to final descent."

"How far off primary are we?" came Theo's gruff voice.

"Two thousand kilometers, maybe more, east southeast."

"From Occator?" Santos thought out loud, "mostly lowland plains, good for landing but not target rich."

"Ahuna Mons," Theo muttered, then again louder, "head to Ahuna Mons."

"You want to aim for the tallest damn mountain on Ceres with an uncontrolled ship?" griped Santos.

"What's the matter, Gabby, scared?" Barton shot back. "Your call, Colonel. We're getting low on fuel."

"Make it happen, Sara. Squeeze every drop out of engine three then hand control over to the drone jets."

"Almost there, stand by..." Barton replied.

Everyone held their breath as the five kilometer high mountain appeared on the horizon of the holo display. "Down to 150 km/hr, nearing acceptable range for the drones, 140, 130..."

Silence returned as the last engine stopped. "Jettisoning three, turning the controls over to the drones. Take us down, little friends."

Pia's face went pale as the sheer cliffs of the mountain first filled the holo. They had traveled over the Ceresian nightside and were now the first humans to witness sunrise from the surface. The desolate landscape made the mountain loom like an alien monument, with massive craters to the north and south causing Ahuna Mons to appear even taller in contrast. Quickly rising over top was the same familiar Sun that had warmed Pia's face on countless mornings, only here it was as diminutive as Ceres itself. The ultrathin atmosphere was faintly visible as a halo, making the Sun appear to spit flecks of ash like a campfire.

Dozens of drones fired like welders' torches around the ship, pushing and prodding it towards a flat surface. The seemingly random bursts suddenly became a single chorus as they joined together. If the drones would have had two or three more seconds, Cerex might have managed a gentle landing.

Instead, the leg trusses had barely locked into position before getting crumpled underneath the ship's bulkheads as they were driven into the brittle regolith. Pia's muscles finally gave out and she fell from her makeshift harness, landing on the airlock door which she climbed through less than half an hour earlier.

Chapter 6

"There you go, Pia," Barton whispered, "open your eyes." Pia felt her head throb and struggled to focus. "Where am I?" she asked, then closed her eyes again.

'I should've climbed out of my pod, not you.'

Pia forced herself to look for who said it, but only Sara hovered over her. The rest of the crew had scattered to begin operations.

Then she felt him. A static electricity spread through her, tingling its way from bruised forehead to bleeding shins.

'Zee?' she guessed through her chip network.

'Just checking in on you, sorry,' he said.

'I appreciate it, but keep your sensor checks to yourself.'

The tingling stopped, and Pia sat up. She slid her hands down under a mylar blanket covering her legs. They came back up smeared with blood from where the paneling had scraped and cut her during landing.

"Mostly minor injuries," Sara comforted her. "That was brave what you did. Stupid, but brave."

Pia lay back down carefully, confused about how Zee had entered her mind. She felt utterly exposed, all her barriers tossed aside like a child's toy lock.

'Clearly he hacked my mind,' she thought, *'and easily. Is he still...here?'* The possibilities were terrifying, disorienting, and exciting all at the same time.

The ship was a swarm of activity in the days following the dawn landing. Plans hadn't changed despite the new landing site. Reconnaissance was the first order of business. A fleet of microdrones made constant trips in and out of the cargo bay. Gabriel drove three remote drills towards the looming monolith, while Theo installed stationary mining rigs around the landing site. Lara unfolded great expanses of solar paneling that had been pulled in for atmospheric entry. The pilots were with Miller and Coburn recording their first transmission back to Earth.

Meanwhile Pia began the process of converting her forest. The plants had to be reoriented now that Ceres provided natural gravity. The walls all folded down into platforms, so what was once a circular forest floor now became a vertical greenhouse. Her muscles were accustomed to leisurely strolls through dirt pathways, and they ached at the thought of daily watering climbs, even if it was in low gravity.

Ahuna Mons kept watch over them like a sleeping titan, always drawing their attention and curiosity. Two days on Ceres had brought multiple sunrises due to the nine hour day. The going theory was that an asteroid impact had originally pushed Ahuna Mons up out of the ground like a seesaw. The crater had pressed down on a slab of planetary crust, forcing the other end up into a steep cliff nearly the height of the Rocky Mountains.

Pia visited the labs just as Gabe's bots climbed out of the crater and began ascending the base of Ahuna. As opposed to the reconnaissance rovers first used to explore the Moon and Mars, Gabriel's designs were a work of art. They looked more like fully stocked trucks with drilling equipment and storage spots for collection.

A thousand meters up, the surface became too steep and brittle. The rock wall broke apart under the wheels, sending debris floating off in explosive arcs across the landscape. A small ledge was located where the rover could anchor itself, and then the drill was deployed.

The outer layers of rock were pulverized before the drill met any serious resistance. Back onboard Cerex, Gabe sat at his desk directing the operation. He turned to Zee, who was monitoring recon drones at the next desk, and said, "We've got a problem, come take a look at this."

Pia stared at Zee, watching his hands work like a conductor manipulating the holo display that surrounded him. Zee linked into the direct data feed and saw what Gabe was worried about immediately. The drill had stopped progressing, but appeared to be operating normally. "Could the depth sensor be broken?"

Gabe shook his head. "Cameras verify the depth, it's only three meters. No other sensors show any errors, the drill is working fine."

"Maybe it just hit a hard deposit," Zee suggested.

"That drill can go through anything."

"You picking up that vibration pattern?" Zee pulled up a display of the seismographic sensors and swiped it onto a screen for Santos. "The drilling is making the surface unstable."

"It's still minor. When she pushes through it'll dissipate quickly." Minutes passed but still it refused to budge, and the vibrations only grew stronger.

"You need to shut it down, try another spot Gabe," Zee decided.

"Good idea," Santos relented, but just as he said it the sensor warnings stopped. "There we go, broke through after all. Wait, now what's wrong with the sensors?"

Zee ran some diagnostics, then opted for a visual with one of his drones. Pia had been watching from across the room, but marched over after one look at the drone feed. She stood in disbelief for a minute while Santos tried to regain control over his drill bot.

Eventually Zee put a hand on Gabe's shoulder, "the sensors are gone."

"What do you mean, gone?"

Zee swiped the video to the room's holowall, then turned Gabe's head towards it with his hand. "A big chunk of the mountainside too." There was a gaping hole and a rumbling landslide slowly bouncing its way downhill.

"Great, first dig, already lost a bot," Santos griped.

"Maybe we can salvage it, I'll take a look." Zee redirected an incoming microdrone back out towards Ahuna Mons. There was no sign of the drill near the base of the landslide, so Zee flew up slowly in a zigzag pattern. Still nothing. He got to the drill site before halting the flight. A bright LED was activated and panned along the scarred fissure. "Gabe, take a look at this."

"Found my bot?"

"Not even close, but we need to get another up there right now."

"What's up?"

"Tell me what that looks like," Zee gestured at the holo.

The landslide had opened a fifty meter long gash in the mountainside. The uncovered section looked smooth and glassy, and when the light shined a certain way it almost looked like...

"Diamond, or quartz most likely, it couldn't be diamond," Gabe stammered in disbelief.

"Does quartz usually break tungsten carbide drill bits?"

Gabe bolted up out of his chair. *'Commander Miller, we need you down here immediately, sir.'*

'What for, Santos?' Miller came through via chip.

'I think we may have just paid for the trip.'

Miller never moved so fast in his life, getting down to the tech labs just as Gabe was sending out another drill rig. One look at the exposed wall and Miller jumped up, forgetting the low gravity and groping awkwardly for a chair to pull himself back down. His normally strained face was actually relaxed and smiling. It looked as if his huge gamble on Ceres was going to pay off. "Time to change that report to Earth," he joked, "damn good work Santos." Then switching to comm, *'Theo, get your ass back to Cerex.'*

The news spread and everyone soon gathered in the tech labs. As they jostled for better views, Pia found herself pressed up against Zee's back. She tried to slide off him to the side when she felt him shaking. No one would have noticed unless they were actually touching him as she was.

Pia concentrated on the systems connecting them all, sifting through ship computers, wires, terminal displays, and finally the chips of the crew themselves. As her uniform rubbed across his shoulder, she could feel the presence of Zee's mind.

His electrical signature glowed much brighter than any of the others, flashing outwards into numerous networks at once. She reached out with her thoughts, directing their energy where she wished, and gently scanned his outgoing signals. His mind was organized, and powerful, but also heavily shielded. *'You're nervous,'* Pia realized.

'And you're more surprising by the minute,' Pia heard Zee's voice in her head. She gave his shoulder a firm squeeze, then backed up out of the main group.

Theo was like a big kid, dancing with nervous energy as he took over the controls. Determined not to lose this bot, he found a few meters of iron based rock above the gash, then shot a piton in as an anchor. With a line in place Theo positioned the drill off to the side of the exposed wall.

"I learned this move in Antarctica clearing away ice walls. Should work here, especially with the density gradient from diamond to this slop on the surface."

Pia went and sat down on the side of Zee's desk, tucking her knees up to her chin as she watched the main holo. Zee glanced up at her and smiled before returning inward to his displays.

Theo continued explaining himself to Miller, who in turn kept asking obvious questions to seem engaged while doing profit calculations in his back channel thoughts. "When the first drill hit diamond, its computer cycled through different speeds and pressures trying to bust a hole through. It couldn't do shit to that diamond, but it did find a resonance frequency for a few seconds."

Miller nodded dumbly, his handsome face squinting in fake understanding. When it came to finance he was not to be messed with, but remained out of his depth in most other situations.

Theo got the drill up to speed and everyone held their breath. At first nothing much happened, with Santos merely calling out the depth periodically. Slowly a rumble could be heard in the lab, at first through the video feed, but growing more pronounced until the ship itself began to vibrate.

"Lot of movement here Theo," Miller said nervously, "are we in safe ranges?"

"Hell yeah, sir, same as a gentle earthquake, ship takes much worse anytime we fire the engines." Theo turned back to the displays. "Wooooooo, we got her shaking now though, don't we? C'mon, Ahuna, drop that dress."

"Language, Theo, you're not on an oil rig anymore."

"Sorry, boss."

Just then all of the monitors and feeds went blank and the ship itself began noticeably shaking. Pia instinctively looked for a window, but found only gray walls. She impressed herself by mentally retrieving a station camera with the appropriate view. What appeared on the wall holo made an icy panic flood her body as she instinctively reached out to grab hold of something.

"Anyone else seeing this?" she managed to blurt out. All eyes that had been glued to the scrolling data monitors whipped around to see the projection. The whole screen gave an impression that the ship was launching back up into space, but then turbulence on the mountainside betrayed the true cause of the illusion.

The entire near side of Ahuna Mons was sloughing off in slow motion, a million tons of rock coming down like an avalanche. No one moved for what seemed an eternity, frozen in place watching the scene unfold.

Pia was the first to voice what they all must have been thinking. "Is that going to reach us?"

Theo's normally booming voice was now closer to a whisper, "Shouldn't, a slide that size on Earth would pancake us, but here it just won't have the steam. Shouldn't..."

Zee was rapidly doing the math with his enhanced network implants. "Theo's right. Most of the material will pile up at the base, which will slow the rest even more. We're good."

Slowly the debris settled and the dust scattered, some even escaping the gravity well entirely, but what remained staggered the senses. The brain can often process something long before the mind is ready to accept it as reality. They all could see the mountain shining with countless reflected suns, each no brighter than a full moon due to Ceres' distant orbit. But with no comparable sight existing, their minds simply groped for the words to describe what they plainly saw.

This time Miller was the first to find his voice. "It's fucking beautiful."

"Language, boss," smirked Theo.

Miller ignored him completely. "This is it. Game over. Earth belongs to Natocorps." He ran both hands back through his gelled hair, disrupting the carefully manicured look. "I'm gonna be so fucking famous."

Pia felt her stomach drop into her feet. *'Why did I ever agree to be a part of this?'* she thought. In her head she had convinced herself this mission was just another step in an endless struggle for resources between soulless corporations. But she was looking at a diamond the size of a city, the consequences of which were staggering.

Back on Earth most precious gems had long since been mined, processed, and stockpiled. This discovery would let Natocorps buy out every last bit of competition several times over. Natocorps really could now become the sole Globalcorps. For the briefest of moments, Pia wished the landslide would have crushed them, along with the greed and ambition of Miller and all men like him.

'*No, there are good people on board too,*' she thought. No matter how self righteous she might be feeling, that was no excuse for what would essentially be murder.

Just then amid the growing jubilation, she noticed Zee staring at her from across the terminals. He often wore a glazed over look as he interfaced with his networks, so his current stare was dismissed by the rest of the crew. But this time his dark eyes were studying hers, causing Pia to force her glance down towards her boots as she shuffled in amongst the crew.

Theo was particularly gleeful and picked her up in one of his signature bear hugs. When he let her down, Pia retreated as soon as she could without drawing undue attention to herself. She climbed down to the lowest platform and flattened her back against the cold metal wall.

She randomly remembered those vapid twins from training and tapped her temple three times. "Standby mode," she managed to whisper. Her fists came down hard on her thighs, then again and again until her hands ached and her thighs screamed for mercy. She threw her head upwards and pressed her hands into her face until she began to sob. She sat like that for nearly an hour, then abruptly got back up, smoothed out her uniform and went to work.

DAVID COLELLO

Chapter 7

The euphoria from discovering the immense diamond deposit quickly evaporated as soon as the reality of life on Ceres came settling over the crew.

Pia fought hard not to show her relief when the news broke. They were parked next to the largest diamond mine humanity had ever seen, with no way to extract it. With no diamond drill bits onboard and manufacturing capability nowhere near up to the task of forging new ones, it would be years before they could start mining. Things were made even worse by surveys of the surrounding regolith. Despite the vast wealth in Ahuna Mons, Cerex had landed in a virtual dead zone for resources.

Coburn and Santos were tasked with finding a more suitable mining spot. CereSat data suggested their original landing site near Occator was still their best hope of finding useful amounts of what they would need to quickly produce fuel, water, and food. However, Occator was located some 500 kilometers away in the Hanami Planum highlands, so Santos' two remaining operational rovers began lumbering their way there. Meanwhile, drones flew off to retrieve tiny scoops of loose material for analysis.

Pia found herself in uncomfortably high demand at a time when she wanted nothing more than to curl up on a cot and listen to rain beat down on a heavy canvas tent. Since their improvised landing site contained nothing useful beyond a few trillion carats of raw diamond, Pia's forest remained their sole source of oxygen and water.

As the official steward of the life support systems onboard Cerex, Pia was constantly having crew come to her for requisition approvals.

Lara needed water as coolant for the rapidly expanding solar arrays she was constructing. Theo was clamoring to get to work drilling for subsurface water, but needed water to help cool his machinery as well. And of course everyone wanted to go out in their exosuits to explore on foot. But all of it used resources, and even if fully recoverable or reusable, only a certain amount could be used at any one time while still maintaining critical systems.

Pia lay back on a mossy ledge, letting her bare feet and dirty blond hair dangle over the sides. She let out a deep sigh, closed her eyes, and listened. But there was no rain, no tent, not even a comfortable bed where she could hide out.

'Maybe Zee could make canvas with his fancy 3-D printers?' she thought. He hadn't said a word to her in the week since the big discovery, but something had changed between them.

Maybe it was all in her head, she was never very good at reading other people, but she would catch him glancing sideways at her during meetings. Every so often she would be alone and swear that he was watching, that he knew what she was thinking.

Rather than getting more freaked out, Pia decided to go visit him and get a better feel of the situation. While her domain at the center of Cerex had converted to life at Ceres gravity, most other areas were now spun up artificially, so she waited in the air lock as it matched speeds with tech deck. Under her arm was a narrow golden colored tube which she began tapping on the walls. As she neared Zee's station she paused to collect herself, took a deep breath, and then blew it out hard with an intentional body shimmy.

Zee sat tilted impossibly far back on his chair with hairy legs up on the desk and his hands resting on an old t-shirt. His eyes constantly darted around at invisible screens, and it was difficult to tell if he was dreaming or working. As had happened with many of the crew before, Pia went to wake him only to have Zee be the first to speak.

"Pia, I was hoping you'd drop in."

"You did?" She straightened up and began searching awkwardly behind herself for the nearest chair or desk to lean on.

"It's about the Ahuna diamond," and with that she could feel the sweat beading on her brow.

"Lucky find, huh? This trip has got a horseshoe stuck up its ass." The nervous laughter came flooding out of her now. What was she so scared of, that she wasn't super excited and he saw it? That absolute global domination for Natocorps didn't exactly thrill her? Zee was probably so lost in his stupid Datanet that he didn't care what happened to Earth.

"A what? A horse's shoe?" Zee had a much gentler laugh, and it was disarming to see him staring at her, just her and not with the usual sideways glances at holo imagery. "Anyway, you're our resident expert on chemistry and I wanted to see what you make of this."

Pia was relieved to find the conversation going along professional lines. "I'm not sure you need my expertise to classify a diamond. Miller has probably called a thousand gemologists back on Earth for that."

Zee rolled his eyes and leaned closer to her. "Yeah, no, that asshole is only worried about himself and money, in that order." His eyes lit up when he laughed this time, and Pia felt like she was finally connecting with him for the first time.

"Then what's so weird that you need me?" she asked.

"Awww, but you like weird, don't you?"

Now Pia didn't know what they were really talking about anymore. "Yeah," she chuckled, "It's mysterious, no? All the best things are weird somehow or other." She couldn't tell what Zee was feeling, but he kept rolling with the banter, and it was a relief to talk casually with someone after the stress of the last week.

"Well here, this is what a typical spectrometer readout from a diamond looks like," he said, and began pulling up graphs on a nearby screen, "and THIS is what we're getting from Ahuna."

As he moved aside, he took her hand and pulled her over to his station. Pia scanned the readouts quickly, then furrowed her brow and leaned closer. "This is just from one sample? One site?"

"3cm wide circle, yep. And we've checked multiple sites, all have unique signatures but roughly equal percentages of these trace elements."

"Corundum, beryl, iridium," Pia rattled off as she examined the spectrographs.

"Impressive, or as us laymen call them..."

"Ruby, sapphire, emerald, there's half of the periodic table here. How?" Pia was stunned.

"How is this possible? Simple oxides or carbonates are always found in diamonds, but these are entirely different elements, which form in vastly different ways, all just sprinkled through a diamond the size of Paris."

"Gold, platinum, yeah, damn near everything. And that's not all." Zee swiveled in his chair and brought up a new chart. "Most diamonds on Earth are ancient, we're talking one to three billion years old. Care to guess how old Ahuna is?"

Pia examined the chart, then dropped down and sat on the floor to steady herself as her mind raced. "This is impossible, all of this. What the hell is going on here?! A diamond less than a million years old, oh and it has every precious metal known to mankind riddled throughout it like blueberries in a cake."

"I would have gone with chocolate chips in a cookie, but yeah, basically this is insane." The two of them sat and thought for a minute as Zee smirked at Pia sitting on the floor with her knees tucked in under her chin.

"Does anyone else know? What does Theo think, or Gabe?" she finally asked.

"Gabe and Theo showed me, and they're as baffled as we are. Miller has a meeting about it set for sundown Ceres time, four hours from now. You have to start using your chip more," he said casually.

'How did he know whether she was using her chip or not?' Again she felt an overwhelming panic strike her that he was able to read her thoughts.

"I think Miller will flip his shit if you ignore another one of his comm requests," Zee laughed, not seeming to notice her fear.

She began to think she was overreacting again. She had avoided tech for so much of her life that she imagined the worst most of the time. Still, Zee was no mere tech user. He was a genius, and when his eyes bore down on her she felt utterly naked, like her every thought and feeling were being recorded, cataloged, and analyzed.

"Honey?" Zee asked, startling her back to the conversation.

"Excuse me?" she said defensively. Zee pointed at the golden tube Pia had laying beside her on the floor and raised an eyebrow. "Oh, yes! I had nearly forgotten. For saving me back at landing."

She handed him the tube of honey freshly harvested that morning. "And thanks for saving us at launch. You do a lot of saving...and not a lot of talking."

"Well talking is usually just wasted breath. We need to be careful with our air, which you and your sprouts so kindly provide, so thank you right back."

This time it was Pia who couldn't help but smile. "My sprouts?"

Zee pursed his lips. "The others call them that...or your minions."

Pia stood and got up in Zee's face, still grinning. "Is that all? What else do they say about me?"

Zee's hand slipped on his desk as he leaned backwards awkwardly. "Well, you're always hidden away in your hab. Theo says you like plants more than people."

"Not true!" She pretended to take the honey tube back. "I only like plants more than *most* people."

"Well if it helps any, he's got plenty to distract him now with this megadiamond."

"Oiu, c'est magnifique. No honey for him," Pia smoothed out her uniform before realizing what she said. "Don't even say it, no honey for anyone."

Chapter 8

This time Pia made sure she kept her chip linked in before the meeting, and even managed to pull up the various supporting files and charts that Miller had attached. There were soil composition readouts from all over Ceres, along with inventories of their available equipment.

She almost didn't recognize the command module when she got there, because a holo of Ahuna Mons took up most of the room and all movable work platforms were folded back towards the walls. The Spine itself was hidden at the center of the holo mountain, and Miller waited at the shimmering base, right where Pia emerged from the airlock.

The Commander knelt down in his beautifully tailored flight suit and offered Pia a hand up off the ladder.

"Why thank you, such a gallant Commander we have," Pia said warily, "I should start arriving early to every meeting."

"Yes you should, because it's your job." Miller said, smiling through the barb.

"Ahhh, now that's the Commander I know. I was beginning to worry you might be running a fever."

"Cute, but I have no time for our little games, have a seat please."

Pia somehow resisted the urge to gag, and took a seat at the end of a row farthest from Miller. She busied herself estimating how much power was spent by printing out eight single use chairs. In the next few minutes the others filed in and chose seats as if they were a grade school class. To Pia's surprise, Lara made a point of sitting next to her, while Zee went over to the seat beside Miller.

Lara leaned over to her before the meeting began. "I need a break from these tech boys. You don't know how lucky you are to have a separate hab that doesn't smell of B.O. and desperation."

The two of them laughed a little bit too loudly and drew a glare from Miller, who was looking for a quiet moment to begin. Soon all eyes were on him, and he gave a signal to Zee, who wordlessly began to animate the hologram.

Sunlight pierced through the diamond wall, illuminating the whole room with a warm blue glow. The tiny circle of Sun came to rest behind the peak as the animation paused.

"Dawn...a new type of dawn for a new era in human history. No other human beings have ever been this far from Earth before...let that sink in for a moment. With all the excitement of our mission to date, it's easy to lose sight of that monumental fact."

He paused a moment in what looked like a bit of dramatic flair, but which also allowed the next part of his display to continue. The mountain began shrinking as the view pulled quickly back across the landscape of Ceres. It settled over a huge crater with a blinding white splotch at its center.

"Occator," Miller continued, "this crater is the key to it all. Right now we're sending drones and cargo bots to scrape away at the surface and bring it back to Cerex. But at our current rate, it could be years before we have a self-sustaining base able to properly mine Ahuna and begin refueling for the first return flight. This is not acceptable."

Miller paced in front of the seated crew. "Right now we have a brief window of opportunity before the other Multinats attack. We've been fortunate beyond our wildest dreams, and yet cursed as well. If we let our temporary advantage slip away, it could mean a multiworld war."

"You have a plan then, I assume?" Colonel Vineland challenged. He rarely spoke, and it drew considerable attention from the crew when he did.

Miller motioned to Zee again. The holo zoomed out to encompass most of Ceres. It looked ancient and strangely beautiful to Pia, its ash gray surface covered with craters and specks of bright white.

"What I propose..." Miller scanned the room slowly while trying to detect any opposition, "is flying to Occator."

"Fly Cerex?" Barton asked incredulously. "The anchored spacecraft with no engines and no fuel?"

Gabe and Theo started brainstorming simultaneously, "The engines are printable, but it will take months for even the first one to be completed," Gabe started, then Theo jumped in. "Fuel is just as long a project, maybe longer. Shorter for a jump to Occator I guess, but we still need a fuel burst for liftoff."

Zee was next to speak, "If you're counting on the mini thrusters for anything beyond flight control, I wouldn't. They mostly just know how to keep things vertical and how to slow them down."

"That might be enough," Miller countered. "We just need to set an explosive charge big enough to kick us up off the surface and then the minis could take over..."

"An explosive charge is not going anywhere near this ship, Commander, with all due respect, " Vineland interjected sternly.

"Well it doesn't have to be an explosive charge, I don't know, I'll leave the details to you. The point is, this is happening. It has to if our mission is going to succeed."

Barton was next to object. "It's way too risky, even for me. As you so lavishly pointed out," she motioned to the hologram, "this ship is stable, on the surface of a dwarf planet, tens of millions of kilometers away from the next nearest human, and by some miracle we're all alive. Not to mention we're parked next to a jewel the size of Chicago. Our first priority *has* to be safety."

Miller waited for support, but only silence filled the room. Sarah tried to drive home her argument. "There has to be better options...sir. We could cannibalize other equipment to build more bots and accelerate the retrieval process from Occator."

Gabe chimed in, "I'm sure I could find parts for half a dozen more rovers."

"I could drill deeper exploratory holes to see if any resource rich regolith is nearby," suggested Theo.

The mood was turning against Miller, and he sensed it. "These are still all much too slow," Miller announced. "We need to start thinking of the big picture. With enemy ships incoming, everything we have now is at risk.

Miller was on a roll, "They'll send military ships and attack drones to eliminate us and buy them more time. Those ships launched shortly after we did, meaning they could come rain down laser fire on us any day now. We have equipped ourselves with some defensive capabilities, but with the resources at Occator we could manufacture safer habitats and greater weaponry in a matter of weeks."

The crew looked around at each other searching for some sort of consensus, but found none. Now it was Miller's turn to go for the kill. "I know that this is where I'm supposed to take a vote and see if you all agree with my plan...but that's just not going to happen."

He glared around the room, and his eyes were already imagining his future wealth and power. "In order to prevent a massive war, finally bring peace and stability to Earth, and because I damn well say so, we're taking Cerex to Occator. You're the best at what you do. Figure out how we make it happen."

Miller walked over to the Spine, clicking a button which made the holo mountain disappear. He quickly climbed up to his command platform, leaving a stunned group scattering while starting to brainstorm via their chips. Pia began retreating back to her garden, then stopped and turned back. She walked with purpose now, more and more convinced that she would never see Earth again. Her target was lingering while he formatted the room back to normal.

"You talk big behind his back, but you're just another yes man, aren't you?" she confronted Zee.

He tried to ignore the insult and pretend he was lost in his work, but Pia gave him a shove right in the chest.

"Wake up, will you? Miller is going to get us killed, if some drone doesn't do the job first apparently, and you scurry off to program pretty mountain holos for him?" Pia raised her shaking fists between them.

Zee was silent for a few seconds, then took her hands into his. "Some things can't be changed, no matter how much you or I wish it was different."

Pia's eyes opened in wild confusion as she started for the ladder exit. Before stepping onto the top rung, Pia looked up one last time, her face flush with a few tears. "What the hell does that mean?"

"It means I'm on your side, whether you believe me or not. And I need you to trust me."

Pia's face became calm, and she swiped the tears off defiantly. "Stay the hell out of my chip, asshole."

Chapter 9

After two days of protests and arguments, a plan was finally agreed upon. With Ceresian gravity being so weak, an initial kick off the surface could replace a sustained engine burn. To everyone's great relief, no explosions were required.

The engineers devised a collection of piston tubes which they welded to the hull all around its base. When triggered, the pistons would drive meter long rods down against steel plates anchored beneath each tube. Once all thirty tubes were charged and linked for simultaneous firing, Miller gave the word for launch prep. Everyone settled into G netting and chipped into their data streams. Since everything was well within safe limits for the life support systems, Pia signaled she was a go for the jump.

Pia found herself longing for ground beneath her feet. Whenever she felt nervous, the softness of soil on her bare feet calmed her mind. Now in the confines of metal and plastic, she felt completely adrift. She closed her eyes and felt soft blades of grass brushing her toes. With the help of her chip she conjured up vivid memories and made them seem real. Cool wet grass at dawn. Walking barefoot through the forest undergrowth.

Her focus snapped back as Vineland finished his final checks. Miller took his moment to be the center of attention. "Alright people, time is not on our side. Let's get this done so we can start mining. Go for launch, Colonel."

Vineland merely glanced at Miller before returning to his work. Thirty awkward seconds later he said, "Thank you, Commander. Engaging pistons now.

Pia braced herself for an initial slam into the netting, but nothing happened. She looked over at Theo and Lara, and they both seemed equally confused. Against her better wishes her eyes shot to Zee, who was working as if everything happened as planned. "Are we...?" she asked no one in particular.

Sarah came to her rescue by projecting a holo wall with an outside camera. "We're up."

Pia stared at the video and didn't notice much at first, but then Ahuna seemed to shrink steadily into the background.

"Solid lift, speed at ten meters per second vertical, forty lateral," Vineland announced.

Without an engine blast, the launch was more of a jump, but with the extremely low gravity that jump was enough to send them flying. If not for Zee's drones, Cerex might not land for months, stranded in orbit with no fuel to maneuver. Zee seemed intensely aware of his role and was openly sweating as he made minor adjustments to the thrust of particular drones.

Most of the crew had nothing to do, and yet for the next three hours of flight they had to stay in their nets. Gabe was the first to break the tension.

"So no inflight meal? Peanuts?"

"Shut up," Theo grumbled, his hulking mass resting uncomfortably like a huge caterpillar stuck on a spider web, "you're making me hungry." Everyone relaxed a bit watching Theo squirm.

The initial jump could barely have gone any better, with Cerex only having to correct course by two degrees. The thrusters slowed momentum until just enough remained to provide a gentle rainbow arc ending at Occator. The terrain began getting more rugged and cratered as they went. Cerex had to skim the four kilometer high southeastern rim, then slow to a vertical descent inside the crater.

"Let's put her down in the northwest quadrant," Vineland decided, "gives us the most gradual drop."

Coburn suddenly lifted his head above his netting. "What's our path through Occator?"

"Dead center almost," Zee said proudly, "we had a perfect jump."

"There's such a thing as too perfect, you know?"

"What's your point, Geoff? Kinda busy here."

"My point is Cerealia Facula," he said heatedly, "the haze." No one seemed to have a clue what he was talking about, so he added, "CereSat tracked consistent haze caused by outgassing, with a density reaching..."

An intense flash came from all directions, followed by a brief but violent shaking of the entire ship. All crew went to work assessing damages.

Zee reported first, "no response from the drones...wait, some are coming back online."

"Life support has us losing air down on the tech deck. Must have a breach, tiny based on air loss rate, but definitely there," Pia said out loud as she read the data herself.

Miller looked frantic, his hair roughed up by his gyrations in the netting. "Where's the attack coming from? Who has eyes on any ships?" He was nearly screaming out questions as rapidly as he thought of them. "McKinnon, swing us around and return fire!"

"We're less than five minutes from landing, there's no room to maneuver," Vineland objected.

"There's no maneuvering, period, full stop," Zee clarified. "Only seven drones are functioning and able to help slow us. We're gonna hit, hard."

Everyone fell silent as they processed what that meant, then resumed their feverish pace of mostly useless data checks. Theo glanced at the flight holo and his heart dropped down through his stomach.

"Screw the gods, we're spinning," Theo said.

"Eloquent as always," Zee responded, "but yeah, trying to find out which part of Cerex is gonna impact."

Miller demanded answers. "If it was an attack, where are the follow up strikes? What the hell is going on here?!"

Coburn was bracing as if he expected a crash at any moment, but pried his eyes open following Miller's outburst. "We're not under any attack, Commander. It was the goddamn haze."

"Start making a whole lot more sense in a hurry, Geoff."

"The haze over Cerealia Facula," Coburn went on, "had tons of free hydrogen. We just flew dozens of pilot lights through a gas leak and blew ourselves up. The only thing that stopped us from being obliterated was the super low density of the atmosphere."

Zee was desperately trying to stop the spin so impact would happen where he chose, but he was clearly angry. "How was that not brought up at any meetings? Come down at this descent angle, slow at this rate, and oh yeah, don't fly over this spot or you'll blow us all up? Unbelievable!"

Vineland stepped in to regain control. "Zee! Get us stable if you can. Everyone else is going into pod lockdown in ten seconds. Try to relax while the pod system does its thing. We have just over a minute until impact, so there's no time for debate. Pods engaging now."

Pia felt cold gel fragments spraying against her body from all angles, pressing her suit uncomfortably against her skin as it locked every fold and crease in place. In a few seconds the gel ceased and she lay there encased in a thick shell of what looked like blue jello. Only her face remained uncovered by what her chip informed her was a hybrid of ballistic shock absorbing gel and a rudimentary life support system.

The outer layer stiffened to Kevlar strength to protect against shrapnel, while the rest used advanced medical nanotech to treat injuries. The netting separated smoothly, with half the straps tightening to grip the hard outer gel. The other half widened to become a solid graphene egg with the inner netting anchored at various points. All this was done in under thirty seconds, a thoroughly impressive and disconcerting feat.

It was hard to concentrate on anything other than getting egged, but Pia noticed the ship had nearly stopped spinning. Just then time ran out.

The crash began with a thunder of slow motion violence. The ship hit going a mere 20 km/hr, but its massive bulk wouldn't give up without a fight. The bottom hull furrowed deeply into a surface untouched for billions of years, causing the helm to lift up dozens of meters in counterpoint. It reached nearly a 45 degree tilt before letting out a terrifyingly loud creak which had Pia convinced the ship was going to break in half. But sure and steady the helm dropped again, until it landed hard on the scarred path Cerex had created.

Chapter 10

Pia was afraid to check the data streams, but from the lack of panic in the crew who called out she knew the ship was at least intact.

"Way better than the diamond mountain, boss," Theo groaned.

Barton was first to snap back into the lead. "Systems show a slightly enlarged crack on the tech deck, but it seems to be in a section that's buried at the moment, so that buys us some time. Ship integrity is holding, no other signs of breach. Cerex is a tough bitch," she smiled proudly, "initiating pod release on your command, Colonel."

"Go ahead, Sarah, get everyone out."

The reversal began immediately on Pia's egg, with the inner shell pulling back out and taking most of the jello mold off with it. Pia sank downwards and was gently caught by a handful of support straps, which held her briefly until the egg cracked itself open. The others were all being dropped out of their respective eggs as well.

Zee had been thrown hard against the central spine anchor point after keeping his netting loose enough to project all of his holo screens. His left arm hung limp at his side, but as he sat there he was furiously issuing commands to his microdrones about the ship.

Vineland had kept his netting loose as well; the webbing had left his face with long scrape marks. In his element, his body moved in the rapid but relaxed bursts of someone trained to react without panic.

"Let's get out and work this problem, people!" Vineland leapt from egg to egg in the low G, issuing commands. "Good work on the landing, Zee. Full status check with visual confirmation on every wire, bolt, and panel on Cerex."

A distracted grunt of approval was all Zee managed, but he hadn't stopped working since before the piston launch.

"Coburn, take the Commander and reestablish a link with Natocorps," Vineland ordered. Let them know we're still alive."

Miller was a bit dazed. Coburn had to grab hold of the Commander's uniform, lift him from his harness, and guide him towards the unfolding Comm Center.

"Sarah," Vineland said, "I need you with Hixley, Santos, and Koeniger. You and Koeniger suit up and take a rover to patch Cerex from the outside. Hixley, Santos, you two head to Tech Hab C and seal us up from inside."

As Sarah and the STEMs went off through the ship, Vineland turned to Pia.

"Secure life support and assess any soft damages. But take a look at Zee's arm first." With that he was off, heading to inspect each deck himself.

Pia never thought of herself as a doctor, but she had spent her mandatory service year trained as a field medic. She hadn't treated more than the occasional broken bone or cuts in over a decade, but the work always excited her. Muscle memory kicked in as she bounded in Ceres gravity across the tilted room to Zee's pod.

To her surprise, he was using both hands again, with his left arm ever so slightly tucked inward. "It's nothing. Don't worry about it, Pia, I just gave it a good smack. It's feeling better already.

She rolled her eyes and smirked. "You damn men. Just give me your arm, dummy." She held her own hand out and flapped her long fingers inwards demanding his arm. "Give it here, let me look."

He realized she wasn't going anywhere, so he lifted his arm up to her. He winced a little as Pia gently rotated his arm in various ways. Then suddenly she stopped and her moss green eyes shot him a serious glare.

"Your ulna is broken, Zee. Not a hairline either, this one is partially displaced. How are you even using it right now?"

"It's fine, it doesn't even hurt much," he protested.

"Miller's gonna lose his shit if I don't get your arm set."

"Why, because he cares about us so much? If we can't stabilize this ship, we lose all mission capability. The arm is broken, I get it. The adrenaline must be keeping me going, but until it stops working, I keep working."

"I'm heading to the garden, and then I AM coming back to set this arm, understood? You won't be much good to us if you can't keep flailing your arms around like always."

He didn't even look up as she turned and bounded back towards the exit, but before she closed the hatch he heard her yell back.

"Be careful with the arm!"

Zee grinned. He quickly opened a private line through their chips in response.

'As you wish, princess.'

Pia worked her way back into the forest core through a mess unleashed by their crash landing. With Cerex laying on its side there was no artificial gravity, making her little kingdom more of an odd donut shaped tunnel. She opened the airlock only after rechecking with her chip that the area was intact. Once at the top of the entrance ladder, Pia peeked out to survey the damage.

The recent impact made her forest look like it had been through a hurricane. She glanced upwards again at the glowing Spine which shone like a greenhouse light, and suddenly she had a plan. Debris blocked most of the normal pathways, so she would try for the Spine instead. Ten meters was an easy hop in Ceresian gravity.

'Now I really do look like a superhero,' she thought as she flew up and grabbed hold of a narrow ladder running the length of the Spine.

The damage looked less severe from this height. Pia climbed along the ladder until she neared the end of the tube.

Just then Zee came through loud on the shipwide comm. *'Hold onto your butts, people. We're going vertical.'*

Before Pia could respond, the ship began vibrating. Her perch on the Spine tilted until she was clinging to it like the crow's nest of a mast. Outside the hull, Zee's tiny drones had all been rebooted and were working to get Cerex upright again.

"Holy shit," Pia spat out, as she recoiled from the view. She found herself looking down a hundred meter chasm with metal platforms interspersed along the way. It was like a tree house built up the sides of a giant redwood, with the Spine as the glowing central trunk. Looking down at the newly defined ground floor, Pia saw a great big claustrophobic mess.

As she planned how to get safely from platform to platform, her ears pricked up. *'Some wiring must have shorted out'*, she thought as the noise grew louder. Then as the first bee flew by her nose, she realized what had happened. From her vantage point she could only see two of the ten hives onboard, but one of them had its inner slats knocked open and bees were streaming out.

The emergency lighting of the Spine acted like their daily sunrise beacon, and soon dozens of bees were buzzing nearby. One landed on her face causing her to instinctively swat at it, momentarily releasing her handholds. In the hasty maneuver, she accidentally pushed off enough that she couldn't regain her grip.

The gravity was slight, and Pia might have easily jumped her way carefully down the tube. But without a big enough kick off the Spine, she began to drift downwards. At least the bees were no longer an issue, with most already crawling along their artificial beacon at the central Spine.

Slowly, imperceptibly at first, she picked up speed. While trying desperately not to look down, Pia stared at the lush greenery of her garden which passed in front of her faster by the second. Panic took hold, making her limbs rigid and her throat tight.

'Ready to set my arm, Pia?' Zee asked casually in her head.

'Fuck, fuck, fuck,' was all she could respond. Zee was silent for a moment, then returned.

'Just ran the numbers, you're gonna be ok at impact...I think you'll be fine.'

All she managed was a low groan, eyes locked downwards and kicking her legs wildly as the floor approached. *'You THINK? I'm going to punch a hole through the floor in a few seconds!'*

'23 seconds by my count,' Zee said seriously, *'no more than 8 m/s at impact.'*

'Don't you fucking say impact again, you hear me?'

'You got this, Pia, gonna be a rough landing, but doable. Can you reach anything to grab and slow yourself?'

'Stop talking now,' she barked out, instinct kicking in. She focused down on the point where her feet would hit, where there was a jumbled mess of tools and branches. She quickly formed a plan. *'If I extend my legs to absorb the initial hit, maybe I can push sideways into a roll.'*

The instant her feet made contact, they promptly slid sideways as soil underneath gave way. Her planned tuck and roll transformed into a full length body slam as her head smacked the steel floor, knocking herself out cold.

'Pia, are you ok? Pia! Pia?' Blackness settled comfortably over her once more as she felt the pleasing coolness of soil on her face.

Part 3
Occator Unleashed

Chapter 11

THE LAST THING PIA remembered was falling, and the ache throughout her entire body let her know the landing must have been rough. As her eyes slowly opened, she scanned her surroundings and found she was no longer in her forest hab. She didn't recognize the room at first. It was much too clean for a tech, but not nearly nice enough to be Commander Miller's, thank God. Then she saw Barton's freckled face and red hair hovering nearby.

Sara's expression softened after seeing Pia awake. "You've really got to stop falling off shit, ok? I'm rusty as hell at working these autodoc kits." She motioned for Pia to stay laying down. "Rest, you have some time, and a concussion by the looks of it. Couple hairline fractures in your ribs. Sprained your ankle something fierce. I thought the least I could do is give you my bunk for a bit."

Pia began to speak but nothing came out. She collected her thoughts and concentrated before trying again.

"Th....thank you, Sara," she finally managed to say, "make sure my cast is cooler than Zee's."

"Zee was just here checking up on you. He looked pretty torn up about you getting hurt. Said he should've made sure everyone was ready for the shift. Didn't you get the comm alerts?"

Pain streaked through her head as she instinctively tried to roll her eyes. As she regained her composure she made herself a promise to stop being so stubborn and just embrace the Datanet chip.

"But wasn't he hurt? I don't understand, how long was I out?"

"About an hour or so. He looked fine to me, little skinny for my taste, though," Sara winked at her. "I'm probably just jealous since I don't get any bedside checkups."

As the fog in her mind persisted, Pia gave up fighting and decided she must have imagined Zee's injury.

Recuperating was not nearly as boring as she anticipated. While she was healing, the rest of the crew had all lurched into high gear, filling the comm lines and Datanet with plenty of interesting information. As she lay in Sara's bunk, her mind flew through the cables and networks of Cerex. Her implant let her expand her thoughts wider until data came to her as easily as breathing. Inhale: the data was scoured, organized, threads followed, records made. Breathe out: requests sent, comm links established, old data purged.

Soil samples had come back off the scales for useful volatiles. There were numerous salt compounds and ice layers that extended for nearly ten meters in depth at spots. Cerex herself had helped by gouging a path that deep during landing. Now the walls of the crash impact looked like a layer cake.

Despite Miller's insanity, the new location really did set things in motion for the Cerex crew. The entire spacecraft had been coiled up waiting with all her real talents hidden in deep storage until now. As different parts of the ship came alive and stretched their gears and circuitry, Pia's chip could follow it all in beautiful detail.

After the initial reconnaissance phase that mirrored what had happened at Ahuna Mons, this time the activity kept ramping up with each passing hour. With so much raw material right on the surface, Theo skipped the drill rigs and set up one large plastic domed processing station.

Gabe had a growing fleet of rovers to scoop up a cubic meter at a time of the soft upper layers of Ceres. They delivered their load to Theo's station, which in turn began heating and separating the soil.

The real magic began once these initial processed materials were brought back onboard. The entire STEM labs were buzzing with excitement as they could finally get their hands on the industrial size 3-D printers waiting on the lower storage decks. Bulk supplies of basic materials such as carbon, silicon, and hydrogen were transformed within minutes into parts for everything from rovers and drones to solar cells and simple buildings.

The only setback in moving from Ahuna Mons to Occator was the mist from the frequent geyser plumes. It didn't seem like much when viewed from CereSat, but at ground level the mist gathered in the crater basin and made everything look a bit blurry and faded.

Some began affectionately calling their new home the Fog Bowl, but Lara was not among them. Solar generation was cut in half by the gauzy atmosphere, and she was devising a battery charging station to be installed high up on the nearest crater edge.

Lara couldn't keep up with the energy demands, so Theo fashioned a rudimentary engine to brute force some extra energy for the printers.

Once her concussion had cleared, Pia was eager to get back to her forest. There was so much to clean up, starting with the bee colonies. After overruling some objections, she decided to go take a look and get back to work. Much to her surprise, the bulk of the debris had already been cleared away.

Looking up from the entry hatch, the full scope of how far she fell really sank in for her. Pia said a little prayer thanking Ceres for such weak gravity, or else she would have been a pancake.

She decided the best way to get over any fear she still had was to get climbing again right away. Even on only one healthy foot, she could do her Wonder Woman jumps from platform to platform. Fear was quickly replaced by embarrassment that she managed to get herself hurt in this gravity. Literally the only way to do it was to fall straight down where you can't reach anything to push off of...just as she did. Her playful grinning turned to a grimace each time she caught herself on a platform and her broken ribs were flexed.

The bee hives had been her biggest concern, but other than an overabundance of honey they were doing fine. Better than fine, in fact, as the two colonies which were destroyed during the crash seemed to have joined up with the remaining ones. She had barely finished clearing the honey from the hives when Miller barked at her through the comm.

'Enough playtime. If you're clear to work, you need to ditch that garden and come help Zee with the life support systems.'

'So much for resting up,' she thought. *'On my way to STEM deck, Commander.'*

'Try again. Down on storage deck two, I'm updating your ship map...now.' Pia bristled at his tone, but was distracted by an update warning as her current ship maps changed suddenly. They were showing three entire new floors down in deep storage.

'How the hell did that just happen?!' She struggled to make sense of it while sliding down a plastic wire zipline she had set up to ease the climbing.

Now that she was fully adjusted to her chip, the idea that the information it gave her could be wrong or hidden seemed unsettling. Though it immediately made sense logically to her, the thought had naively never crossed her mind before now.

When she arrived at the right deck, she had to wait as Zee unlocked an impressive door security panel to let her inside. The room was one cavernous whole, with only the central Spine obstructing the view across. This was beneath her forest floor level, close to where the main engines had been anchored.

All around the level there were enormous machines of the sort that only exist in the secret labs of nameless corporations. They reminded Pia of the hulking computer mainframes from a century ago. She was getting ready to search out Zee at some hidden terminal when out he slid from underneath the one by her feet.

"Holy hell!" She spit out, startled half to death, then groaned as her ribs protested the sudden movement.

Zee jumped up and rushed to her side, gently placing one hand on her shoulder and the other on the small of her back to help steady her. The gesture could easily have been unwanted, but he seemed so genuinely concerned that it came off as very caring. Once she had ceased tightening her lips in pain, he stepped back again, slowly this time.

"It seems I can't stop hurting you. I'm so so sorry for the ship tilt. It won't happen again, I promise. I'll do a quick verbal check with everyone to be sure next time I make a move like that."

She let out a sigh and blew her hair up out of her face. "Maybe just check in with me. The rest of the crew seem to be well aware of these things."

"I will," he promised sweetly. Then off he went to the nearby terminal of the machine he had been working underneath. "C'mon, you've gotta see this."

He hopped into a leather swivel chair and began typing in instructions. She leaned over his shoulder, but whatever he was telling the computer wasn't in any language she knew.

"This is life support?" Pia asked. "Miller told me to help you out, but I'm afraid I don't know any computer languages."

Zee was momentarily lost in thought, but then swiveled back around towards her with a giddy grin on his face.

"You're our resident plant expert, chem genius, all around Bio Pia, right?

"Bio Pia," she chuckled, "I kinda like that. But yeah, I know nothing about these beasts though." She patted the side of the impressive machine beside them.

"Maybe not, but you had better start learning. These babies will be feeding us soon. Absolutely the edge of the cutting edge in tech. I would stay here all day if I could, but Miller is getting paranoid about our defenses not being ready."

"Zee," she grabbed his face carefully with one hand, steadying his focus on her, "what are they?"

"Sorry, food printers! Remember the terminals back at the Natocorps facility? Tinker toys compared to these. Most food printers take complex organic molecule chains and sort of paint with them. These are a game changer. They can synthesize almost any molecule or substance, as long as they are provided the raw materials. Imagine being able to produce food on demand using inorganic base materials."

Zee was excited, and paced around as he explained, "Theo and Gabe have already begun to process serious amounts of hydrogen, along with lesser amounts of dozens of other chemicals. Air and water generators are up and running. As beautiful as you...it is...your hab I mean, it's going obsolete."

She ignored the slip up and pressed her case. "So what am I supposed to do, flip a switch and watch a screen or something? If this is Miller's way of punishing me, he can shove it."

"It's not like that, Pia."

"Bio Pia," she teased.

Zee smiled widely. "He really does need you. These printers are astounding, but they're also temperamental as shit, pardon my French. The chem tech that goes on here is way out of my league. You're the only one who'll be able to follow what's going on and make any adjustments."

Pia sighed long and slowly. "So...what, am I supposed to start reading, I don't know, a manual or something?"

"You always underestimate the power you have right at your fingertips. Try to calm your thoughts, this is going to feel weird."

Before Pia could object, suddenly her mind felt like it got sucked down a deep well, with the real world quickly falling away. Schematics and instructions flooded past her, on their way to some storage spot in her chip.

Her face collapsed, mouth hanging open in a numbed ecstasy of pure thought. Slowly, life returned to her green eyes, blinking in an effort to claw her focus back to her physical surroundings.

"You ok, Pia?" Zee sounded far off. "Pia...can you hear me?"

The voice sounded odd coming from outside of her mind, but eventually she managed to respond.

"What. What? That was...what?" She stammered, as her mind was witnessing her mouth's pathetic attempts to communicate with a mix of amusement and terror. She had never thought so clearly in her life, but it felt as if it had come at the expense of her entire physical well being.

"Oh shit, you're not ok, are you?" Zee's scruffy face was beginning to go ghostly white.

"What the hell did you just do to me, Xander?" She came out of her torpor as suddenly as she had entered it, to the great relief of Zee.

"Holy shit, quit scaring me like that!"

"That's not a fucking answer, Zee!" But as she protested, the answer was already becoming apparent to her. "The machines, I know everything about them now. Jesus, I could build one from scratch if I wanted."

"Direct File Transfer, DiFiT for short, and I'm assuming this was your first time?"

"Yup, you just took my DiFiT card," she laughed. "You can do that again anytime, by the way. I've been meaning to learn Latin."

"Listen, you have no idea how important the data is that I just gave you. Treat it with the proper respect, ok?"

Pia was slightly hurt at his cold shift. But she saw an earnestness in his demeanor that totally diffused the tension.

"Ok, well I'm sorry to DiFiT and run, but I really do have to go. Miller is gonna have my head for taking so long down here with you." And with that he turned and strode toward the open hatch.

But before he climbed the ladder up out of the area, he hesitated and turned back.

His first steps were halting, then grew more confident as he got closer. Just as Pia thought he was going to collide into her, he did. A warm strong hand slid behind her back as he pressed up against her jumpsuit. Pia was stunned, but met his lips with hers without a second thought as his other hand grabbed up through her hair and held her close.

Then as he released her, he stepped back, unsure. Her reddened cheeks and fire filled eyes buoyed his confidence. "I've been wanting to do that for a very long time." He shot her a knowing smirk with a raised eyebrow, then turned again for the exit.

This time it was Pia who stopped him in his tracks, as she called out, "Hey, McKinnon!"

"Yeah?"

"I've been waiting for you to do that for a very long time, too." Then her hair swung out widely as she flipped down onto her back and slid underneath the nearest printer. From underneath the machine she chided him. "Now get back to work!"

Chapter 12

THE NEXT FEW WEEKS were a blur. The settlement grew exponentially, with resources coming in faster than they could be used. There were no immediate plans to ship anything other than precious metals and rare elements back to Earth, so all the rest was being flipped directly into construction.

Pia spent the hours split between her newfound role as printing guru and her twice daily visits back to manage her treehouse, as she'd taken to calling it. The bees had fully assimilated to their new orientation, and the orphaned hives were all adopted successfully. The plants kept thriving, but for now the rigorous measurements and adjusting could stop.

The printers became an astonishing new challenge for her mind to tackle. She quickly ran through prints of all the basic macromolecules in the only available manual, even managing to shave some time off most of them. Simple sugars and fats were appearing out of thin air, or at least it seemed so.

But most of all she thought of Zee, or at least she tried hard to not think about him. Cerex was a big ship, but not big enough to sneak off easily. In fact, the two hadn't spoken since their kiss.

At first she worried he had withdrawn back out of embarrassment or fear of getting caught. Then on the third day of hearing nothing at all, she felt his presence in her chip.

'Hey there, Plant Queen.' She heard his voice as clearly as if he were right there next to her.

She concentrated just as she had practiced a dozen times before, and reached out with her mind until she found him. She sensed him through the electric maze of the ship, and saw his extensive glowing techno aura.

'Found you. And it's Princess Printers now.'

'Ehh, maybe just Princess.' Zee said.

'What are you doing? Need a break?'

'I wish. Trying to keep us safe here, how about you?'

'Well, I'm on track to figure out sucrose by this week.'

After a short mental silence she pushed on, *'that's right, I'm bringing sugar to Ceres! Aren't I sweet?'* She was flailing awkwardly like a teenager on her first date, only worse because she couldn't even see his face. More silence.

When Zee finally responded, his voice came clipped and urgent. *'Pia, I think we're under attack. Get to the nearest exosuit and hold on tight.'*

The now familiar icy panic flowed through her veins, but she did as he asked, and heard him repeat the warning on a shipwide channel as she searched for a suit. Near the exit ladder she found what she needed, a sturdy exosuit with helmet. They were not meant for prolonged work outside, but would keep you alive during emergency exposures. She slipped quickly into the suit and jumped up into the ladder tunnel for cover.

She focused on the metal rungs near her face and managed to calm herself down. When she reached out with her mind towards Zee, an open link was awaiting her. Like a security feed, it showed Zee at his massive holoterminal on STEM deck, but also numerous other system feeds to which she didn't normally have access.

Long range radar and drone fleet orbitals flashed up for her, even the shipwide lockdown controls. *'I need you to have my back if things go badly, Pia. If I can't for any reason, I'm giving you my access codes to stabilize the ship and its life support.'*

Pia was glad to hear Zee's voice again, but recognized that distant tone instantly. He was concentrating on multiple different areas, and his voice came out as a hollow side note to his overloaded mind.

At first there didn't seem to be much to see. Topographical maps of Ceres speckled with what she imagined were exploratory rovers and drones. Orbital readouts from CereSat. Ground layout of the expanded Occator base camp. The camera shot of Cerex herself caused her to do a double take, as it was completely encased in what looked like gray mud. Apparently a lot had changed while she tinkered in the basement with her printers.

In her periphery a growing series of flashing yellow circles caught her attention in the widest range cameras. They didn't appear to be moving, but it must have been because of the scale. As she watched closely, she spotted more highlighted specks slide across an imaginary line and gain their own yellow halos.

They seemed to be spread out across thousands of kilometers of space, but all came from the same direction, and all were heading their way.

She flipped onto the crew channel, expecting a now tiresome scolding from Miller, but also curious for any new information. The voice she heard was not Miller's, but Vineland's, confident as always but searching for facts like the rest of them.

'And we have no visual at all yet on what they are?' Charles asked.

'They're not ours,' Miller responded, *'which means they're hostile.'*

Theo unexpectedly broke through the chatter with his own update. *'Zee, defenses are primed and at your disposal.'*

With so many objects to track and control, only Zee could handle the complexity. His voice was everywhere: in a private link to Pia, over the main comm, and in person with the techs near his terminal. *'Commander, I'm showing three groupings, each with a main ship and a few dozen subs. Still too far for detailed visuals, permission to engage at will?'*

'Granted. Blow those bastards out of our sky.'

'Let's see if any of them have a brain.' Zee's thin hands flew through virtual displays. *'Firing cannon now.'*

No big explosion followed, which Pia realized was silly to expect in a virtual vacuum. Her private access showed her the cannon in question up on the rim of Occator. A simple machine apparently rigged up by Theo, it looked like an oversized potato gun. It built up pressure with gas, then released it to fire a projectile from a long rifling tube. Whatever it shot couldn't have been more than the size of a soccer ball, but in the absence of atmosphere to slow it down, it was moving at nearly three hundred meters per second.

The incoming objects were still several hundred kilometers out, so as the first cannonball traveled, Zee proceeded to fire off one after another from around the crater rim. Each shot followed about twenty seconds apart, and a few dozen shots were on their way by the time the first was approaching its targets.

Pia hadn't been able to look away from the lead cannonball, watching as its tiny blip sped out from Ceres like a worker bee. As it approached to within twenty kilometers of the incoming attack line, the nearest object began adjusting its path to avoid an impact.

'Got their attention,' Pia thought.

Zee updated the crew, then began entering new instructions. Theo's cannon was apparently firing some sort of sturdy mini drone. Zee had the next closest cannonball drone light up like a flare, burning brightly for over thirty seconds before running out of fuel.

'You missed! What the hell, McKinnon?'

Zee barely even registered Miller's yapping. He was examining the screens and holos intently, watching for something.

Pia was actually the first to see it, and quickly alerted Zee. *'They moved towards the heat. Jesus, they'll track onto Cerex too!'*

'Keep your head on, that's a good thing. Trust me, ok?'

The line of incoming attackers were at the four hundred kilometer marker when Zee's next flare drone went off, this time behind the approaching line. The entire spread out net of drones began moving slowly inwards as they attempted to track onto the flare.

'I don't like the looks of their formation, too spread out. And they're moving way too fast for mine to match speeds,' Zee complained.

Pia, along with the rest of the crew watched as drone after drone flew right past the attacking line and then ignited..

'I swear to God,' Miller began, *'if you keep missing, I'm going to come find you and make sure to kill you myself before the rest of us die.'*

This time Barton stepped in and said what the others were thinking. *'Commander, he's saved our butts more times than I can remember already, please just let the man work.'*

Miller was fuming, both at Zee and how Barton made him look scared in front of everyone. *'What the hell was that about,'* Pia began asking Zee, but he cut her off early.

'He's a petty, arrogant, insecure little man, that's what.'

After ten drones all flared up and died behind enemy lines, the purpose seemed more clear. Zee had lured the entire dragnet of incoming attackers to within about a ten kilometer wide cluster, and made them slow themselves considerably as well.

'Time to get up close and personal.'

The next cannonball fired its thrusters in full reverse until it came to a halt and then began fleeing the nearest main enemy craft. The gap between them closed fast at first, but by the time they collided there was only a five km/hr difference in their speed. Zee's drone latched on and began inspecting its counterpart.

This enemy drone was clearly a weapon of some sort, and appeared to have dockings where its much smaller companions had only recently detached. It made sense that the mini swarm wouldn't have the fuel or thrust to manage a trip from either the Moon or Earth on their own.

The suction grips on Zee's cannonbot made it resemble a remora attaching itself to a passing shark. It drilled holes through the outer casing and inserted a handful of cameras, sensors, and miniature laser cutters. Pia could see wiring inside, with a second inner hull which kind of looked like a torpedo.

Time was quickly running out as the nearest missile was now under a hundred kilometers from Ceres. Zee feverishly worked the controls to attempt a breach of the inner casing. This second material was much sturdier, causing him to send his robot sensors sideways between the inner and outer hull.

Pia stared at the feeds intently as beads of sweat built up at her hairline. She went to swipe her hair back out of her face when she heard a faint click and then, for the briefest of moments, she imagined she saw a thin curl of blue flame.

Suddenly all of her external feeds flared brightly and then blinked off. It's a strange feeling to be blinded in your thoughts, but not in your eyes. It was as if half of her mind was simply switched off. The cannonbot sensors, the long range CereSat data, even the perimeter cameras around the ship, all showed nothing but static. The only thing left intact was internal Cerex hardlines and shipwide comm channels, which promptly filled up in pandemonium.

'*Are we hit?*' Vineland asked incredulously.

'*Of course we were hit, you son of a bitch!*' Miller screeched back.

The rest of the crew all yelled over each other to be quiet, wanting to hear from Zee.

'*I thought so,*' was all he muttered to himself. '*Where are you all now?*'

'*Jesus, what was that?*' Pia pleaded with Zee on their private channel to explain.

'*Releasing sensor net Gamma,*' he stated flatly. A hundred specialized microdrones spewed out of partially obscured holes in the mud encrusted surface of Cerex.

Then to Pia, quickly he said, '*EMP, from a nuke.*'

As the new sensor array deployed, the crew struggled to make sense of the neural blackout.

Geoff was next to chime in. *'Sir, a blackout like this had to come from an EMP blast. But with no apparent damage to Cerex itself, it must not have come from a nuclear bomb.'*

Theo knew explosives, and called bullshit immediately. *'This is space, Burnsy, no air.'*

'Yes I know there's no air, and no rocks either, so maybe you let the big kids talk, huh?'

Theo was about to go find the sniveling little twerp when Zee finally controlled the situation again. *'Theo's right, at roughly a hundred kilometers, there's nothing left of a blast wave. No air means no extra material to heat, only the mass of the bomb itself is available to spread out in the explosion-'*

Miller cuts him off, *'So there was an explosion?'*

'Oh yes, my probe tripped a defense mechanism on one of the main incoming. I figured as much, they wouldn't want me to take them apart like I did when we left lunar orbit. New array is operational now, the other two nukes were blown up and triggered in a cascade. All bogies appear to be neutralized. Firing another flare now.'

All eyes and minds turned to the new feed which popped up showing the radar array. The flare drone lit itself up, but there was no movement from anything in the area.

Pia scanned her own more detailed feed which showed lesser circles around suspected debris. Some were going at a tremendous speed, pushed along by the leading edge of the nuke's shockwave. As she saw a stray target lock pop up almost overlapping that of Cerex on the screen, instinct kicked in.

'Exosuits, everyone, impact any second.'

'What are you seeing, Pia?' Zee began, but stopped as a collision shook Cerex down to its carbon fiber Spine. The hull seemed intact, and only a few sensitive systems were blinking warnings. There was a sound like heavy rain all around, and for a brief moment Pia imagined her field tent back in Pando.

By now Zee had retaken the lead and jumped back onto the main comm with confidence. *'Now that we've once again somehow managed not to die, I'd like to direct your attention to the eastern side of the plane. If you can find a window nearby you'll see the newly formed Occator geyser spouting what looks to be organics rich sleet in tremendous amounts. Everyone be sure to thank our thoughtful competitors if they still exist upon our return to Earth.'*

Theo and Sara were first to a window while the others tried accessing any outside cameras. Sara let out a gritty shout of joy as Theo picked her up and spun her around. She grabbed two handfuls of his dirty blond hair and messed it up playfully.

"Now no more excuses for taking a bath!" Sara laughed.

Chapter 13

IN THE AFTERMATH OF the explosion, Zee confirmed that each main attack ship had been a sizable nuclear missile. When Zee leveraged their heat seeking ability and gathered them close, setting off one nuke had destroyed them all.

All but one. The stray rocket had torn its way into the bottom of Occator, no farther than a couple hundred meters away.

"It must have locked on to Cerex, but was moving too fast to adjust in time to impact us directly," Zee had explained at the briefing following the celebration. "That explosion was large but definitely not nuclear. It opened up a fissure roughly 10 meters wide and must have tapped into whatever source has been causing the periodic geyser action that we were unlucky enough to experience during descent."

"As for our own beat up but beautiful ship, if you were wondering...while you science nerds were off doing experiments, me and Theo were improvising some defenses. Theo played in the dirt mostly...typical, while I built the flare drones." He winked at Theo. "The EMP risk was diminished nearly a thousandfold by the mud bath Theo gave Cerex and the substations. Each is coated with a foot or more of dense clays formed from the crater regolith mixed with water. The chip blackout should be temporary, too. The substations, assuming they're not damaged from the explosion or light sleet we're experiencing at the moment, should just require a jump. In Cerex herself, we're good."

Miller interjected, but more mildly than with his usual bluster. The repeated heroics by the crew had effectively minimized his role as commander, and though his massive hubris remained, he had been forced to narrow his focus considerably. Fame and power beyond reason lay waiting for him back on Earth, while on Ceres he was becoming a tolerable nuisance. Thinking of home made Miller suddenly panic.

"Oh God, CereSat! We lost our only link with NatoCorps?"

Zee grinned widely, "As soon as the first missile blipped up on radar, I sent CereSat to wait it out in high polar orbit. You can thank me later."

Relief washed over Miller's face, but was quickly replaced by shock and anger.

"How exactly did you bypass my personal controls, McKinnon?"

Silence all around. Miller couldn't run this operation without Zee, but refused to be blatantly disrespected in front of the crew.

Finally Zee smirked. "I didn't, technically. I had parked a few heavy thrust drones nearby after we first landed. Just in case we lost comm link with it, of course. Hope that's ok...Commander."

Zee could see the battery acid running through Miller's blood, but somehow he kept his composure.

"Alright. Well, we're lucky we still have our satellite link. Geoff, find it and let's set it back into its usual orbit. Now," doing his best to reassert control of the conversation, "tell me about this geyser. Are we in danger from the spray?"

Pia jumped in, angry at how Zee was being dressed down. "I think we'd all be in trouble if Cerex couldn't handle a little snowstorm Jared, no?" Then she scrunched up her nose and upper lip in the way French women have mastered for centuries. "I've been monitoring the outpouring, and it's already slowed considerably. Less than half the volume is coming out compared to immediately following the impact."

"Stage fright in front of an audience," joked Sara.

"Lara, is it obstructing the solar arrays?" Miller deadpanned, ignoring Sara.

"My arrays are most likely garbage," she let out with a sigh. "Unlike some of you, my equipment couldn't get treated to Theo's little mud bath, so it's probably toast. The materials can be reused of course, but our power is going to be way down until we get the arrays back up again."

Pia interjected again. "With all due respect, forget the arrays. We need to get a bot down there immediately. If we manage to get access to whatever water source is powering that geyser, we'll have more power than we can ever use."

"We can't just send a bot over to get launched off planet by the outgassing." Santos wasn't onboard with risking his machinery, understandably so.

"We can't just sit here and wait for the damn hole to freeze back over!" Pia said.

Theo didn't get mad, but he came over and gently held Pia's shoulders, squatting down to her height.

"That's exactly what we have to do. We'll send a melter, don't worry." He laughed at not being the most excited one to start digging for once.

"But first the fissure has got to stabilize. Then we melt our way down, and the water refreezes behind us. As long as the ice is 10 meters thick or more, that should give plenty of strength to prevent it from cracking open again right away."

Pia wasn't sold yet. "But then what good is the water if it's stuck under 10 meters of ice?"

"Oh ye of little faith. Theo has already thought of everything. I had to do a similar job once in Norway setting up a bunker for the President of some..."

"Theo, how?!" Pia growled anxiously.

"Alright, alright! We install a valve to handle the pressure and let us control the outflow. As long as we can get down deep enough and anchor the valve into the surrounding ice, we're good to go. Simple job."

"How long?" Miller asked.

"Harder to say, with the repairs and power losses. But I can get a test melter ready by the time she freezes solid enough to get near her. Tomorrow, likely."

"Make it happen, Theo." Miller charged out of the room, determined to be the first to leave.

The prototype Theo came up with was crude looking at best. Measuring nearly three meters long and almost a meter wide at the base, it resembled an enormous tear drop with nanomachinery crammed into the entire tail of the structure. The front was a miniaturized nuclear reactor, which Pia was concerned to learn was one of many already in use onboard.

The geyser had slowed considerably in the first hours after the attack, but didn't cease entirely for another two days. At Vineland's urging, they waited one more day to be sure the area was frozen solid. Santos repurposed an ore collection rover to shuttle the melter into place, but Theo rode along for the placement.

The land surrounding the eruption lay buried under a few meter[6]s of snow. A second rover ended up being necessary to plow a road and uncover the original blast site, with icy spears jutting out in a frozen explosion. The plow shattered these fairly easily, sending a storm of ice fragments flying away in slow motion arcs. Eventually Theo was able to outline the main circular depression, a new scar on a surface largely untouched for billions of years.

Between the low gravity and his massive Nordic frame, he was able to lift the nuclear teardrop with ease out of its makeshift harness. He carried it down the gentle slope, placing it in the snow as if it were a baby carrier.

To Pia's chip the melter looked lit up like a mini sun, reminding her of what it contained. She watched as he triggered the device to begin heating up, and felt Zee on the edges of her thoughts, a playful reminder of their connection that passed as the digital equivalent of flirting.

Zee had been busy as usual with the clean up and repair work following the attack, but still managed to surprise Pia with small signs of affection. Once while she was arms deep in the wiring of a food printer, he overrode a nearby sensor panel and had it play birdsongs. She slid out from under the machinery when she heard it, and saw the entire open floor of the printer subdeck had been holographically transformed into a beautiful forest stream.

Pia shook off the memories for the task at hand, monitoring Theo's life support readings, frustrated at how often her thoughts of Zee had begun interrupting her work.

'I've got some movement.' Theo's voice boomed out through the comm with nervous excitement. While others may have been nervous, he was like a kid about to open up a birthday present. *'Wiggling her into place, then she's all yours, Zee.'*

Sara was abnormally quiet as she watched on the main holo wall display along with the rest of the techs. Everyone was waiting to see how far down they would have to go before reaching the fissure, but Sara was concentrating more on making sure Theo didn't do anything stupid.

The melting probe sank, imperceptibly at first, then picking up speed to about a centimeter per second by the time it went fully into the ice. If the fissure was too jagged, the melter would get stuck before long. If the probe got too hot, then it ran the risk of hitting the fissure before the ice above it was sufficiently solid again.

Theo retreated up the slope on his way back to the ship, grinning so widely his beard was scratching the sides of his helmet as he hopped along. The entry looked spot on, with his extensive drilling knowledge helping him choose a perfect temperature to ease the melter down gradually.

There was chatter on the open crew comm, until Miller cut through with an executive override. Only he and Coburn were up in the pilot module, leaving the rest of them free to grumble their frustrations to each other out loud in the STEM bay.

'That's it, Koeniger, just as we discussed,' Miller said. *'If I can get this probe down to ten meters, we'll park it there for a few hours. McKinnon, you keeping tabs on the depth for me?'*

'If HE can get it down, huh? Someone's in rare form tonight,' Pia laughed on her private link with Zee.

'Yuuuup.' Then to the main comm, *'Coming up on 5 meters, still at a steady rate. Damn nice work, Theo.'*

'Oh, Miller will love that," Pia told Zee.

'Nice touch, right?'

Theo was entering the airlock and Sara helped him remove his exosuit by the time the ten meter mark was reached. Zee triggered the slowdown, sending the reactor back into the center of the probe while flooding its outer hull with supercooled ethane. This effectively put the probe into neutral while it waited, not sinking further down, but still warm enough not to freeze solid itself. The nuclear reactor was in no rush; it could run for a few thousand years before giving out.

"Just in time to wait and do nothing?" Theo began as he watched the readouts on one of Zee's consoles. Sara pulled him back by the belt away from the screens.

"You've been working for days, you big ox. You can afford to get some sleep."

"Coming to tuck me in?" he suggested, grabbing her by the waist and lifting her up to his height. Sara simply glared at him and pointed a finger back to the ground. "I don't think so, tough guy. Sleep, now."

"Aww, no fun."

Her face worked hard not to betray her true emotions, and she kept him at arm's length with one hand while pointing to the bunks with her other. "Plenty of time for fun later. In the meantime it'd be great if you don't pass out on us from sleep deprivation."

As Theo pouted, she jumped up and gave him a quick kiss before slapping him hard in the ribs, sending him off.

'Speaking of sleep deprived, when's the last time you slept?' Pia asked Zee.

'I'm ok, once I get this programmed up for monitoring the freeze, I'll probably try to take a nap.'

'Probably? You aren't a vampire or something, are you?'

'No, no space vampires here. Although if you want to come give me a kiss goodnight like Theo got, maybe I'll go take a nap sooner.'

'Get your shit done, McKinnon. Then get some rest.' She was excited and more than a little bit scared at how close they were becoming, but wasn't ready to let the rest of the crew see. Even while they were in the same room as they were now, their private comm link kept their relationship anonymous.

In fact, the whole secrecy of it was intoxicating. For someone who had kept herself isolated most of her life, this was the perfect blend of vulnerability and professionalism. He could reach her mind at a moment's notice, and she went through the day feeling his constant presence. It was incredibly freeing to be so independent in her work, while knowing he was always just a thought away.

An hour later she practiced her skills by attempting to check in on him. She found where he was easily enough, in his bed down in the outer ring hab modules. He could still be working from bed trying to fool her, though. The next part was trickier. She shut off any automated alerts and attempted to stretch her mind out into the channels which he normally used. No activity in the holocomp screens near him. Nothing being inputted under his ID. Satisfied at last that all seemed quiet, she left him to sleep.

A few hours later all sensors confirmed that the tunnel above the probe was solid again, and work began on expanding the bubble of melt water to make room for a valve.

Nanostructures extended out as rods in all directions like the spines of a sea urchin. Zee had the probe heat up again, but this time held it in place by burrowing nanorods further out into the surrounding ice.

Once there was enough room, the probe itself expanded, first doubling, then tripling in diameter, allowing the melt water to siphon in between inner and outer hulls to relieve the pressure.

The whole process took less than ten minutes, at which point the reactor core separated itself from the now assembled valve. Tiny drone engines powered by the reactor's heat fired in unison, pressing the core back upwards through the ice at a breakneck speed of a few centimeters a second. When it finally broke the surface the whole crew cheered.

"Now we can get to the real work," Theo grinned as the noise settled down.

"Gabe, you're up," Zee tapped Santos on the shoulder to give the go ahead. While the probe was in standby ten meters below, Gabe had set up a ring of bots on the surface.

Now they went to work in unison, some blowtorching the top layer, while others vacuumed up the water into enormous tanks. This industrial excavation continued until the entire blast cavity had been cleared out down to within a meter of their target. The last bit of ice was chipped away pneumatically to reveal the matte black nanotubes of the valve ring through the ice.

Next up to work was Barton, who was ready to remotely pilot their modified submersible through any cracks or caves which it might encounter. Sara was up in the pilot bay at Miller's insistence, despite her obvious grumbling.

The goal was to find a pocket of liquid large enough to replenish their tanks and begin making fuel. The submersible was equipped with its own heater, but this time a conventional induction nose cone to save space. Once she was in command of her tiny vessel, training took over and she was all business.

'I'm gonna see what this heap can find for us. Firing full power.'

The tiny sub lurched against the ice in the valve core, then gradually sank down beneath it. The cylinder sealed itself at both ends and expelled the excess slush. A meter of crude tunnel was left behind as the sub melted its way deeper. Not until an hour and nearly sixty meters later did she encounter any obstacles. Pia marveled at Sara's focus, as she seemed as fresh and determined now as she did at the start.

'Some bedrock ahead of me, seems to be coming in at an angle. Rotating and beginning a new pathway at thirty degrees west. Standby...'

As the craft began its maneuver, the crew roused themselves back to the screens in hope of some action. More ice followed the turn, and a trial cutback revealed that the angled bedrock remained shadowing the new diagonal tunnel.

'Ninety meters and no liquid in sight except for my snail trail,' Barton sighed.

The sub had dropped sensors along its path to light the way and test for conditions. To Pia's surprise, the entire tunnel back up to the valve had remained mostly liquid. A quick diagnostic on the sensor trail revealed them to be more than they seemed at first. Each was a little floating motor, keeping the ice around itself at bay with a small heating unit. When the sub fell into open water, no one except for Sara even noticed.

'Take a look at what I found!'

Vineland had stayed by her side throughout the exploration, and he was the first to help assess the situation.

"Throw it into neutral Sandy," he told her quickly. He had the stern quiet authority that reminded Pia of her father. He never seemed to say a thing that didn't need saying, and the crew respected him and his advice without question.

'Switching to manual,' Zee jumped in, *'let's see what we've got.'* Zee had taken full control of the sub's sensors, and systems began humming to life by the dozens. Pia tried keeping up with the flood of data streams, but had to pull herself out of the feeds when it became overwhelming.

'Open water, we've definitely got open water!' Zee said quickly, *'it's unusual though.'*

Miller began asking for more details, but Zee cut him off mid sentence, *'there are some strange signatures here. It's almost,'* and he trailed off again.

'What the hell are you seeing, McKinnon?'

The pause of a few seconds seemed interminably long, until Zee came back on over the comm, *'it's warm. Well, relatively. 50 degr-, I mean 10 degrees Celsius.'*

'How big is this pocket?'

Zee hesitated, then briefly reached out to Pia. *'You looking at the main holo?'*

'Oiu.'

'Good, you're gonna love this.'

Zee switched back to the main comm and simply said, *'Ladies and gentlemen, let there be light.'*

The wall holo screens in every hub were taken over by a single data packed video feed from the sub. The camera was washed out for a second as it compensated for the sudden glare. When the glow faded, the resulting view brought everyone into a stunned silence. At the top of the image was a bright ceiling of rock and ice shelf, but most of the screen was filled with sparkling water that seemed to dance with activity.

'What the hell is that?' Miller exclaimed.

The water was full of tiny flecks of light which darted suddenly a few centimeters at a time. Pia was immediately struck by the comical memory of sea monkeys she had as a child. The movement was small and fragile, but not entirely random either. They almost seemed to be moving towards the sub as it got nearer.

'Is all that...alive?' Pia asked the question on everyone's minds.

'Who cares, how big is the damn pocket?' Miller came through jarringly.

Zee punched up a depth overlay, and this time even Miller grew silent. The numbers only came up across the top sliver of the shot at first, with the lowest among them in the hundreds of meters. As the sub waited on the sonar pings to return, the resultant depth readings sped higher and higher. A thousand meters, two thousand, three, until the entire lower screen filled with infinity symbols.

'Depth is...unknown, sir.' Zee sounded utterly lost for the first time since Pia met him. *'Out of range for the sub's sensors, it can't read anything beyond three kilometers. But I've done a diagnostic check and even rebooted the sonar equipment. There's no doubt about it. The sub is now swimming free in a Ceresian ocean of some kind, and it may not be alone down there.'*

Chapter 14

BARTON HAD TAKEN THE mini sub down nearly a kilometer before it gave out. The little explorer had glided down through shimmering water, sending more tracers fleeing from its path. Eventually the pressure built up too high and the live video feed blinked out.

For Hixley the ocean was a bittersweet discovery, sealing the fate of her solar arrays. Abundant water in this volume would fuel not only the rest of Cerex's mission, but entire future mining colonies. Miller tasked her with getting the arrays back up, but just long enough for Theo's domed factory to start producing at full capacity. By pulling a double shift and concentrating on just two arrays on the nearby rim of Occator, Lara was providing power to the ship again within the day.

Theo was equally busy ramping up his hydrogen engines using the water gathered from when the ice tunnel was excavated. This left Santos and the pilots busy designing a sturdier sub for the next mission into the ocean. Pia dropped in to see the progress firsthand, and was surprised to see Zee in the middle of their huddle.

'Psst,' Pia whispered into Zee's mind. He didn't turn from the conversation, but she could sense his smile from the way it made his big ears lift up.

"I know that you just forgot to invite me, so I took the liberty of checking your schedules and came on over.

Vineland and Barton stood up quickly, their military backgrounds on display as they looked like cadets who got caught sneaking booze into their barracks.

"At ease soldiers," Pia saluted them. "I just figured you might need the mission biologist since we may have, you know...found some sort of alien bugs swimming in a freakishly warm and inconceivably large ocean on a tiny frozen rock in the middle of the asteroid belt."

To her credit, Pia held a straight face for her entire speech. Not until Zee came up to her laughing and pulled her over to them by both hands did the pilots relax.

Zee came in close to her face and she panicked for a moment thinking of him kissing her in front of other people. At the last moment he veered to the left and gently pushed her hair back behind her ear before whispering back to her.

Pia quickly tapped her temple and shut down her main chip functions. Only the main channel was kept open one-way for emergencies.

"What's going on? Why the secrecy?" she asked after making sure that she was disconnected.

"To be honest, I'm not sure." Vineland took the lead, eager to explain his actions. "That's also why we wished to keep the others, and you, out of this talk for now."

Sara had served with the Colonel long enough now to sense when he was going to beat around the bush. She sat down in front of Pia and balanced herself on her balled up fists.

"Miller is going to get us all killed. You must see that, right?"

Pia quickly scanned the room, but found only expectant faces watching her right back. She closed her eyes and took in a deep breath, letting the inhaled air cool her parted lips before opening her eyes again.

"Laisse tomber, il ne sait rien faire de ses dix doigts, celui-là," she rattled off quickly, suddenly letting the French flow out to relieve some of her stress.

Sara sat back and grabbed her knees as she snorted loudly. "My god, we brought a lady to a mutineer meeting!"

Pia's cheeks reddened before translating, "Miller's an idiot, he's completely useless." Then checking herself, she continued, "no, not an idiot. Letting ourselves think that would be a mistake."

"I agree, mademoiselle." Vineland winked at her. "I dealt with him for months before our launch, making preparations and designing Cerex. He may have a paper thin ego and the empathy of a dung beetle, but he's sharp."

"Ruthless," offered Pia.

"Dangerous," Sara repeated her claim, this time more conclusively. "Between the rushed zero-g launch, the risky maneuver getting to Occator, and the Multinat attack, it's a miracle we're still alive. Thank god Zee has pulled our asses out of the fire more than a few times, but that luck won't last forever...no offense Zee."

"None taken. We need to stick together and get base camp up fast. Miller will do whatever it takes to get back to Earth with his treasure. I say we get everything stable, gather enough to fill the ship, then find the first excuse to get the hell back home."

"Not good enough," Sara shot back. Vineland raised a hand in a calming motion, but she continued, "what? Nothing is ever stable with Miller in charge. I say we tie him up to one of her bee hives and leave him there until we get back home."

"Not that simple, unfortunately," Vineland said, "he's not alone. Coburn is attached to his hip. No way he goes along with removing Miller from command."

Zee grimaced as he thought out loud, "I could nudge CereSat around, but controls for it are linked directly to Miller and Coburn's chips. We mess up a hair on their heads and they'll call home to rat us out. We'll be in prison once we return. Even if we took them both out quickly enough that they couldn't send a message home, then we wouldn't be able to either. CereSat is our only link with Earth, and they hold the keys."

They all sat in silence for a moment, each coming to terms with what they already knew before the meeting. Vineland finally gave their thoughts a voice.

"Keep your heads down and let's get to work. That's our only choice right now. We still have a submersible to build."

"And an ocean with bugs or something floating around in it." Pia bounced up out of her seat. Everyone else looked depressed and Sara rolled her eyes, but they all began standing up to join her over near the schematics holo.

"What?" Pia asked. "We can handle Miller. There's a damn ocean under our feet, so get excited already!"

After a few different craft redesigns, they ended up building a ship Pia nicknamed the Sting Ray. The electronics and sensors were all packed into a central sphere small enough to fit through the airlock, and strong enough to keep working in the crushing depths it would encounter. The ship had a long whiplike antennae trailing behind it like a tail.

At Theo's suggestion, mechanical propellers were scrapped in favor of a magnetohydrodynamic drive. After learning how to pronounce the damn thing, Pia promptly gave up trying to understand how it worked. Something about using magnetic fields to control the water flow, but after that it was above her pay grade. Zee seemed excited about it though, and got to work making it happen.

The pilots had insisted on wing structures, a feature missing on most Earth submersibles due to technology restraints at the time. Gabe managed to come up with a beautiful pair of flexible graphene flaps which were controlled by varying the current passing through them using a gridwork of wires. They could travel wrapped up tightly around the core while getting through the tunnel, but extended to over a meter from core to tip on each side.

It was a week of constant struggle printing ship parts and wiring while the rest of the crew kept asking impatiently when they could get something back into the water.

The massive increase in their water supply finally let Pia stop policing every project that needed it. She regularly searched for excuses to go ask Zee some technical question in person, tiring of the disembodied flirting that made up most of their relationship so far. She was as physical as he was digital, and craved the feeling of his hand in her hair again more than she could logically explain.

Sara and Pia were assigned the task of controlling the Sting Ray's first mission. Both were jumping out of their seats to get on with it, but Vineland managed to delay them long enough for some basic debugging and diagnostic checks to get done. At last, nearly ten days after discovering the Ceresian ocean, they once again had the greenlight from Miller to return.

The valve had been kept scraped clean of ice build up, while the surrounding area got upgraded with rudimentary stairs and an equipment conveyor. Theo and Gabe took the Sting Ray out to the fissure and carefully dropped a smart flare down through the airlock. Resembling a cross between a backyard sparkler and a soccer ball, the flare cooked its way down nearly ten meters. It reopened the original pathway and then halted momentarily. Guided by Zee back on Cerex, the flare shifted sideways and burrowed out of the way into the surrounding ice wall.

The Sting Ray was placed carefully into the airlock, where it splashed into the meltwater, and then was sealed in by Theo's manual control. The sub came down through the bottom end of the valve lock and extended its own more powerful nuclear powered melt plate.

After getting the sub down past the flare, Sara signaled Gabe to continue his work at the surface. Out of a large military style duffle bag he began scooping handfuls of tiny mechanical gadgets. For a few minutes Gabe piled the machines into the airlock, then sent them through into the tunnel.

Pia had been briefed on the nanotech by Zee, but it was still a marvel watching them begin their work through the chip feeds. With so much of the landscape around the ship emitting no electronic signals, the tiny workers shined like fireflies, even deep within the ice.

They were attaching themselves to any ice wall surface they could find and flattening out to form a tube. Starting out no more than a centimeter in diameter, they were capable of expanding several times that width, anchoring into the ice like vines on a tree trunk. As the sub melted through the ice pack, the nanomachines combined to create a permanent tube in its wake. This would ease future access to the ocean considerably.

Sara elbowed Pia in the ribs, snapping her out of the distracting feed and back to the mission at hand.

"Sorry, what?"

"We're almost to the end of the ice pack, you ready?"

"Of course, I'm with you."

'Still regret coming up to this rock?' Zee teased. Pia's body tightened involuntarily at his voice, but recovered quickly.

'Regret is for girls. I'm a goddamn biologist. Now build a nice strong tunnel so you boys can follow our lead.'

'That's my princess.'

'Not yet I'm not. Now leave me be, the women are busy making history here.'

Chapter 15

SARA EASED UP ON THE controls as the last of the ice began cracking loudly around the sub. Suddenly a full meter of surrounding walls broke apart, leaving the Sting Ray floating free in the ocean. All system checks came back healthy, so Pia commenced with her top priority for the mission. A tube protruded out from the top of the sub, taking a sample of water back into the craft for analysis.

"It's going to take some time to run the necessary tests. Let's get going Sara."

"Finally. Let's see what this baby can do. Diving her now, 30 degree down bubble."

So they wouldn't end up too far away from the entry point, Sara took it down in a slow arcing corkscrew path. The ship maneuvered surprisingly well considering they had designed it from scratch not long ago. The initial kilometer was uneventful except for the constant flickering particles dancing across the headlight beams. Depth soundings were still coming back off scale high, despite the upgrades put in place for this journey. Not until after passing the 3 kilometer mark did Sara hear the loud ping she had been anxiously expecting.

'Holy shit,' is all she managed to say.

'Do we have a problem, ladies?' Miller asked sharply.

'No, no problem,' Pia answered for her friend. *'Do you want to tell him? Or should I?'*

'Ten kilometers at least! It's an abyss down there, deeper than most trenches back on Earth.'

The corkscrew grew steeper and wider as Sara's excitement translated into more speed. The only noticeable feature change as they hit five kilometers was a rather large increase in the amount of light streaks flitting away from their path.

'Getting some preliminary readings from the sample,' Pia announced on the main comm. *'There's a bit of everything in this water. It looks a lot like the makeup of Ahuna Mons. There's no way this should be here. All of these metals should be ten kilometers down collecting mud.'*

'That's exactly what I'm hoping for.'

'Diamond mountain not good enough for you, Commander?' Pia asked.

'The fact that you have to ask disappoints me.'

'Heaven forbid, I just thought that a diamond mountain—-right turn, now Sara!'

The ride had become monotonous, but Sara's trick flying experience came in handy as she responded with lightning reflexes. Coming in from the left of the sub's sphere of light was a rapidly flashing object which blinded everyone for a moment before chips compensated their fields of vision. The Sting Ray managed to turn in time to pull up even with what appeared to be a rotating torus of enormous crystals.

Sara matched speeds and turned every available light in the direction of the anomaly. The side nearest to them reminded Pia of a wood chipper's blades, with the crystal shards whirling in an interlocking pattern too fast to follow but never grinding against one another. Every surface was shining with mysterious iridescents in endless cycles, and so far the creature seemed oblivious to their presence. It stretched out of view both above and below them, causing Sara to back them away slowly.

'I really hope the rest of you are seeing this, because your silence is less than reassuring for my sanity,' Sara said.

For a long moment there were no answers, as the entire crew watched slack jawed.

Vineland finally broke the reverie. *'Alright, good job Barton, back her up a bit more so we can get a better look.'*

When they were ten meters away, the scope of their find began to sink in. Stretching thirty meters across, the crystal torus traveled slowly through the shimmering water. It moved like a vortex, with thousands of gemstone teeth pushing the water inwards. The overall movement was powered by a hydrojet effect as the torus opening narrowed towards the back.

'Still want to study those bugs, Princess?' Zee asked.

'It's alive...that's a living...something,' was all she could manage.

'Doughnut?' offered Theo, only half joking.

'Plenty of time to go sightseeing ladies, keep going to the bottom.'

'Is he serious right now?' Pia private linked Zee.

'You just want us to keep going?' Sara asked. She looked sideways at Pia to see if she was onboard for a fight, but was disappointed to see her shake her head in dismissal.

"Pisser dans un violon," Pia whispered to Sara in the next chair.

"You know I don't speak French, right?" But then her chip must have come through with a translation, "piss in a violin?"

"It's useless to argue with men like him, let's just press on and send more drone subs in after us."

'We just discovered alien life, right there, on camera! Anybody else freaking out?' Sara continued.

The crew, with the exception of Miller, were all flooding the main comm with protests. Even Coburn made a case for a prolonged observation period of the torus. Suddenly the comm was cut off, before Miller came back on in a measured tone.

'Let's all take a moment and reflect on what we've just witnessed.' The chatter in STEM bay halted momentarily.

'I don't have any idea what that is down there, or whether it's alive.' A new flood of exasperated crosstalk never made it onto the main feed.

'But whatever it is, it looks to be made of similar composition to Ahuna. Which begs the question, what else is down there? I intend for

us to find out, and I want it to happen now. If this thing is alive, and we found it accidentally less than an hour into our first dive, then it stands to reason it shouldn't be too difficult to track one down later. Barton, dive now, or you'll be relieved by Colonel Vineland. Let's get down as far as we can before getting our sketch pads out, shall we?'

The massive gem doughnut kept trudging along through the water, as oblivious to the sub's departure as it was to its arrival. The headlights slowly turned down and away, leaving the strobing light flashes to blink out into the vast darkness once again.

Pia kept quiet as Sara chipped off and let loose with a stream of curses that few outside of the military could appreciate. As momentous as the crystal torus had been, Pia found herself agreeing with Miller. If that creature was so easy to find, imagine what else could be waiting below.

'Do me a favor and get started on some mini botcams with Gabe, will you please?' she asked Zee.

'As you wish.'

'How is the Sting Ray holding up, Barton?' As always, Vineland got the crew back on track with a simple but necessary question. They were passing the six kilometer mark by then, and the ship had only limited testing. One loose joint or poorly printed piece of equipment could end the mission in a hurry.

Theo took the lead on this question. *'Shouldn't be a problem, boss. We aren't in Kansas anymore, if you know what I mean.'*

'No, Theo, I'm afraid I'm going to need a little bit more from you.'

Zee came to his friend's defense. *'He may look like a caveman, but Theo's right again. Gravity, Colonel.'*

'Ahhh, so what kind of range are we anticipating for the craft?'

'Well, give me a moment.' Zee began. *'Pressure is gonna depend on a number of factors including temperature, density, gravity...'*

'Fifty kilometers or so,' Theo beat him to an answer.

'Our caveman savant, ladies and gentleman.'

'All else being equal,' Theo explained, *'only difference is gravity being thirty times weaker. Figure a sub like that would last maybe two kilometers deep back home, so yeah, fifty kilometers or so here.'*

'Good enough for me,' Vineland replied. *'Take her down slowly. Full sensor array at the ready.'*

The floating streaks grew larger by the minute, darting away from the sub in all directions like a shock wave. By seven kilometers the streaks were pencil thin crystals, and they no longer floated passively waiting for the Sting Ray to come scare them out of the way. Now the little needles of light seemed to be traveling fast and dodging their craft at the last moment. No obvious form of propulsion could be seen, and they only moved the bare minimum necessary to avoid a collision.

'We're officially surrounded down there,' Pia remarked.

Sara had begun slowing their speed once the fly bys increased, afraid of getting pierced by them. No impacts had been registered on the sensor array yet, but their field of view was narrowing by the second as the number of crystals grew.

'The spaghetti are all swimming parallel, none from above or below,' Zee offered. *'How is that possible? We've been seeing some form of them since the surface. When we get that ocean sample to Cerex, I bet we'll see microscopic versions of the same shape.'*

'Spaghetti?' Pia laughed. *'So where are they coming from?'*

Vineland cut in, *'Wrong question. Not from where, but where to?'*

'You think they're attacking us?' Miller got concerned all of a sudden.

'Not attacking, there's been no contact as of yet. But it definitely doesn't seem random either. Sara, you up for some evasive maneuvers?'

A mischievous grin split the young pilot's face, but she was calm over the comm. *'At your direction, Colonel.'*

'Pull up hard and put her on her tail in 3, 2, 1, now...' he directed.

The spaghetti swerved in closer to the sub on the turn, but immediately resumed their familiar pattern. This time however, they were moving vertically along with the sub.

'Parallel with us still,' Pia confirmed.

'Now dive, straight at the floor.'

'10-4.'

The same brief adjustment from the bogies, then parallel straight down with the sub. Vineland paused for a couple seconds, then asked, *'the magnetohydr-...the engine, can we restart it remotely?'*

This time it was Zee who paused. *'I don't see why not, the antennae can be put into standby and receive any signal we send.'*

'Commander Miller, with your permission,' Vineland asked, *'I'd like to shut down the sub briefly.'*

'Is this really necessary, Colonel?' Miller responded tersely, but even he must have known Vineland never asked anything on a whim.

'Not sure we'll make it intact much further down with this much company. Have to see what options we have.'

'It's your ass if we can't get it going again.'

'All due respect, Commander, but there's no need for that. And if the time ever comes when you have a problem with my judgement, you and I can have a nice little chat about that.' Pia and everyone else onboard could hear from his tone exactly what kind of a chat Vineland had in mind.

'Zee, you ready to help with the reboot?' Sara intervened, eager to get on with the action.

'Ready when you are.'

'Let's shut her down then, on my mark...engine off.' The sub slowed to a halt quickly, and everyone held their breath as the sub's systems began blinking off. As they watched in amazement, the streaks halted course. They began retreating from the Sting Ray, and were almost completely out of sight by the time the feed went black.

'Did we lose them?' Pia asked anxiously.

Vineland was as unflappable as always. *'Let's not get ahead of ourselves, people. Zee, let's try to light her up again.'*

'Already in the process, Colonel.' Pia couldn't help noticing how Zee and Vineland seemed to command immediate respect, and made a mental note to give Zee a hard time about it later so he didn't get a big head. Even in the most tense situations, her thoughts kept wandering to that wiry little genius, and not always in the most professional of ways.

'Onboard computer is restarted...just a moment. There.'

The video flicked back on to a black screen that rapidly filled back up as the spaghetti returned to their original behavior.

'We've got fleas again, boss,' Theo snickered.

Vineland responded before Miller, not intending any offense. *'The engine, its EM pulses must be attracting the buggers, but repulsing them once they get within the engine's direct magnetic field.'*

Pia jumped in, *'Can we keep the sensors on battery power of some kind but keep the engine off?'*

'We'll drop like a stone, sir,' Sara said. *'Takes all my fun out of it, but I'm game.'*

'Make it happen, Zee.'

'We didn't plan for this, Colonel,' Zee protested. *'I can't guarantee how long the sensors will operate on the limited system we installed. Pia, you ok with shutting off everything but the lights and camera?'*

'If it means I get to see some action,' she joked.

'Going silent now,' Zee said.

As the sound of the water jet ceased, the sub coasted to a standstill. Its alien chaperones stopped rushing past as well, and just drifted in a cloud surrounding the Sting Ray. The camera view tilted down as the sub sank head first into the abyss.

Less than a minute later the view cleared suddenly as the sub dropped out the bottom of the swarm of visitors. For the first time since they were near the surface, the cameras were able to see beyond the immediate surroundings, and it was beautiful. In every direction they saw lights in the distance. Blue, yellow, and purple flashes kept drawing Pia's eyes.

'Are those torus...es, tori...oh hell, crystal doughnuts?' she asked.

'Can't tell how far the lights are, and no idea how big they are without distances,' Barton answered.

The sub sank quickly now, wings tucked in as it went. As it passed ten kilometers, a strange new glow began to build up from underneath. Unlike the multicolored flashes, this was a deep red spreading out in all directions.

Theo read out depth markers. *'Eleven kilometers, showing signs of a bottom finally, maybe at twelve.'*

As the red brightened, Pia squinted to make out what appeared to be columns of bubbles rising up nearby. With the sub's engine offline, they couldn't move any closer to investigate. As more columns reached out of the crimson fog beneath them, the sub sank less than five meters away from one of the smaller bubble tendrils.

'What are those?' Pia wondered out loud. *'Can we zoom with this thing?'* Zee began punching up the camera subsystems, but Pia beat him to it. *'Nevermind, here we are.'* She allowed herself a prideful grin before slipping back into intense curiosity.

The view raced forwards towards the nearest column. As the bubbles grew closer, they appeared to glimmer and waver. Trailing under each one was a huge gossamer fan of impossibly delicate fibers. These iridescent jellyfish creatures floated up out the top of their red haze conveyor belt, to drift steadily away in various directions. The sub passed several more jelly columns before the light from below grew so intense that it overwhelmed the hazy columns.

Theo alerted them all to what was already apparent. *'Seabed, or whatever is down there, approaching in less than two hundred meters.'*

What emerged out of the blinding red depths was a titanic archway twisted into braids of different colored crystalline structures. It formed an uncanny rainbow lifting fifty meters up off a seabed alive with countless creatures of every size and shape imaginable. From their distance all they could discern was constant motion and the unmistakable hallmarks of life. The archway stretched in either direction so far that the ends were swallowed up by the fog of color. The sub fell directly onto this crystal bridge, slamming down with enough force to crunch its way through a meter of unknown alien terrain.

Not a whisper could be heard throughout all of Cerex, and even the comm channels were silent with the reverence and shock of what they were witnessing. Pia felt Zee open a private link, but no words were exchanged. Just the connection was enough.

The sub was scuffed and battered, but largely intact. The camera watched as dozens of tiny emerald insects rolled like spiked wheels over the damaged area. As the went, each of their crystal spikes seemed to plant itself and break off. Within seconds a glowing green grass emerged, and at its center sprouted a gorgeous diamond flower ten centimeters in diameter. It swayed in the gentle current, a curious mix of soft inner structures and incredibly strong exterior.

Miller cut through the reverie like a drunk stumbling into church. *'Jesus, will you look at THAT! Sara, we still have access to that engine?'*

Sara grimaced at his request, but answered. *'Yeah, should be able to fire them up.'*

'Get me that diamond. Gabe, please tell me you installed a sample retrieval method of some kind.'

'Yes, the tail actually. It can wrap up and secure something that size I think.'

'Now, do it now, and then bring it back up, Sara.'

Sara initiated the tail, causing it to snake out towards the diamond flower which was shooting a fine powder of some sort out through a central tube. The flower stem snapped off easily, and was rolled tightly into the tail of the sub as the engines began coming back online.

'*Full power available,*' Sara said, but she was drowned out by a sound like the deep tolling of a cathedral bell.

'*Get up out of there, Sara,*' ordered Miller.

The engine was at top speed in under two seconds, but it was still too slow. The archway had broken a single blue braid away from the main structure and swung it upwards with terrifying speed and accuracy. It plucked the sub out of the sky like catching a troublesome gnat and sank back down into place once more. As the braid rejoined its archway, tendrils grew out and enveloped the Sting Ray. Then as the sub was held in place, still more creatures swarmed slowly through the gaps in the cocoon.

Pia was overwhelmed by it all; the beautiful trip down towards the seabed, the abundance of alien life, and the violence of the protective maneuver. It was all connected, from the tiniest spaghetti near the surface to the emerald seed layers. A planet sized Gaia creature had grown on Ceres, and the sub was caught like a fly in its web.

Then she had an insane idea. She quickly drove a connection into Zee's systems and concentrated as she searched frantically for a way to enact her plan. Zee got the message loud and clear, for within a few seconds he had patched a reversal into the sub's audio microphone and switched it on.

'*STOP,*' Pia yelled into the void. '*PLEASE STOP!*'

Immediately there came an echoing response, this time higher pitched and sustained for several seconds of varied tones. The crew watched in awe as the swarm of tiny creatures halted in obedience to the command. Everyone held their breath as motion across the entire visible seafloor came to halt in unison.

Zee let out a nervous laugh. '*Well, Pia, I think you have their attention. Now what?*'

'Exactly,' she gasped, *'now what?'*

Part 4
Rebel Uprising

Chapter 16

After first contact with the alien, the crew of Cerex demanded an emergency meeting to discuss their next steps. Commander Miller was forced to come down to the tech deck ring, swallowing his pride in the hopes of maintaining some form of leadership for the mission.

Since Pia's shouted plea, they had lost contact with the Sting Ray probe nearly twelve kilometers beneath them. The crystalline cage holding it had sealed over entirely, cutting off their ability to communicate with it. The last video recorded was a kaleidoscopic array of gems fluidly knitting themselves together into a thick wall.

Pia took the lead once Miller arrived, eager to get on with the necessary next steps.

"This is beyond anything we've discovered so far—beyond anything in human history. Before we do anything else, I think we need to get the consensus of the scientific community back home."

"Along with the politicians, I'm sure," added Lara.

"And whether we like it or not, military will likely be taking the lead on this." Vineland stood up as he spoke, then sat back down when he was through, having said his piece.

Miller had walked to the head of the makeshift table, although no one had noticed except for Coburn, who was ready to assist.

"Commander, what are your orders, sir?" Coburn asked dutifully. Eyes rolled, but everyone turned to give their attention to Miller.

"No one will know about this. No Multinats, no techs, no one except the board of Natocorps." Shocked silence gave way to outbursts from the crew, but Miller cut them off.

"You will take this knowledge to your graves, whether that be decades from now, or significantly sooner..." He stared pointedly at each of the eight people in front of him.

They maintained composure in spite of the fire coursing through their veins. Miller laughed, then pulled his face into a childish pout.

"C'mon, this is no fun without a little resistance. I thought you scientists live and die by your principles. Turns out, you're all chickenshit. Oh well, don't be too sad. You still get to investigate the anomaly."

Pia stood up, a picture of defiance. Then she took a deep breath in, and with a grace and sadness well known to women throughout history, she accepted the situation and continued with her jaw clenched tightly.

She managed to spit out the words, "you'll allow us to investigate?" The rest of the crew were still regaining their composure, and all looked to Pia with respect.

"Of course, we must find the extent of our discovery, and what it contains. Our primary mission is to inventory and extract all available resources on Ceres. This includes whatever the hell that thing is on the ocean floor."

"At least admit it. That thing is alive down there. And it shows signs of intelligence."

"I know it's alive. I just don't care, sweetheart. As for intelligence, I guess we'll just have to see who's smarter."

Zee was lost in his networks, but bristled at the word "sweetheart." Pia reached out and ran a digital hand across Zee's shoulders. Zee responded by flashing a series of futile search requests he had run, looking for ways to bypass Miller's Natocorps hardlink.

Until they found a way around Miller's security clearance, they remained under his control.

Ideas were begrudgingly called out and approved by Miller, who seemed bored by the lack of confrontation. He left the meeting as abruptly as he had entered, appointing Coburn to take over the logistics.

Once Miller was gone, their creative juices started flowing again, and within half an hour their plans were made. Five more probes were designed and built, all similar in design to the Sting Ray. They were meant to fan out and explore the depths as far away as the ocean extended. Dozens of mini water drones were also produced. They were slender machines built for speeding along the ice pack, all the while building a map of the subsurface.

To complement their submersibles, a massive antenna was installed on the underside of the ice beneath Cerex, then wired through its own mini tunnel and directly up into the ship. This gave tremendous power and range to communications with the probes throughout the ocean.

With the Cerex encampment now running at full power and expanding daily, the probes were completed quickly. First to see action were the torpedo bots, lowered one after another by Gabe into the airlock, and then down the ice tunnel.

Just as CereSat had methodically uncovered swath after swath of the dwarf planet's ancient surface, these torpedo bots sped off taking detailed measurements about the water composition, temperature, and depth of the newly discovered ocean.

The first surprise came as the bots left the Occator region and began steadily descending along with the bottom of the ice pack. At first it was a gradual slope, ten meters or so down for every kilometer away from their base camp. This pace quickened exponentially until it seemed the bots were speeding straight down a vertical wall. Theo was concerned they were reaching abort depth for the shallow water probes. Then, as suddenly as the ice pack had thickened, the wall ceased.

The torpedo bots leveled out and took side rader readings. The wall had opened into a vast circular gap, with crystals jutting like broken teeth from the edges. Once through the gap, the foremost bot headed upwards once again along the ocean roof until it reached a depth similar to that near Occator.

It was the same with the other bots, with gaps ranging from a couple hundred meters across up to over a kilometer. They seemed to be spaced fairly regularly in every direction, except not all circular gaps were open. Instead of ragged crystal shards, some gaps were completely sealed by a nearly translucent sheet of green hued crystal. Whenever a gap was sealed, the probe would inevitably find an open one within a few kilometers.

It didn't take long for the probes to travel out of communication range of the main Cerex antenna. No matter how powerful the signal, the constant honeycomb of separate ocean chambers would always make contact impossible for more than a few dozen kilometers away. They were left with no choice but to let the probes continue on autopilot to continue their mapping project.

While the torpedoes had not been able to detect anything at the ocean floor, their readings offered a few promising leads for the sturdier Sting Ray subs. Wherever there were sealed over wall gaps and lowered ceilings, the crew reasoned that there must be some sort of increased crystal activity down below.

All five of the larger subs were sent out simultaneously to their assigned areas, with one tasked with heading back down to the previous first contact point. As each made their slow corkscrew descents, they encountered the spaghetti creatures at a much earlier point.

The incredibly thin crystal rods would repeatedly dart directly at the subs' engines, only to be repulsed by the strong magnetic fields. Whereas the first probe had not been swarmed until several kilometers down, the one tasked with finding its captured comrade could barely make progress as soon as it passed two kilometers. The spaghetti stopped trying to reach the engine after a few minutes, opting to merely shadow the probe at an uncomfortably close meter or so. Any closer and the magnetic fields would repulse them back. Down the probe traveled, flying blind, but confident it had nearly ten kilometers to go before reaching bottom.

Then the spaghetti began doing something odd. Pia watched closely as a few of the rods flashed bright white for a moment while touching. This cascaded rapidly, and each time resulted in an apparent fusing of the touching crystals.

Soon all the surrounding escorts were larger fused forms, which was when another round commenced. Then another, and another, until six large flat crystal shields were surrounding the probe, moving just as silently and effortlessly as ever before.

When the final fusing occurred, the video feed was first filled with an overwhelming series of colored flashes, then blinked off entirely, leaving a blackness as total as the flash was bright.

"What happened, Theo?" Zee asked.

"We just got quarantined, I think," he laughed.

"Can we bust through it?" Sara asked hopefully.

"We can't do a thing about it," Pia realized out loud. "If that crystal cube stays sealed around us, we can't get a signal to the sub."

"Engine won't function either." Zee shook his head in disbelief. "That cube is a closed system, no water in or out, which makes a hydrojet pretty much useless."

"Well shit," Theo said. "Looks like maybe they're smarter than us after all." As embarrassed as he was, he couldn't resist the dig at Miller who was undoubtedly watching the feed from his private hab.

"Two down, but still have four to go," Vineland offered hopefully, but he could see the writing on the wall.

At Theo's suggestion, the next probe to encounter fusing spaghetti didn't wait to get boxed in. Sara directed it to rapidly change both speed and direction, a series of evasive maneuvers worthy of the best dogfights back on Earth. The crystals had difficulty adjusting their own pace, and the sub was able to break away for a moment.

Whatever hope arose in the crew was quickly dashed when the spaghetti reappeared assembled into large squares already. The pieces flew in close and began fusing a mere meter away from the sub's camera. In a last ditch effort, Sara threw the sub into a hard spin, whipping the graphene wing flaps around hard. While the engine repulsed the crystals whenever they got too close, the graphene wings were able to reach out far enough to make contact.

The crew covered their ears instinctually as a sound like machine gun fire at close quarters filled their feeds. Their ears were no more involved in hearing the sound than their toes, but it somehow felt like the right thing to do. Soon their chips filtered the sound down to manageable levels, and they turned their attention back to the wall holos. Shards of crystal were flying in every direction as the sub wings cut their way through the closing pieces like a buzzsaw.

Sara took advantage of the momentary chaos and dove the sub straight down. They were nearly three kilometers from the floor still and the crystals would be regrouping quickly. Sara maxed out the engines, hoping to win a race to the bottom, but was surrounded again in less than a minute. She tried cutting the engine again, but the trick didn't fool the crystals this time. The cube fused into place around them, and the feed went black.

"Three left, any ideas?" Sara asked.

Everyone fell silent as option after option was researched internally, but dismissed just as quickly. Every scenario ended with the subs getting boxed into crystal quarantine.

"C'mon, people," Sara pleaded. "We're better than this. It's time to scrape the bottom of the barrel now and..."

"That's it!" Pia practically shouted.

"That's what?" Vineland asked.

"Time to scrape the barrel, Colonel." She performed scans with the remaining subs to find the one closest to a chamber wall and direct linked her plan to Sara.

"Ballsy," Sara laughed, "I love it." She aimed the chosen sub directly at the nearest wall and maxed the engine. The five hundred meters closed fast, and the wall grew ominously large in the widescreen.

Miller jumped onto the comm line. 'Have you lost your damn mind, Barton?'

Pia looked over and saw Sara practically sneering with pride at having pissed off Miller yet again.

"Time to dance," she challenged herself as she flipped the sub upside down. As it got within ten meters of the wall, the sub dove down parallel to the rock face. The spaghetti were already swarming around it, tiny flashes warning them the fusing process had begun.

Sara drove the sub closer to the wall, impossibly close. Tiny crevices and outcroppings screamed past the camera with the lighting only giving her a couple seconds worth of warning. Her insane maneuver was starting to pay dividends, with crystals shattering against the wall constantly.

Pia marveled at Sara's fearless piloting. Her reputation as an elite smuggler was on full display as she took advantage of every feature of the rock wall before Pia could even open her mouth to shout a warning. Try as they might, the crystals couldn't form their cube around the sub.

As an automated chime signaled they had blown past the one kilometer mark, the red glow from the ocean floor lit up the remainder of the wall. The entire area cleared and they were suddenly left alone. Sara tentatively glided the sub into open water, leaving all of the crew a chance to exhale after the breakneck race with the spaghetti.

When the probe reached the bottom, there was no sign of the massive creature they had seen with the first Sting Ray. No creatures making the floor look alive. No gemstone spires. The only evidence of life was the red glow filling the ocean. With the eerie absence of objects to reflect the light, they could detect a direction for its source. Sara cruised the sub close to the ocean bottom, nearing the coordinates of where they lost the first Sting Ray.

"Where the hell is everything?" Pia gave voice to the question on every crew member's mind. "Underground?"

Just then she saw the faintest glimmer of something dissolving into view in the distance.

"Sara," she started.

"I'm on it," she replied quickly.

The glimmer turned into a brilliant red line, fuzzy along the edges but almost too bright to observe the center directly.

As the sub grew closer, a signal pinged out strongly. At this depth instructions from the antenna under Cerex could barely be distinguished from the background noise. This was a thousand times stronger, and close.

"Is that, whatever it is, trying to communicate with us?" Sara guessed.

Pia shook her head, unsure. "If it is, there's not much to the message. It's nonharmonic, and seems like it repeats itself every few seconds."

"Move us closer, Sara," prodded Vineland, more to cut off any more speculation. Sara had already visibly increased their speed towards the red tower of light.

Their chip filters were having a hard time adjusting to the constantly increasing light coming from the structure.

"That's no bubble column, that's for damn sure." Theo's attempt to break the tension fell flat.

Now details begin to emerge about what the source was for the light. There was a couple meter thick crystal snaking up out of an opening in the ocean floor the size of a small crater. No structures could be discerned past the opening, because the glow was too intense. Pia kept picturing childhood stories about the gates of hell...

"The signal is on the move," Zee said. "It's traveling up with that tendril."

Sara swooped the sub upwards and parallel to the structure, but gave it a wide berth just in case it made a grab for them. Even though the crystalline formation must have just been erected, it looked ancient and unmovable. The light from inside it pulsed like a current, shifting in color slightly as it brightened and dimmed in turn. The sub had followed it up for more than a kilometer when the signal began to grow noticeably stronger.

"Any sign of our tiny chaperones?" asked Vineland.

Lara had been constantly scanning the surrounding environment since reaching the ocean floor, and was ready for the Colonel's question.

"Not a whiff of them, Charles," she said. "I never thought that I'd miss the little devils, but this quiet emptiness is almost worse."

Two more kilometers passed by without incident. The structure remained the same thickness and pattern, as if it had been there a million years. Now the signal came through stronger, yet was still indecipherable.

Gabe thought otherwise. "It's the Sting Ray. That's what we're hearing. The sub must be inside the structure still, hitching a ride upwards."

"Why the hell is it taking it up with it?" Pia wondered out loud.

"Maybe it doesn't realize it's there?" Theo suggested, but even he didn't believe his theory.

"Or maybe they're taking out the garbage," Zee said.

Five, six, seven kilometers passed by, and now they showed signs of catching up with the leading edge of the crystal tower at last. The Sting Ray still pulsed its futile emergency beacon that got refracted and garbled endlessly by the crystal surrounding it.

Now Vineland was showing signs of concern. "Everyone who is able should find an exosuit and put it on, please."

Pia was caught off guard by the Colonel's order, but realized the reasoning immediately. As a scientist, the idea of a crystal lifeform growing to such epic size was staggering, but she hadn't even considered the possibility that the tower might not be stopping at the ice pack.

Along with the rest of the crew, she grabbed a suit from the nearby equipment rack along with another for Sara. Zee's eyes nearly popped out of their sockets as Pia stripped down to her underwear right at her station in the middle of tech deck. Everyone else soon followed suit, changing into their exosuits but leaving the helmets off for the time being.

"Your turn," Pia told Sara as she hip checked her out of the pilot's station. "Don't worry, I've got this. Fly straight, don't hit the alien, easy."

Sara balked at first, but under the circumstances didn't have much of a choice. She too stripped down and changed, shooting warning glares over towards Theo. To his credit, he restrained himself to a slow wink at her, having already put on his exosuit.

As Sara took back over the controls, they were pulling up equal to the leading edge of the tower. Still nearly a kilometer beneath the ice pack, the crystals were forming at an incredible rate. As the energy pulsed rhythmically up through the column from the abyss below, new crystal seemed to grow out of nowhere at the top. With a rate of ten meters per second, they had less than two minutes before it reached the top.

All eyes were on the sub's video feed as the tower showed no signs of slowing. What did begin to change was the top of the tower, which flared out wider and wider.

"Pulling back, not sure what's happening Colonel," Sara said.

"Maintain a good visual, Sara. If it was going to grab this sub it would have done it already," he responded.

In the final seconds before impact, the crystal suddenly disappeared from view. Sara had to break hard and pull even with the ice pack before looping upside down again to regain visual. It had decelerated in a split second to a slow crawl, covering the final few meters a leisurely few centimeters per second.

There was no mistaking its target now. The exit to their ice tunnel was directly above the crystal, reflecting a dark crimson from below. The flared top expanded further until a half dome collided with the ice in an ear splitting crunch. All around the edges, tiny crystals branched out and into the nearby ice, welding itself securely in place.

As the dome was complete, Sara's sub blinked offline, followed by the remaining subs out exploring the deep ocean catacombs. To their surprise, a new feed reopened on Pia's monitor. The original Sting Ray was broadcasting again, seemingly intact. Pia punched up the video to replace the wall holos, and a rainbow of light danced across the hab. The little resurrected sub had been brought up from the gates of hell and held gently in the half dome.

"Return to sender?" Sara guessed.

"More like taking out the trash," Theo said.

"I think it's safe to say we are officially no longer welcome in the ocean." Zee summed it up.

"The hell we aren't," Miller snarled.

Chapter 17

An emergency meeting was called in the tech deck, mostly because everyone was there already yelling at Miller all the reasons why it was insane to continue attempting to mine the ocean floor. Miller leapt up on top of Zee's station, right in the middle of his active holos. Even in the middle of such chaos, Pia burst out laughing when she saw Zee's face. Miller gave her his best death stare, and she managed to suppress most of the following giggle.

'Oooh, he's gonna get it now, messing with your precious screens,' Pia teased Zee over their private link.

Zee glanced over at her and the frustration melted off his face as he tapped his holo pendant off entirely. While the rest of the crew gradually found suitable chairs or desks to sit on, Zee walked right over to Pia and held her by the waist close to him. Miller stopped mid sentence as he noticed the gesture, then continued on.

"We're not going to just stay up here on the surface twiddling our thumbs while there's a goddamn money farm growing beneath us. That thing is intruding on our mission, and that cannot, and will not, happen on my watch."

Wild protestations and waving arms were plowed right through by Miller's barking speech.

"Now clearly this thing is alive, and can react to its environment, but that's hardly cause for us to start being afraid of it."

"I'm afraid of it," Vineland said. Everyone waited, not knowing how to respond. "I don't know what that creature is either, Commander. And I don't have a clue what else it is capable of doing, but I just witnessed it carefully carry a probe up a twelve kilometer extension of itself. And it did it in under an hour. Quite frankly, you'd have to be a moron not to be a little afraid of a creature like that." There wasn't a shred of embarrassment or regret in the Colonel as he sat down calmly.

His response may not have fazed Miller much, but it gave a massive morale boost to the resistance. They gathered their outbursts into an orderly wave, not letting Miller get another chance to interrupt them.

Lara jumped in first. "The energy required to build that tower is off the charts. We're talking gigawatts of power."

"That tower is nearly straight the entire way up. It came up out of the seabed, nearly exactly under the ice tunnel hole twelve kilometers above it," Santos added. "We couldn't have done better ourselves given a week to prepare."

"We need to know more about it before we make a decision that could kill us all," Pia said, then Miller was finally allowed to respond.

"That's the first semi-rational thing any of you have said. Of course, I'm in favor of learning more about it. How we can get around it, how it reacts, what will we need to suppress it? Natocorps sent the first unmanned resupply missions as soon as we landed safely on Ceres.'

"Nice that we're hearing about this now, and not before we supposedly HAD to make the jump from Ahuna Mons to Occator." Sara was livid, so much so that Theo actually got between her and Miller. Her eyes were wide, and she was ready to hurt Miller, consequences be damned.

"The jump where we almost blew the ship apart, you mean?" Pia was not far behind Sara in anger. Zee didn't step in to stop her though, he got right in front and in the face of Miller.

"And when Pia almost got seriously hurt?" Pia flinched at the memory of falling all the way down the forest hab, but more from embarrassment than anything else.

"Oh calm down, it's not my fault your girlfriend can't hold on to a damn railing. I mean, seriously, who gets hurt in this low gravity?"

Zee shoved the Commander without thinking, sending him soaring backwards precisely because of the just mentioned microgravity. Miller tried turning to face where he was flying to get his bearings, but ended up flailing awkwardly before slamming the lower half of his body on a desk across the room.

This impact only spun his torso downwards, scraping his chest against the far side of the metal desk before flipping his feet up and over him. He grabbed hold of a chair and scraped to a halt, aided by the magnetic grips on the chair legs. Silence ruled the previously raucous meeting for the few seconds it took Miller to regain his footing.

Zee began laughing loudly, not seeming to care anymore what Miller might do to him. The absurdity of it all washed over the room, and Miller watched as everyone either began laughing or smiling at the situation. Only Coburn refrained, and he looked mildly terrified as to what his leader would do in response. Before the Commander opened his mouth, Coburn jumped into action, surprising even himself.

"Colonel, get Zee out of here and into solitary confinement. Restrain him if you have to. Put him in a storage locker to cool down."

At first no one moved, and Miller looked confused as well. He was being robbed of his revenge, even if some sort of retribution was being carried out.

Pia rushed in front of Zee to block them, but heard his voice in her head as his hand held hers firmly. *It's okay, let him have his justice. I shouldn't have pushed him.*

Colonel Vineland was hesitant to be anybody's lackey, but the look on Zee's face reassured him. Only once Zee started walking off with Vineland did Miller seem to exhale.

"Yeah, take a walk, you fucking holo head." Zee looked back at the grade school insult and smirked. Miller continued, "take his comp pendant too." This time Zee was genuinely concerned, but tried not to let on. He took it off himself and handed it to Vineland.

"Pissing contest aside, that's not a wise decision," Vineland said. "Zee's interface with Cerex has saved our asses more than once. Commander, I ask you to reconsider, for the sake of mission security."

"Well all I ask is for you to do as you're told, Colonel. Surely, you must be used to taking orders by now at your age."

The Colonel didn't dignify it with a response and merely turned and walked out with Zee.

"Now back to the task at hand," Miller continued, despite the fact that the room had a mood like ice water. "To further study this creature, I propose we do some sort of experimental drilling into the dome structure with a bot."

"That's insane," Hixley burst out. "I'm sorry, sir, but how do you think that's a safe action to take?"

Miller barely looked concerned. "So far, it hasn't taken any hostile actions. It even returned the Sting Ray to us. You're clearly afraid of it, I understand that. But how can you be sure it's not the creature that's afraid of us? We have to make a show of force to demonstrate that it's right to fear us."

Sara marched up to Miller again, then quickly lifted her hands up to signal she wasn't going to hit him. "You said it yourself, Miller." She expressed her anger by at least refusing to show him respect. "The creature has not shown signs of hostility...yet. We've already riled it up by plucking that stupid diamond flower off the ocean floor, and now you want to make another hostile move towards it. After seeing a tiny speck of what it's capable of doing, even at twelve kilometers away, you have to assume it could destroy Cerex. I know you like to think that you're all about the greater mission, but you don't want to die here on this rock, do you?"

"No, of course not." He placated her like a child. "And soon you'll see that it will move away from us when we reclaim access to the ocean. And even if the worst happened, the incoming backup missions will know better what they're dealing with and how to take it out. We'll be martyrs for a greater good."

"We don't want to be martyrs, you shit. Sorry for the language, Commander." Theo's voice boomed out in the room, the last word dripping with sarcasm.

Pia took a deep breath in with her eyes closed, then opened them with calm resolve. "How is this going to help future missions, anyway? You haven't even tried any other ways, yet. Declaring war on an unknown alien species might make any settlements on Ceres much more difficult and slow going than they would have to be. Figuring out a solution, however, could be vastly more useful to Natocorps."

Miller clearly hadn't thought this all the way through yet, and he grudgingly accepted her point. "And do you happen to have such a solution?"

"I go and talk to it," Pia said with a straight face.

Chapter 18

No one seemed particularly optimistic about the idea, but no one could think up anything better, either. Later that day, Pia was suiting up in the lower cargo bays, preparing to head out the tunnel. She tried reaching out to Zee, but it was nearly impossible for her to locate his electronic signature without his pendant. She was worried about him, and she figured he would be even more worried about her if he found out her plan. She shook off the distracting thoughts and focused on the task at hand.

'*No big deal*,' she told herself. '*Just going to climb down an ice tunnel near the top of a twelve kilometer high alien and say hi.*' Her feet had been tapping rapidly on the metal floor, but they stopped suddenly as her composure returned.

Sara was waiting at the outer airlock with a large bag full of rope, half hoping to talk Pia out of going. One look and she knew that would be a waste of breath, so she handed over the bag and did a manual check on Pia's equipment before opening the airlock.

Pia nodded her readiness through the airlock window, then stepped out and down the hull ladder. This was the first time she had actually been on the surface, and for a moment she froze. The absurdity of her boots crunching into Ceres made a tiny nervous laugh burst out.

'*You okay so far, Pia?*' Vineland asked.

'*Oh, I'm peachy. Heading to the tunnel site now.*'

She kept picturing old footage of when the Lunar colonies were first being set up. An endless desolation of grays and whites filled the landscape in front of her, yet each step she took brought flashes of red in her mind.

Deep beneath the ocean, somewhere there was an intelligence lurking. Whatever it was, it dwarfed even the Pando forest organism she had been fighting so hard to preserve back on Earth.

She crossed the distance to the tunnel before she knew it, bounding down the makeshift stairs leading down to the tunnel entrance.

Although she had seen the airlock a few times by now on the camera feeds, it still surprised her how small it appeared up close. Not much bigger than a sewer grate, the airlock was a tight squeeze with her oxygen tank and exosuit. After unlocking the top cover and sitting with her legs dangling over the side, she had a small moment of panic.

'Everyone still with me?'

'We're here, Pia,' multiple voices answered, all but the one she cared most to hear.

'Entering the airlock now.' She lowered her body as slowly as possible down over the edge, careful not to tear her suit on the rim. She knew they were strong enough to withstand much more intense impacts, but being out in the near vacuum had put her nerves on high alert.

The top hatch slid closed above her, and for a few seconds she was crouched into a ball. She checked the air feeds on her pack, then checked again. The tight squeeze was strangely comforting to Pia, and she hesitated just long enough that she wouldn't start getting asked if something was wrong. Then she triggered the lower hatch.

Seawater began gushing upwards through the expanding gap, swallowing her legs in seconds. Soon the entire hatch was full, and visibility returned once the bubbles and turbulence subsided.

'Solid lock confirmed, going down into the tunnel.'

'We read you, Pia,' Vineland answered calmly. *'Video and audio are live.'* Pia held onto the rim of the lower hatch and pulled herself down through it. As her helmet cleared the hatch, she could see the light from the microdrones much brighter than she anticipated. They were bright enough to shine off the tunnel walls, and helped Pia keep her fear in check. She kept imagining a crystal tendril climbing up through the tunnel to grab her feet and pull her down into the depths.

'We still have eyes on the seal?' Pia asked as casually as she could manage, hoping the rest of the crew didn't have access to her pulse or breathing rate. She busied herself by clipping her rope onto the lower hatch handle.

Gabe jumped on the comm. *'We have the Sting Ray's camera operating. Not seeing very much except a great closeup of reddish tinged crystal, but no movement either. If it knows you're coming, it's not showing it.'*

Pia exhaled slowly through her dry mouth, trying to picture Pando forest back on Earth. She began walking her way down the tunnel by pressing her gloves and boots against the far wall. *'Just like climbing down a tree,'* she thought to herself. After a minute of steady climbing, she reached the turn in the tunnel where Sara had originally gone around the rock wall. The shaft opened out wider here due to the change in direction, and the light from the microdrones was being drowned out by the red glow from the bottom.

'Going to switch it up for the lower half,' Pia said. She placed her feet back and wedged them into the deepest corner of the turn. Her arms pushed herself down until she was crouched as tightly as possible around her boots. She had to wedge her helmet sideways a bit, but managed to clear the far side of the wall and began straightening out her body again headfirst.

'Better view, thanks Pia,' Sara joked.

Once she was upside down, she lost all sense of orientation. In Ceresian gravity, up and down were fairly similar. Pia swam forward, hoping to let momentum build up her bravery as she dolphin kicked her way down the bottom stretch of tunnel. The red light became so bright near the exit that the water seemed alive with the shimmering.

Panic hit her at the thought of all the microscopic spaghetti creatures which must be swarming all around her exosuit. Her body wriggled and spasmed upward involuntarily as the insanity of her plan was sinking in for her.

'*Get it together, Lamotte,*' barked out Vineland. '*It's alive, so are you. If you panic, you die, and I'm not going to let that happen. Understood?!*' The last word came out like a drill sergeant, and got the intended response.

'*Yes, sir,*' Pia said. Her voice was timid, but she managed to calm her movements. She groped out into the Datanet for Zee, but came up empty. She was on her own, just as she had been most of her life. Her eyes jumped back to the steady sunset glow, so close now she could almost touch it. She made her way downward, until at last her head poked out from the bottom of the tunnel.

The Sting Ray sat at the center of a magnificent crystal dome, seemingly undamaged despite its travels. The dome itself looked smooth in every direction, yet was made up of thousands of separate pieces. Its surface was fused together like a fiber optic cable, and despite the red glow there were numerous subtle colors shifting underneath.

'*Beginning descent into the dome,*' Pia managed to squeak out, and she pulled herself out of the tunnel entirely. A single graceful flip downwards and her boots landed softly against the crystal next to the Sting Ray.

'*Down in front,*' Theo joked. Pia flinched at the noise, but relaxed when she realized who said it. She moved her boot out of the way of the sub's camera before lifting it up and turning it towards her own face.

'*Is this better?*' Pia said.

'*He's not allowed to answer that,*' Sara interrupted.

'*So now what?*'

'*It's your rodeo, you're the biologist.*'

Pia turned back toward the dome, but with no obvious features to focus on, she didn't even know where to direct her attention. First she attached the end of the rope she had been carrying to the Sting Ray. She was very interested to see what kind of footage it recorded during their comm blackout.

After pushing the probe back up into the ice tunnel, she left it with its camera facing down into the dome. While she knew that the question she wanted to ask was ridiculous, she couldn't help herself. She lifted her arms out into a welcoming pose and simply asked, '*Hello?*'

After seeing what this creature had already shown itself capable of doing, Pia was not about to assume anything. However, five seconds of holding the pose produced no response, except for a heated one by Miller.

'*Seriously?! That's the best you've got?*'

Pia knew Miller was trying to bait her into reacting, but she honestly was embarrassed. '*Sorry, had to try, right?*'

'*Did you?*' was all Miller responded.

Pia gathered herself as quickly as possible, then tried to figure out a new tactic. She scrutinized all parts of the dome, but very little varied along its surface. '*Math,*' she thought. '*Anything able to make a dome this precise must understand math.*'

Saying a silent prayer that she wasn't about to start a fight with a living skyscraper, she brought her boot up before slapping it down once on the crystal. Nothing. This time her boot came down twice. Nothing. Three times, five times, seven times, all nothing.

'Strike two,' she deadpanned.

The comm made her rethink her approach. She accessed her chip's settings to emit a local broadcast into the surrounding water. This time, instead of simply stomping her feet, she broadcast out a series of numbers and 3D models all referring to hydrogen: its atomic weight, its structure, along with the images of a star and a gas giant planet. When she got no response, she pulsed the data again, and again, each time with the same message.

Then, after the fourth time broadcasting, she finally got a response. She was suddenly deafened as the entire crystalline dome vibrated strongly, overwhelming her chip's dampening features and dropping her down in pain. The noise halted, then pulsed again two, three, four times. She could only hold her head and hope her chip could ease the volume.

She finally gave up on fighting the sound, and began trying to listen to it through her chip as the energy flowed brightly in all directions. She instinctively reached out a hand to the nearest wall and spread her gloved fingers out wide. She could feel a tremendous stream of electricity coursing through the crystal, drawing its source from the tendril beneath them.

Pia couldn't tell if any of the crew were talking to her or not. For her, all that existed was the sound. Unable to resist it or hide from it, Pia was forced to struggle through. She reached out with her chip and felt further for the source. Normally, she'd be limited to signals in fairly close proximity to her. Not with this. The power was so immense that she followed it down for kilometers, until it reached the sea floor.

At this point, Pia expected it to expand out into whatever form the main body of the creature had. Instead, the signal branched out in every direction, braiding and intertwining itself around any natural features. At regular junctions, the path dove deep into the subterranean material. Following the channels of energy became hypnotic, as they seemed to endlessly grow in complexity and length.

When she reached the end of the pathways, she was struck with a moment of sheer panic as the reality set in. The end of the pathways was a central core stretching across the entire interior of Ceres. Over five hundred kilometers in diameter, the energy source holding Pia cupped in its tiny dome was a majority of the dwarf planet's mass.

Pia fell back in shock for a moment, then pushed up hard for the exit. The Sting Ray was still there, and she planned to push the sub the rest of the way to the airlock as quickly as her limbs could take them.

'Pia, I repeat, are you okay?' Vineland pleaded, breaking through as the dome sound ceased.

'On my way up. Have to get away. Can't be down there anymore.'

'It's okay. Just come on back to us. Good first steps.'

'Yeah, great...' she muttered.

Only she didn't make it to the top of the tunnel.

She barely made it out of the dome before feeling a tugging at her legs. Convinced she would look down and see crystal fibers curling up to wrap around her suit, she tried kicking and swimming up as hard as she could. The pull got stronger until she was noticeably sinking back down.

Finally, Pia worked up the courage to look, and to her surprise what she saw was not tendrils, but bubbles. Powerful streams of bubbles were pouring up out of unseen gaps in the dome. However, instead of being blown upwards, her and the bot were getting sucked toward the bottom.

'You have any idea what's happening right now?!' Pia yelled over the ship comm.

'Water level is receding,' Gabe said, *'few feet of tunnel per second is emptying out. Pressure readings are normal.'*

'The bubbles, they're filling the tunnel!' Pia exclaimed. Swarms of gas swirled up past her legs, causing her to lose her grip on the Sting Ray. As the last of the water got drained out of the dome, the sub crashed against the floor, breaking its camera in the collision.

'Pia, you okay down there?' Sara asked.

'I think so,' she replied, unsure if the creature was done whatever it was just doing. *'What is the tunnel filled with? Air?'*

'I doubt it,' Lara said while she checked the sensors. *'It's...hydrogen. All of it. You need to get the hell out of there before you explode.'*

Pia clutched at her air supply hose. *'My air supply is detachable, right?'*

'I'm not sure who you were directing that question towards,' Vineland intervened. *'But I'll jump in here and suggest you keep your air hose attached right where it is.'*

Pia laughed. *'Thanks, Charles, but just the facts, please.'*

'They're detachable, rotate the hose and pull firmly. Repeat it in reverse to reattach. But why do you—'

'Thanks, Colonel,' Pia cut him off. She quickly detached her air hose and touched the end down into the crystal floor at her feet. She stayed crouched until her head started to swim, then rapidly reconnected her air. After gasping for air momentarily, she gathered herself together and repeated the experiment.

Hose pressed down to red crystal while air rushed out, then a slightly panicked reattachment. The thinnest of bubble columns came up from the crystal where her hose had been. Pia was sure it was remnants from her expelled air, but it gradually grew stronger, and it was joined by several other microfissures. Soon, gas was flooding out of the floor once again, even faster than before.

Pia didn't need to wait for spectroscopy to know that the tunnel was filling with breathable air, a chemical copy of the exosuit's own air mixture. She also knew to quit while she was ahead. She rechecked the sub's tow line and began climbing back up out of the now claustrophobic dome, only stopping briefly to navigate the sub through the turn.

When she returned to Cerex, she had to enter through the decon suite, an automatic cleaning airlock. She dragged the sub in after her, and immediately wished she was back with the creature.

Her heart rate was still pounding as she remembered the staggering size of the alien, and was filled with a deep primal terror. As the doors closed and decontamination procedures kicked in, Pia started to reach her hands out in front of her. Blinding flashes of UV light strobed her and the sub. Her eyesight was still recovering as a series of liquids sprayed her exosuit. A final airjet dried the room, then the inner door unlocked.

Once she finally got inside, she threw off her helmet and dropped to her knees. Sara got waved off when she went in to help out, and sure enough, Pia was on her feet in a few seconds. Not only was she up on her feet, but on the move.

"Where is he?" Pia asked Sara.

"Storage room 4B, Deck 2. Theo has been by to check on him."

"Thanks to you both." And off she marched to find her prisoner boyfriend, or whatever he was.

As she neared the storage bay where Zee was supposedly being held, she saw no one else around. She was expecting something, not a guard necessarily, but *something*. As she reached for the handle, she was startled backwards by the laughing voice of Miller over a hallway speaker.

'Awww, have you come to fluff his pillow?'

'Let him out of there already, you've proven your point. You're in charge.'

'That's right, I am in charge. And he forgot that.'

Chapter 19

The crew went into a nervous series of secret meetings: Miller huddling with Coburn about options for completing the mission without Zee, the rest hurriedly checking with each other to see if they should try to mutiny. Pia went right to Vineland for advice, since she trusted his judgement.

"No Coburn, no way," he said as soon as she turned the corner into his area.

"Nothing's changed. We touch Miller, and Coburn can sink us all. As long as Zee is not being harmed, the only real option is to wait it out. Miller will cool down, and then we can get Zee back in action."

Pia came prepared, since she was fairly sure what the Colonel was going to say. "And what if we need him before that happens? What if the Ceresian decides to get rid of us and we need to leave quickly? This is petty and ignorant, and it needs to stop."

"Come sit down," he said.

"I'm not some schoolgirl who needs to be calmed down, Charles."

"No, just listen then. I've been in a chain of command nearly my entire life. Want to know what keeps it all running smoothly? Power. Or fear of whoever has the power. Miller may not amount to much as a person, but he has full control of this mission."

"That's great, we just do nothing and wait for him to stop being jealous?"

"Instead of going behind his back with talk of mutiny, why not go talk to him?"

"Oh, I intend to." Pia was nearly growling out the last words. She turned abruptly and bounded away, determined to confront Miller. Before she could make it up to his office, she heard his voice in her chip comm.

'Pia, meet us in the lower cargo hold.' Miller's voice made her stop and change direction yet again, and she made it down to the cargo bay in under a minute. Miller was flanked by Theo, Gabe, Lara, and Sara. They all appeared to be busy building another drill.

Sara turned and gave a resigned shrug. "Welcome to Plan B."

"Aren't we up to Plan Q or R by now?" Pia countered. "Besides, what's wrong with our current plan?"

This time Miller jumped back in. "Too slow. Hold off on any more contact with the creature for now. We're going to drill a second tunnel in a thinner section of regolith and try to sneak past it."

"What the hell is that supposed to do?"

Gabe tried to be a peacemaker. "Let's just give it a shot, Pia."

"You should know better...Gabe." She shot him dagger eyes for going along so willingly with Miller. She suddenly felt all alone in her struggles now that everything was starting to fall apart. The crew had all been onboard for a mutiny, then Miller locked up Zee and no one lifted a finger to help.

"Even if we drill a tunnel and miraculously it has clear access to the ocean, how long do you think it will be until the Ceresian blocks off that tunnel too? The only way to gain access to the ocean indefinitely is to make peace with the creature who basically controls the entire planet."

"So you think you can get your best friend down there to make it rain some diamonds on us?"

"That's what I'm afraid of happening, we do something wrong and it decides to flick us off its planet, whether it be an accident or not."

"Ceresian? Its planet? You sound like a Free Earther. If you want to stay out of confinement like your boyfriend, I'd suggest you fall in line and stay out of our way."

Pia was so mad she didn't even respond. She stomped a boot down sharply in front of her and flipped into an expert aboutface. She was out the hatch before anyone could respond. Once she got out of the hab, she rushed into the nearest corner and began breathing heavily, nearly hyperventilating from the stress. She recovered quickly, afraid someone might leave and see her.

She paced around aimlessly for a minute, having no choice but to keep moving from the emotion. Unfortunately, there were few rooms in the spaceship good for rage pacing, until she remembered the printer deck. After she returned to her central forest core and took the short cut down to the cargo bay, she slipped through the hatch and lost her breath.

Down around her ankles there were endless varieties of wildflowers, waving in an imaginary breeze across fields which stretched off towards impossibly distant horizons. The holographic sun beat down from straight overhead, possibly due to the cargo bay's low ceilings, but also because it was the best for shining on every petal of every wildflower, all at once.

Pia smiled at the thought of Zee having to research wildflowers in order to program such an exquisite scene. Despite all of the frustration boiling away inside her, the field seemed to wash over her, eroding her anger by the second. Pia didn't want to march around anymore, so she sat down, right there in front of the hatch. As she ran her hand across a hundred nearby blooms, she wondered how long this holo had been running.

She reached out with her mind to find Zee, but even when she knew where he was, the security programs in place to block his chip were too much for her to overcome. He appeared to her now only as the light green blur on an electric field map.

Her gaze focused back to the fields surrounding her, and how peaceful it all felt. A piece of her wanted to run off and find a comfy nook in her now backup status greenhouse. It would be so easy to simply give up and let Miller take the lead.

'Fuck that,' she thought. *'This insanity has to end.'* She stood and walked for the ladder, making all the flowers glitch as she passed through them. Before she started to climb, she swiped towards the main control panel and caused harsh gray cargo flooring to replace the fields.

Pia was determined to get back down with the Ceresian before Miller managed to piss it off for good. If she was going to do this without being noticed, she would have to move slower than she would like. Once the drill team was finished with their assembly, Pia could sneak down into the launch bay room. With a quick step against the top ladder rung, she lept and flew towards the exosuit station. She landed with more noise than intended, and rushed to get suited up.

Just as she was halfway through changing, she realized that she needed someone to lift the air tank in place. She slowly zipped up past her chest as she sighed at her own stupidity.

"You feeling as dumb as you look right now?" The Scottish came out thick as Sara enjoyed catching Pia in the act.

To her credit, Pia did not entirely freak out after getting scared, although she failed miserably at playing it cool. When she was able to form words again, she muttered, "will you just come over here and help me with this tank?"

"Damn, you're cranky as hell. You on the warpath for Zee?"

"It's not just that, it's all of this." Pia swept her hands in all directions. "Zee got in trouble for something any of us might have easily done. You can't just turn your back on him and follow Miller, no matter how much power that prick has. You're better than that."

"Whoa, tiger." Sara came over and pulled the stretchy exosuit into place over Pia's torso, then started on the air tank. "I was just busting your lady balls, alright? We're all on your side, now more than ever. Even Coburn is starting to see the light. Figured you'd come up with a plan, so we're distracting Miller with his own ego."

A wave of relief washed over Pia, just knowing that her friends were still supporting her. She checked the readings on her air supply which Sara just finished clicking into place.

"So what's the plan?" Sara asked.

Pia looked down and continued her safety check. "Well, I'm going back down there."

"Uh, no shit. What are you going to do when you get down there?"

"I wish I knew."

"Nice plan, you sure you're not American?" Sara grinned.

"Fous-toi." Pia laughed, and it echoed in the cramped space of the airlock Pia was climbing down into.

"Fuck you, too. And good luck, Pia."

Pia signaled for Sara to close the hatch door and start the depressurization inside. The process only took a few seconds, but seemed like forever while Pia thought of Miller noticing the outer door hatch opening. She stepped off the ladder and, for the second time, felt the crunch of ancient regolith beneath her boots.

She glanced over in the direction of the second tunnel they were drilling, but could only make out the floodlights shining on the dig site. There's no way anyone could've seen her exiting. She hustled across the distance between Cerex and the ice tunnel, checking every few steps for signs on the crew comm that she had been spotted.

When she finally reached the opening and climbed into the airlock, she was immensely relieved. Then she remembered the rest of her plan, or lack thereof. This time she opted to descend head first the whole way. The climb was easier this way, and she was terrified of not being able to see if a crystal or tendril was coming toward her. The low gravity let her lower herself gradually using her hands. Beads of moisture were sweating out of the pores in the ice walls, yet another reminder that the tunnel was now full of alien produced copycat air. Pia had run spectroscopy on samples gathered by the helmet's filtering system, and the air was chemically identical to the high oxygen mixture which is fed through the exosuit tanks.

There were no surprises as Pia glided her way down the narrow passageway, and her determination grew with each second. By the time she finally reached the entrance to the dome, she had even managed to work up a bit of confidence. *'After all, I'm the one who's actually communicated with an alien,'* Pia reasoned with herself. *'That was me, no one else. While Miller finishes off his stupid second tunnel, I'll be...'*

Her brain stopped working momentarily as she saw what was waiting for her at the bottom of the dome. A small nuclear core had been detached shoddily from a generator bot and surrounded with an odd contraption attached to industrial wiring. *'Bomb,'* she thought.

She had been logged out of the shipwide comm before now, worried that Miller would stop her from going down again. With nothing to lose at this point, Pia switched over to the main channel.

'I need help here, people. I'm back in the dome, but now there's a bomb in here with me.'

Miller jumped into the lead unexpectedly. *'Jesus, Lamotte. Okay, let's get you back home safely before we deal with your monumentally poor decision making.'*

'What kind of a bomb is it, Pia?' Theo's voice was much more reassuring, and it was around then that she finally realized the absurdity of her asking for help with a bomb. There were only a few crew members, and Pia didn't have to do much thinking to decide who the one person was who would ever consider doing this. Miller

was still playing the innocent hero, probably embarrassed that Pia caught him before he could blow up his bomb.

'The blinking kind, I don't know. What do I do?'

'What's blinking?' Theo asked.

'The goddamn bomb, Theo! The...oh Jesus it's not the wiring, it's the nuclear core.'

'Get the hell out of there, Pia, right now.' Vineland sounded worried, which freaked out Pia more than anything else.

Pia turned back to climb up the ice tunnel, then froze. *I can't. I need to take it away from the Ceresian.*

The comm was flooded by protests and demands for her to drop everything and leave, but she had made up her mind. Pia carefully lifted the entire bomb up off the dome floor. It was less than a meter wide, and she was able to push it ahead of her as she climbed up the tunnel. The elbow turn got a little scary when the bomb took a hard bump into the wall.

Once she reached the airlock, Pia couldn't open it. She punched at the trigger panel, but nothing happened. The power was cut to the entire unit. The same could not be said for the bomb however, as the core started visibly pulsating with energy as the core destabilized.

She tried shoving the bomb into the small side cutout dug beneath the airlock by the original bots. It wasn't much, but enough to lodge the bomb in place while she fled down the tunnel. Pia let herself fall straight through, picking up some speed even as her exosuit scraped its way along the ice. She took a serious ding to her shoulder while she made the turn, but managed to make a strong push off for the bottom.

Her speedy descent allowed her time to reach the dome just before the bomb detonated. The shock wave sped down the tunnel after her, rocketing towards her battered suit. When it hit, Pia was thrown down against the crystal floor, leaving her gasping for breath. A few panicked heartbeats later, all of the air rushed up into the tunnel, hissing as it left the room. Absolute silence blanketed the dome for a split second. Pia thought her eardrums had been punctured, but then she heard the rock begin rumbling.

Pia could barely move when she saw the flames start to speed down the tunnel at her. They glowed strangely and emerged out of the tunnel like a liquid blow torch. Her face stared transfixed at her coming death, not noticing as the dome began warping.

Rapidly thickening stained glass seemed to rush up around her, with vivid orange flames dulling into much darker maroon, then deep purple as the explosion enveloped the crystalline egg that had grown out from the dome floor to surround her. When the light finally ceased, Pia felt what was left of her senses falling away into a blissful rest.

Chapter 20

When she woke up, Pia could barely see. Even if she was capable of standing, which was doubtful at the moment, the crystal pod that saved her remained less than a meter around her body. She could only manage to prop herself up on an elbow before her helmet bumped into the ceiling.

An alarm was going off in her suit. Pia glanced at her chip display to find the cause, and saw her air was nearly out.

'What happened?' she thought at first, then, *'The explosion! How long has it been?'*

Datanet said only an hour had gone by since she was knocked out. Her air tank must have been damaged to be running out already. She was out of options, so after making a silent prayer, she unlatched her helmet. When no spontaneous explosion or flash freeze happened, Pia leaned forward and wrestled her helmet completely off.

The first breath came against her body's strong objections, but her mind, and desperation, prevailed in forcing her lips open. She gulped so hard she choked like a fish on the dock, but soon her face relaxed and normal breathing took over. Now that she was officially alive, Pia decided it was a good idea for her to share that news.

Only when she went to access the comm channels, she realized she had been locked out entirely. Everything but her internal memory and functions was shut off. *'Miller covering his tracks,'* she thought. Wonderful. *'No way to call for help, check. Dwindling air supply, check. Trapped under rock, ice, and an alien, check check.'* Her thoughts were slowly being drained of energy as the shock of her situation wore off.

'Never going to see the sun again...check. Never going to be with Zee...check. Going to die, alone and terrified...like my parents...check.'

Suddenly she laughed loudly, her eyes glazed over by the dazzling reflections around her. She grabbed a glove and twisted to unlock it. As it came off and away, Pia reached out and touched the smooth inner walls with her bare hands.

When her fingertips made contact with the glassy surface, all sensation fell away from her mind. Or more specifically, all Pia's senses and thoughts were drowned out by the cacophony of energy currents streaking through her body. She thought she had felt the vast power coming off the alien before, but that had barely scratched the surface.

What she felt now was a primal force, not causing any pain, but taking over her completely. Her bruised limbs pressed uncomfortably against the inside of the exosuit, attempting to escape the onslaught of energy. As she became a conduit for the creature, her chip struggled to adapt, eventually making some progress after a few turbulent seconds.

The white flash gradually subsided and her vision cleared. She said a silent apology to the twins back at Natocorps in France, because the technology in her skull was worth every penny. Endless branches swept through the planet from the very core up to the geysers at the surface. The full extent of its reach couldn't be measured in terms of individual lifeforms. Instead, Pia could feel the movements of whole ecosystems within the coded energies of the crystal. The oceans allowed the Ceresian to grow to such gargantuan size; it provided resources, a way to move its otherwise fragile structure, and a defense against predators. At one point there must have been other lifeforms on Ceres, but the Ceresian dominated from the safety of the deep.

Once Pia felt under control of her mind again, she tried reaching back toward Cerex; a brilliant blue and gold lattice of energy highlighted the spaceship she had called home for the last year. This time the static of blocked signals was easily brushed aside.

'Zee.' She spotted his electronic signature, but not in the cargo bay where she expected to find him. He was up in Miller's private hab. She pulled up the room footage, despite those files usually being strictly locked out.

"I knew you were a Free Earther since before we left Earth," Miller was telling Zee. "Now, you're going to take the blame for this explosion, say you wanted to stop me from reaching the ocean."

"You son of a bitch," Zee responded. "How much is enough for you?"

"It's not about me, it's all for Natocorps. We have to maintain our edge against the competition, and that creature is blocking us from taking what we need."

"What competition? There's enough on the surface to buy out every Multinat a dozen times over. And your printers, they actually work! You could feed the planet, end the wars."

"Why? Conflict is good for business. Sure, we'll let a little tech trickle out, at a price, but-"

"You killed Pia!" Rage filled Zee, and Pia immediately reached into his mind and brushed away the lockout Miller had placed on Zee's chip. She had no idea how she did it, but she just thought it and it happened. Zee's eyes flashed wide as he realized what had happened, but he didn't let on to Miller.

"An unfortunate act, but she wasn't going to stop fighting me. I had to get her and that thing out of the way. Two birds with one stone."

"You're not a god, you don't choose who lives and dies."

"Oh, calm down. I know you were sweet on her, but get with the program. It's done. You do as I say and live like a king back on Earth, or rot in prison until you die."

"And what if the rest of the crew disagree?"

"Oh, they're welcome to step out of the nearest airlock. Crew can be replaced, and most things here are automated anyway. But I think you overestimate their backbones. After all, not one of your supposed friends objected to your arrest when I told them you had blown up the tunnel."

"Maybe we think differently now," Vineland said as he came through the lower hatch, followed by Theo.

"What's this now? Colonel, take this piece of shit out of my hab and lock him back in storage."

Charles undid Zee's restraints and helped him to his feet. "You go help Pia. The rest of us are heading to the blast site already. Zee's chip feed just played on every holowall in the tech habs."

"Pia's alive?!" Miller screeched.

'You sound disappointed, Commander,' Pia said weakly, one slow word at a time. Then she switched to a private link with Zee.

'Hey, you.'

'Are you okay? I'm so sorry I lost my temper. If I...'

'Stop,' Pia cut him off. *'There's no time for normal.'* She braced against the walls of her pod, flexing and contorting to escape the burden of such power.

'About to do something stupid, thought you should know I love you,' Pia blurted out. *'If this works, you'll see me over at the second tunnel. If it doesn't... then you won't, I suppose.'*

'You're gonna be okay, you hear me?'

'No, I'm not. Don't be such an idiot.' Pia smiled through the grimaces.

'Okay, tough girl. I'll see you in a minute.'

'See you soon.'

Pia pried her fingertips off the crystal and immediately fell limp. A few seconds later, her legs curled up a bit as she flipped onto her stomach. She scanned every part of the structure for cracks or seams, but nothing stood out.

She slammed an elbow against the crystal beside her chest. Nothing.

Nerves were beginning to make Pia's moves erratic as she twisted and searched for anything useful. Her helmet might be strong, but damaging that would be a death sentence. Her eyes locked instead on a couple short crystal shards protruding from where the protective bubble was formed.

After slipping her gloves back on loosely, she gripped one shard in each hand, and was able to get enough leverage to crack one loose. Her celebration ended prematurely when ocean water began seeping back in through the gaps. Taking the broken shard, she aimed for the gap where it came from and jabbed repeatedly.

There was a high pitched clap of thunder each time her shard made contact; the pod vibrated as she hammered away. By the time she made a few scratches the pod was halfway full of water and her willpower was starting to fade.

Her face was held up near the top of the pod, and she began to slow her pace as panic and exhaustion were competing to slow her down. As she sat there preparing to drown, she brought the shard up next to her face. It glowed on the side facing her head, but just enough to notice.

"The chip," Pia said in realization. She brought the crystal right up and touched it to her temple. An incredible display of sparks burned like a blowtorch on the crystal closest to her implant. The rising water gleamed a warning back at Pia, causing her to waste no more time. She held her chip implant as close to the pod ceiling as she could, but got no similar response. The shard being disconnected seemed to make it open to new instructions.

Pia held the shard up next to her face again, and this time began broadcasting a strong beacon signal. The shard lit up brightly with each ping, but the pod was nearly full. Whatever she was going to do, she had to do it now.

Pia sloshed onto her side and jammed the shard back into the indent where she broke it off. Instead of another beacon broadcast, she remembered her hotwiring experience from on Cerex. One hand held the shard into place beneath her, while the other hand shook off a glove and pressed its palm flat against the ceiling.

Reconnecting with the Ceresian was like grabbing a live wire, but her bet was working. The current ran through her body and into the shard, completing the circuit. As the torrent of power rushed into the shard, it fused itself back into place, but only for a moment.

Once the shard fully connected, Pia's entire Datanet was streaming a spectacular spider web of lightning quick flashes throughout the dome. The shard, along with the rest of the pod back to the stem, recoiled into itself in under a second, leaving Pia alone in the dark ocean to float around the giant creature.

She whipped her head around, pushing the hair off her face, until she saw a stream of light nearby. From the stem which grew the original dome, there was a side branch snaking off towards another light source. Her strong legs pumped hard one last time, ignoring her pleading lungs, and it was just enough to reach out and grab the side tendril. With no more energy left to swim, Pia pulled herself along hand over hand. Beautiful rainbow patterns of energy sped along their pathways, distracting her rapidly fading mind. She stopped and stared at the colors, sinking into them further with each breathless second. When they surrounded her vision, she felt an intense warmth overtake her body, and she closed her eyes.

She could feel the cool autumn breezes brushing past her face back in Pando forest. 'Such quiet,' she thought, her lips relaxing into a smile. Then birds broke her peace with loud squawking. She tried to ignore it at first, but it just got noisier. *'What's going on that's worth disturbing me while I'm dying?'* she thought as she opened her eyes again.

Blurry and tinted red, Zee's face darted around in a panic. She couldn't make out what he was saying. *'What a strange bird,'* she laughed gently. She carefully tested if she could still move her arm, and was delighted to find out she could. She reached up to grab the little bird and calm all of his frantic movements.

As her hand met the crystal in front of her, it melted away in all directions. Air burst down over her face, along with a huge wall of voices she thought she recognized. A pair of hands reached down and grabbed the shoulders of her exosuit, then yanked her whole body up and out of the opening her hand had triggered.

An emergency air mask covered her mouth and nose, leaving her slowly clearing mind to focus on the face staring down at hers.

'Pia, can you hear me?' Zee pleaded.

'Zee? Is that you?'

'I love you too, Princess.'

When they finally make it back to the ship, they're met at the main entry hatch by most of the crew, except for Miller. Coburn came up to Pia and held her by the shoulder for a moment.

"He's a monster. I'm so sorry, Pia." She nodded her acceptance, but shuffled past without stopping. Meanwhile, Vineland approached Zee and handed him his holo pendant back.

Pia looked at Coburn. "Where is he?"

Coburn's eyes twitched as he accessed something on the Datanet, then told her, "See for yourself. I just unlocked all of your chip restraints."

Zee found him in no time. *'I see you out there, you bastard.'*

'Ahh, McKinnon. Two steps behind as always. I'm on my way to blow a sizable hole in this alien.'

Coburn jumped in, *'you don't have to do this.'*

'You pathetic sap, you caved even quicker than I expected. The rest of you are relieved of duty, by the way. I'll handle this myself.'

'You don't understand,' Pia cautioned. *'The Ceresian is smart. It'll defend itself.'*

'Save your speech, Lamotte. I'm just going to teach it not to mess with us.'

Zee was over at his main terminal again and hacked into the rover's controls to shut it down.

'Son of a bitch!' Miller barked. *'McKinnon, you messed with me for the last time.'*

Emergency alerts began blaring around the crew as the tech deck went into lockdown mode. Vents hissed loudly as air got forcibly evacuated from the area. Theo tried to manually open the main hatch, but it wouldn't budge. Everyone else dashed for the exosuit locker, but it was on the far side of the room. They all staggered to the ground as hypoxia set in. All but Zee.

Pia watched in confusion as she began to lose consciousness for the second time in the last hour. Zee continued working at his terminal, unaffected by the lack of air. Pia pleaded to him for help, but his eyes were glued to his screens.

'This ends now, Miller.'

'How the fuck are you still talking?'

'If I were you, I'd be more concerned with what I just sent your way.'

Miller began cursing in fear, but Zee cut off the feed.

Pia's fading Datanet showed mini drones swarming out toward Miller and the disabled rover. With Miller even going after Coburn, Zee had no choice but to stop the Commander now. He worked his holocomp furiously, and didn't let up until he regained control over Cerex life support.

In under a minute, air returned through the vents. The crew were all out cold, but they gradually regained their senses. Pia went over to Zee and grabbed him by the chest. She climbed up onto his lap, with the holo light shining schematics across her chest as she kissed him passionately. Then as she pulled back away, she raised one eyebrow at him.

"Sooooooo...are you a robot, honey?"

"Free Earth nanotech, in my bloodstream," he blurted out between kisses, "able to produce and deliver medicine, oxygen, repair damage, stuff you wouldn't believe. Multinats keep it all suppressed, so they..."

"You *DID* break your arm when we landed in Occator! God damn it, you had me thinking I was going crazy."

Zee let a wide smile spread across his face, while the rest of the crew watched the wall holo again as the drones were nearly to Miller. He had reached the tunnel and loaded a bomb down into it. In his hand was a small detonator, which he waved back and forth in front of himself.

'Call off your toys, McKinnon. The bomb is on its way, and only I can turn it off. Let me return safely or the bomb goes off now.' Zee didn't flinch as the drones closed to under a hundred meters. Pia reached over to his display and triggered an override.

'He deserves it!' Zee argued.

'It's not worth triggering a reaction by Ceres that could kill us all. Maybe we can bargain his life for not setting off the bomb. It hurts nothing to try.'

The drones swarmed around Miller as he began laughing hysterically. *'That's right. You can't touch me, you prick!'*

The ground began violently shaking, making Cerex sway slightly. Cracks split the ground around Miller as he fell to his knees. Soon steam was pouring up through the multiple fissures and the regolith for several meters around him crumbled.

Zee's drones captured Miller's eyes wild with terror as the rock broke away. An enormous blue crystal spear came piercing the surface, ten meters across and shining with an unnatural inner light.

Miller was impaled on the jagged leading edge as it shot up and out of orbit. Debris exploded out in a slow motion bloom, with some smaller rocks even pelting Cerex. The feed stayed tracking Miller as he receded into the blackness to drift among the stars pinned to his treasure.

With Coburn now technically in charge, he was able to use CereSat to signal Natocorps and inform them of Miller's death. The crew nominated Pia to talk on their behalf, and she delivered a message back to Earth:

'We control Ceres from now on. Release your printer food tech to the Datanet, and we'll supply you with all the riches you'll ever want.'

Pia knew it wouldn't be as simple as that, but she also wasn't prepared for their response, which arrived a few hours later.

'Natocorps is no longer an independent corporation. In light of recent discoveries there, we have decided to merge with the other Multinats. You will not be allowed to land on Earth, and all satellite communications will be intercepted and blocked. We will collect our riches with or without your help. Land on Luna and surrender if you want to live.'

Pia sat there in the command hab, shocked when Zee played it back for her. There was no way this ended in anything but jail or the grave for anyone who surrendered.

Pia leaned back in Miller's fancy Commander chair, digging her bare toes into some soil she had brought up from her forest. She glanced over at Zee before opening the main comm channel:

'We're all in this together now. They can't let us live, and we can't let them continue their destruction. We either get our message to Free Earth...or we die trying. Welcome to the rebellion.'

Part 5
Blue Moon

Chapter 21

A ship the size of Cerex was easy to spot by the defenses around Earth. Long range sensors picked it up on radar nearly fifty thousand kilometers out, triggering a massive reactionary launch of all nearby Globalcorps anti-ship drones.

Fortunately, that barrage never reached its destination. Unfortunately, that's only because ground based lasers got there first.

The ship's hull creaked as it was deformed by the extreme heat. It gave the appearance of an imploding tin can, buckling one hatch and rivet at a time, until suddenly it was all over.

Multiple lasers grouped together as their aim was refined. This tore a hole through the length of the craft, gutting it in an explosion which left nothing but tiny twisted wreckage in all directions. Parts of South America would be dealing with the fallout, but beyond that it was as if Cerex had never even existed.

Long before this all took place however, Pia had been so hopeful after finally reuniting with Zee. The crew had rallied behind her as their new leader, which she hated of course, but which also made her the perfect choice.

Miller's violent end had left a sizable geyser covering much of Occator with snow from the ocean spray. It would be enough to fuel an armada for a decade, but didn't help them with the engines. They were printed as fast as they possibly could, with Zee overseeing their production, but it still took weeks for the new rockets to slowly take shape.

The rest of the crew were busy with other preparations. At first when they were disowned by Globalcorps, Sara and Theo voted to begin building a settlement on Ceres, hoping that they could offer a second home to anyone on Earth who managed to escape. Lara and Charles opted to go back, because as they said, "we're too old to start over on a whole new planet."

Gabe and Coburn, being relatively young and unattached, weren't ready to stay marooned on a barren dwarf planet forever either. This left Theo and Sara as the only ones in favor of staying. Pia had talked privately with Sara afterwards, and convinced her that leaving was the only choice.

"Listen," Pia said. "The only way we're going to be able to pull this off is if all of us stick together."

"You're not exactly selling it as the safer option."

"Who needs safe? You're the bravest woman I've ever met."

Sara sighed and turned away from the compliment. "It's not about being brave, Pia."

Her eyes were set hard in her face, as if she was keeping her emotions in check through brute force. "I've never had anyone like Theo before. I don't want to lose him literally right after I finally found him. Staying here may let us have a life together."

"What kind of life would that be, though?" Pia leaned back for a moment, thinking of her own situation. "I get it, it's scary to find something like that, because then you have a lot to lose. But running away isn't the answer. Come with us. Help us save billions of people, and then I promise you can go play in the dirt with Theo."

Sara kept her face serious, but her eyes darted up to Pia on their own. "You know that's not what people mean by dirty talk, right?"

"I'm French, we practically invented dirty talk." Pia would have missed Sara terribly, and counted on their friendship to stay sane. "Don't we have to go talk with Theo now?" Pia asked.

"No," Sara chuckled. "He'll agree with me if he knows what's good for him."

Despite everyone agreeing to depart, no one wanted to simply hand over Ceres to whomever decided to come next. Preparations for a planet wide defense system were started alongside work on the new Cerex engines.

Zee led the rest of the techs in building a self-sustaining power plant buried deep underground. It was linked to a massive array of solar panels deployed around the rim of Occator, along with one of the remaining mini nuclear reactors.

This became the base camp for a self-replicating assembly line of rovers and drones. Gabe had been inspired by seeing the crystal torus creatures, and adapted the design into large rock worm type machines slowly churning their way through the regolith, bringing back a steady supply of raw materials. Theo had topped it all off with a network of automated anti aircraft drone launchers. Similar to what they had used to repel the Multinat attack, these potato guns were installed by the rover fleet all around the planet. By the time Cerex was ready to launch, they had set up forty stations, and the system would be able to add one more per day after they left.

Pia even managed to do a little more interspecies diplomacy before they left. At her suggestion, Theo had rigged their mining system to sift out all the mixed gemstones, then send them down a tunnel into the ocean far below. When they sent the first load of gems down, the Ceresian sealed off the area with another dome.

Once the gems began filling up the dome, the tendril retreated back down to the abyss. The next loads rained down through the water, and the hole remained unsealed from then on. The peace offering was both a way of apologizing for the bombs Miller had set off, and an indefinite payment system for their presence on the planet.

After a few setbacks, Cerex was retrofitted with her newly printed engines. The power plant was installed, and its rovers were hard at work building their empire of drone launchers. "Not much firepower in any single one, but they're scaleable and damn near impossible to wipe all of them out at once," Theo explained.

Pia transformed her forest hab back up against the walls to be ready for their artificial gravity. *'Traxler would be proud'*, Pia thought. She had doubled the size of her forest, moving extra beds of plants wherever she could make room.

Her first stop had been Miller's personal cabin and office. *'If only I had pansies onboard,'* she thought, before filling his spacious rooms with rows of squash instead. Zee told her that was kind of a messed up joke, but it sure made Pia feel better.

She even managed to spruce up the printer deck with some actual plants instead of the holo variety. Whenever Pia had been stressed in life, she would end up planting something. The feeling of helping new life grow was an instantly calming force for her. Despite the extreme stress on all of them, escaping her central hab in order to branch throughout the ship made Pia genuinely happy. Orchids and other pollinating flowers were added to the tech deck in a possibly futile attempt to class that section up. Grasses lined every floor in the common areas. If she was going to die soon, it would be on her terms.

Finally, despite Zee and most everyone else telling her to leave it be, Pia decided to visit the Ceresian one more time. It hadn't shown itself since the initial dumping of gems into the ocean, but she hoped it would return for her. She had to see it again, and somehow thank it for saving her life. After pulling a metal and nanofiber exosuit on, she went down to the bottom of the tunnel opening.

The ocean looked deceptively empty, with not a single thing in the two hundred meter wide dome of light carved out by their floods. Pia swam down a few meters, then released a handful of holochips. Each glinted with reflected light as they took a zig zag path down before blinking out of range. Pia pulled up the main Cerex controls, and waited as she squinted to look past the light.

As soon as the first projections were emitted from the holochips, Pia cut the lights. What bloomed into existence beneath her in every direction took her breath away. She had told Zee to prepare something for her to show the Ceresian, but left the details pretty vague.

At first came single lights, pin pricks against the endless black sea. More joined in, swirling together until the light all formed into a single sphere. Within seconds the ball of light grew from meters across to nearly the entire width of the holo projection.

The brightness was nearly overwhelming, but eased as suddenly as it came. This mini Sun gathered planets around itself, with Earth taking the main focus. As the projection zoomed in, Pia watched the life history of her planet condensed down into a minute long time lapse.

Corals and fish soon crowded for space, getting lost in a whirl of pastels and fins. The holo stayed with the corals an extra moment, then transformed into a lush forest teeming with wildflowers and birds. Trees towered the whole length of the display, and animals of all kinds wandered through.

Finally a human baby was seen, curled up in a blanket but mostly visible. It grew, sat up, teetered, and ran, then met a new person, causing another baby to appear. The original kept getting older as the cycle progressed, until it died sometime after its grandchildren were born. There was a simple beauty in this display of birth and death, an unbroken chain of humanity.

Above this churning, there came new images like handprints on cave walls, equations on a chalkboard, and rocket launches. Then came the faces of each crew member in turn, lingering a bit longer on Pia as the holo zoomed closer and circled around. Just as Pia was about to message Zee in embarrassment, the holo switched to Miller's scruffy face.

Her initial reaction was fear that somehow Miller had survived, but soon his face contorted into death and faded to dust beneath her boots. Next up was Earth, spinning in glorious blues and greens and whites. Rockets erupted into view and branched out to Luna, then one went on to tiny, ancient Ceres.

'Not bad for a holo head,' Pia teased, floating in the ever darkening sea. As the last of the display faded, a total blackness surrounded her. Nothing happened for more than a few minutes, but Pia patiently waited, her years of field work paying off once more.

She was about to give up hope of ever seeing the giant creature again, when a light began to form from deep in the abyss. It was a single sliver, like a sun ray coming up from below.

'How's telemetry on my visitor?'

Zee was right on top of it, answering almost before she had finished asking. *'It's tiny. Very tiny, and very powerful. It's giving off enough energy to run a city.'*

'I'm just hoping it has brakes,' Pia half joked.

The sliver streamed upwards like a meteor, its intensity growing with every passing second. As it approached Pia, still expanding at a tremendous speed, she began swimming evasively to avoid an impact. The crystal beam tracked and followed her movements, curving in gentle arcs, until thankfully slowing down as it approached.

The water surrounding Pia began to glow, nearly as bright as when the Cerex floodlight was still on. Not stopping for a moment, the light gathered around her. She could no longer see the sliver, or even the ice pack above her. The ocean vibrated as if it were about to start boiling, then held steady in this agitated state while Pia slowly turned to face the growing pressure from the incoming visitor.

Her body trembled in the hard casing of the exosuit, feeling pulse after pulse of strong ocean currents buffeting her around, but she stayed focused.

'You getting all this?' Pia asked.

Static.

'Damn, the energy must be overwhelming our signal,' she chipped, mainly to help calm herself. *'I'm going to keep describing what I see. Hopefully you can replay the recorder from my exosuit later.'*

After realizing her eyes were clamped shut, she forced them open, only to be assaulted by the light once again. She noticed herself shaking uncontrollably from the adrenaline. No matter how hard she tried, her senses simply couldn't come close to handling this onslaught, even with her chip helping.

'Too much, it's all too much. Going to try swimming back. Not sure which direction to head though. Really wishing I just sent a message in a bottle right about now.'

The change in intensity came gradually, and it took Pia a number of seconds to recognize it. The brightest core gathered directly in front of her, with the light tapering off to a dull glow everywhere else. The center grew ever smaller before taking solid form in the shape of an iridescent crystal shard.

'There appears to be an object projecting from the energy source. Not sure its purpose yet. Going to wait and see, and mainly try not to pee myself.'

Time stretched as Pia watched in silence.

'Ok, nothing else happened. The Ceresian must want me to touch the crystal again. And, of course, I'm dumb enough to do it. So, standby...'

Pia remembered the difference when she touched the Ceresian with bare skin last time, and hesitantly unlocked her glove in order to repeat the maneuver. It floated off to the side on its tether, and water rushed into her sleeve through the gaps. Several sensors got fried, but the suit was designed to contain breaches like these.

With the shard only a few feet in front of her, she took one last look downward, imagining the massive crystal lifeform lurking deep beneath her.. Her mind made up, she stretched an arm forward until her fingertips grazed the tip of the mysterious crystal.

She instinctively shut her eyes as she made contact, bracing for another onslaught of information. Several uneventful seconds passed, but still she felt nothing. One eye peeked open, then the other. She swiveled her head around, but there was only the shard shining as brightly as ever.

'If I just died, that was very anticlimactic.' Pia forced herself to keep talking, even if only to help maintain her composure. When no response came, she sighed and took stock of her situation.

'Ok, I touched the shard nearly a minute ago by my estimate, but there's nothing else happening.' Her thin eyebrows arched up as an idea finally dawned upon her.

Pia waved her free hand around, but encountered no resistance whatsoever. *'Wait, there really is nothing. There's no ice pack above me, no Ceresian below me. I'm not even sure I'm in water anymore.'*

She turned her attention back to the only object in sight, her forehead crinkled up in thought. The crystal hung in the nothingness, radiating an intense glow, but was otherwise unchanged. Pia chuckled to herself. *'Well, I'm not about to stop now.'*

She reached out once again to touch the shard, and this time when she touched it the glow dissipated quickly. Now Pia could see nothing except the illuminating gridwork of stripes along the outside of her suit.

'You playing shy now?' she asked the Ceresian.

As if on cue, an enormous blue sphere appeared in the distance and grew larger by the second as it approached Pia's position. It took up an entire hemisphere of her vision by the time it veered in front of her.

Wisps of white clouds streaked across its surface, while underneath there were a hundred shades of blue competing for attention. *'Neptune?'* she guessed as she reached out towards it instinctively. As it began receding off to her left, she was startled by another object smashing into it at a tremendous speed.

The explosion blinded Pia momentarily, but she fought the pain and opened her eyes as quickly as possible to see what had happened. Whatever hit the gas giant, it obliterated both itself and the vast majority of the Neptunian object. For a million kilometers in every direction, a tangle of ejected gas filaments shot out like party streamers. All that remained was a hot metal core, which itself was thrown off course by the explosion.

It moved slowly back towards Pia, while the rest of the hologram fast forwarded around it. The naked core wobbled into an orbit of what looked to be our own Solar System's asteroid belt. It cannibalized rock and water ice as it plowed through the millions of boulders in its path, until the gleaming heated core remnant was lost underneath a muddy slosh.

More time lapse showed a churning planet, boiling from within, as it slowly cooled enough for its surface to freeze over. Suddenly the object split open like a coconut, with one half disappearing out of view, allowing Pia to see the full scope of what was happening inside.

At the metallic core, something strange happened. As the planet settled into darkness, the Ceresian was born down in the hydrothermal geysers at the bottom of a rapidly forming ocean. A suddenly telescoping view showed simple crystal stalks sprouting from the sides of these geysers, all looking identical to each other. Soon these joined together into more varied structures, and the seafloor glowed with new life. With no competition at first and a virtually unlimited energy source at its disposal, the crystals expanded inevitably deeper. The core itself was controlled with elaborate tunnels carrying seawater and acting as rudimentary transistors. The Ceresian directed the movement of all water within its reach, and learned to redirect the planet's heat to exact locations on demand by cooling or heating various convective currents.

Pia stared vacantly, her mind absorbing massive amounts of data. Direct File Transfer was petty compared to this. Whatever the Ceresian was doing through her contact with the shard, Pia could see and feel everything. She was shown the evolution of this amazingly complex creature, as it learned to detach itself into billions of separate iterations, and then reabsorb them at will back into its massive core. The ocean expanded, offering a way to reach the surface. Raw materials from the regolith rained down, and were collected by various types of drone creatures: the crab and spider like creatures on the seafloor, the spaghetti filtering the water, and the torus creatures churning up anything too large for the others.

Then everything disappeared. Only the tiny glow from the shard remained, making Pia recoil her hand out of instinct. The shard floated through the water and stopped right in front of her face.

'To anyone who still hears me...hell, no one hears me. The shard seems to be detached and floating...towards me. Not sure what that means.'

She gently closed her bare hand around the crystal, but nothing seemed to happen. Only something had most definitely happened. Her datanet filled back up with voices and maps, startling her after the intense quiet of the previous few minutes.

'Anything yet, Pia?' Zee asked.

'Energy spike is receding,' Sara chimed in. *'We'll let you know the second we see anything on sonar.'*

Pia's disorientation prevented her from responding at first, but she kept a tight grip on the crystal. Unable to express what she had just witnessed, she looked around for the ice hole and began swimming towards it.

'Coming back.'

After some confused comments, the crew switched to prepping for Pia's re-entry. She didn't tell them of her vision at first, afraid they would think she hallucinated it. Even more than that, she was afraid she really DID hallucinate it.

However, the crystal shard she brought back put all her concerns to rest once they were able to fully examine it. Similar to the diamond matrix of Ahuna Mons, this small shard had all sorts of precious gems. In fact, it appeared to contain every element known to humanity, and quite a few unknown elements as well.

After weeks of hurried planning and construction, Cerex had its full set of engines again. After one last vote, the crew decided to go down fighting. Once all the habs were secured, a date was set for launch, and everyone said a final farewell to their home of the past few months.

Pia fashioned the shard into a necklace she could tuck under her shirt. Zee didn't keep anything but a handful of regolith, which he put into a small container and wore as a necklace to complement Pia's.

The launch itself went smoothly, a welcome change of pace for the crew. As Cerex lifted rapidly away from the dwarf planet, Zee sent a live holo feed to Pia through a private link.

She blushed terribly, laughed, then lay back in her G-mesh netting to wait out the launch. He had carved their initials ten meter high into the side of Ahuna Mons. As Ceres shrank rapidly away from them, they saw the flash of a second launch, even more powerful than their own.

'Decoy deployed successfully,' Vineland confirmed.

For the next six months, they could only wait and hope their plan would work. Luckily, this trip had quite a vigorous recreation schedule, as everyone found plenty of privacy. Even Hixley found the nerve to make her move on Vineland.

If they were facing a death sentence, then they all wanted to make the most of their final days and weeks.

Chapter 22

Before Cerex was officially blown to pieces, it blasted a signal out to all receivers on the near side of Earth. As expected, the SatNet was able to easily block the message using interference patterns.

Before the glowing shards of wreckage had even fallen to Earth, the entire attack was over. Radar stations monitored the debris field carefully, looking for independent movement, but it all crashed uneventfully enough.

Pia and the crew didn't get to see it directly however, because their ship, the real Cerex, was on the far side of Luna and creeping towards its north pole.

Sara had played her part perfectly, keeping Cerex in the radar shadow of the decoy for as long as possible. Before falling into Luna's gravity well, Cerex changed course and cut its engines, giving Globalcorps no reason to doubt their success.

Near the pole, Sara put them down in an unclaimed crater with a rim in perpetual darkness. Water ice was common in these areas, and sure enough, this crater had a great deal of it. The crew could set up rudimentary mining stations to begin producing fuel.

There wasn't much chatter on the comm lines in the run up to the decoy exploding, and even though their plan worked, seeing their possible future fate left the crew a bit shell shocked.

Globalcorps was not interested in talking. The newly formed megacorporation was out for blood, and there would be no going back to their old lives. Fortunately, their landing on Luna appeared to go unnoticed; all of the defenses had seemed focused on ships approaching Earth.

Once safely down, the crew assembled in the loading dock for a quick meeting. Then Vineland gathered a small scouting group to go over their individual assignments. Barton, Santos, and Coburn were all going to various nearby lunar settlements to look for sympathetic miners or lax security; Cerex may not have really exploded, but without fresh supplies the crew wouldn't be safe for long.

Theo and Lara set about powering the ship with simple solar arrays and water ice mining. Zee oversaw the whole operation using his newly retrofitted holo station up in the command module. As usual, Pia found a reason to go off exploring by herself.

The crew nodded at Pia as she passed by, their faces struggling to hide the anxiety they all felt. She strapped into her exosuit, eager to get off the ship after so many months.

Even with Cerex being kept spun up to Lunar gravity for the final month of their journey, Pia still wobbled a bit as she bounded across the rough terrain. Her headlamps cut like knives through the inky darkness, forcing her to keep looking down to see where she was stepping. All around was glistening ice, and it crunched with every boot step. After crossing a short distance, Pia sat down to catch her breath.

'All good, princess?' Zee chimed.

She sighed in return. *'Fine and freaking dandy.'*

'Sorry,' Zee laughed. *'Just checking.'*

Less than fifty meters away there appeared another crater, its tiny rim peeking up and reflecting her light. She was drawn to it, and she knew what she would do when she got there.

Ever since wearing the Ceresian necklace, Pia had been having incredibly vivid dreams. Her connection to the alien left echoes, but she didn't know what they meant. What she did know was that this leftover from a micrometeor was where it would happen. Tucked into a forearm pouch, the crystal necklace was already glowing through the dark suit fabric.

'Zee, permission to do something stupid?' Pia finally blurted out. Now face to face with her dreams, she was getting more frightened of the whole situation.

'How stupid are we talking about?'

'C'mon now. It's me.'

'Fair point.' Zee paused for a few seconds before continuing. *'But sanity is overrated, and we'd all have been dead if it wasn't for your particular brand of stupidity, on more than one occasion. Care to share with the class, though?'*

'The Ceresian, it showed me so much. And it gave me a piece of itself. I don't think it was just a parting gift. Ceres, the Ceresian I mean, wants to expand. We showed it how we came from another planet, and now through my help it has a chance to try the same feat.'

'Could be a powerful enemy if it wanted to be.'

'Or a powerful friend,' Pia came back. *'Either way, I owe it my life.'*

'You owe me a few lives, too, if I recall.'

'Oh, I see how it is. Well, you pick which part you want to break off and give me to wear as a necklace.' She would have given anything to see the look on his face just then.

Pia took the crystal in both gloved hands, and a whole spectrum of light began emanating from within. The dirty tan and grey crescent of Earth kept silent watch from the horizon as she lowered the intense blur of colors.

The crystal pulsed with ever more power, until threads of lightning began to arc from it. Pia struggled to see as the flashes overwhelmed her chip sensors. Finally she let go, and the crystal fell to the surface with an eruption of sparks.

Tendrils of light ricocheted through the ice and into the crater, producing sharp cracks under Pia's boots. As she fell backwards over the rim, she found herself laughing and running for cover.

'Well, it did something!' she squealed with delight.

'Great, now get the hell back in here.' Zee pleaded.

Soon the entire tiny crater settled into a soft blue glow, while a rainbow of light cut jagged paths across the landscape. She breathed heavily in her helmet, straining the air filters to prevent fogging up the glass. Her walk became a run as the cracks in the ice grew louder. Vibrations shook the larger crater, and a beam of light shot out from where Pia had placed the crystal.

'What the hell just happened at base camp?' Vineland asked.

Other crew chimed in with their own reports of feeling vibrations, some hundreds of kilometers away.

'I think...I might have...there's a new... Ceresian just born on Luna,' Pia replied, having to say the words out loud to believe them.

'Nah, not a Ceresian anymore,' Theo said.

'True, now it's a Lunar Gaia, Lunaia?' Zee suggested.

While they debated, Pia was climbing back into Cerex. Just as she cleared the ladder, the ground underneath sparked with energy. Pia turned back for one last look at the rapidly growing creature, then retreated inside.

Drones were picking up footage of the whole polar region coming to life with color. The icy pathways cut across ancient features and filled the polar region with a palpable energy. Back at Cerex, their cozy water filled crater now resembled a brightly lit ice rink. Their ship stood at the center, thrumming with new power.

'Umm, you're gonna want to see this,' Theo added.

Readouts flooded across the main crew feed before anyone had a chance to respond. Ground radar showed a rapidly expanding pocket of some kind.

'Water?' Pia asked as she entered the control room.

'Possibly,' Zee said. *'This expansion is accelerating quickly. Most of the Northern Hemisphere will be covered within the hour at this rate.'*

'Where is everyone?' Pia asked. *'We need to warn the Lunar settlements. People will be scared.'*

Vineland answered for the recon group. *'We're approaching the Meerkat Industrial Colony now. Hundred kilometers to go. Picking up some stronger vibrations.'*

Sara linked her optics feed to the main channel and piped in, *'Lunaia is on the horizon here. I'm within sight of Farside, but looks like we're gonna be overtaken in under a minute. Taking cover.'*

All the crew seemed to stop what they were doing to watch the blue speeding towards Sara's helm cam. It followed fissure lines across the landscape, shining through as the thick layer of dust fractured like broken glass. Flashes sparked out of craters, and shot straight up several meters off the rims.

Sara's feed got choppy as she dove into the harness of her drone transport. The simple machine was essentially a jet pack, but with less power than its Earth predecessors. On Luna, it gave people a quick transport while hovering a few meters up. As she strapped herself in, the video lifted away from the regolith. With the leading edge a mere seconds away, Sara took the jetpack up as high as she could.

The blue streaked across a nearby plain and then, it stopped. From one horizon to the other a glowing edge oscillated rhythmically, running directly underneath Sara.

'Now what?' she panted out in frustration.

'Hold tight, Barton, we're seeing the creature now too,' Vineland added, gesturing past Coburn in the passenger seat of their rover. Coburn had come through for Cerex when they needed him, but some remained wary of allowing him to visit a base by himself.

Multiple holo feeds filled the command hub walls as the feed from the rover with Santos was added to the crew and recon drone views.

'Here too,' Santos added. He was assigned the main Tycho crater complex, a sprawling mining colony nearly a hundred kilometers

wide. LunaComm, one of Natocorps' main former competitors, had developed a self-sustaining colony there with nearly 10,000 workers. If Cerex was going to find any friendly contacts, this was their best hope.

As the crew watched in tense anticipation, the blue line of Lunaia rushed up to where Vineland was parked. Sparks sprayed onto the rover treads, but the progress was again halted instantly upon reaching the rover. Santos confirmed the same happening near him a thousand kilometers away.

'Head back to Cerex, everyone,' ordered Zee.

'But I'm right here,' Sara complained, and walked a few paces towards Farside. As she went, the leading edge of Lunaia followed. Sara wouldn't have noticed right away except for all her crewmates screaming warnings.

'Freeze,' Pia cut through the chaos. *'It's stopped about a meter from you, same as before. Same EXACT, as before.'*

Sara caught on fast as always. *'C'mere big fella,'* she said while patting her thighs and backing up slowly. The blue horizon crept right along after her like a good pet. Sara turned towards Farside and grinned. *'We just got some serious muscle. I'm initiating contact.'*

That was typical for Sara, bristling under anybody else's command, and needing to feel in control again. *'Theo is a brave man to keep up with her,'* Pia often thought.

No one stopped her; since Miller's death they more or less worked without a leader. Bigger questions were voted on, so no one felt left out. But deep down, most of the crew wanted to see what Sara would do anyway.

The holos slowly all shrank away in the command hub, leaving only the three scout cluster feeds. Lunaia stayed a meter behind each team, but Sara was the only one moving. She swooped backwards and up in her jetpack, fascinated watching the deep blue wave keep perfect pace. It was as if there was no reaction time at all, and the alien simply locked itself into formation.

She evened out, then went full speed back towards Cerex. Again, the blue followed patiently.

'You done dancing, darlin'?' Theo's laughs were contagious, coming from such a deep, honest place. His booming voice snapped her out of it.

'Yeah, I'm done. Time to go visit the neighbors.' She turned and sped towards Farside for a moment before pulling up again.

'Shit, sorry.' Sara continued, *'I was going to go scare some Lunars, but probably not in our best interest right now. What should we do?'*

'I'm not sure...' Pia stammered. *'We can vote on a few options when everyone gets back I guess.'*

Zee jumped in, *'alright people, let's call it a day and-'*

'Bullshit. Sorry Zee. Something is happening right now, can't you feel it, Pia?'

'It doesn't matter what I feel. It's too dangerous while we don't know what Lunaia will do.'

'All do respect, boss, but you clearly have a connection with it. Has it done anything hostile, besides taking out Miller in self-defense?'

'No, quite the opposite, you're right. Plus, the element of surprise might make it worth going now. And if we don't know what it's going to do, then there's no point prolonging the suspense. All teams on board for a bit of an adventure?'

Determined cheers let her know they would follow her lead, and everyone was ready for some action after the boring trip from Ceres.

'Ok, Sara. Let's hold until the other two teams are in position. Vineland and Coburn, let us know when you're close. Santos, same with you. I want Gabe to make first contact at the biggest colony.'

'Damn it, why didn't I pick Tycho?' Sara grumbled.

'Because you're impatient,' Santos gloated. *'Any particular message for LunaComm?'*

'We come in peace?' Pia said half jokingly.

'Transmitting trade supply requests through my old back channel frequencies. Let's go see if anyone's home.'

He leapt out of his oversized rover, and bounded across the exposed bedrock in the direction of Tycho. As he jumped down a three meter cliff, floating down while barely breaking his stride, he must have seen the incoming missiles, because he immediately flattened himself to the ground.

Pia called to him, but explosions rocked the hillside behind him, pelting the surface, along with Gabe, in a rain of rocks and debris. Blue streaked across the entire field of vision, a thousand times the previous intensity; Gabe screamed as he stumbled blindly in a panic.

The light burned at their chip sensors, overloading them faster than they could adjust. Through the storm of blue came Zee's steady voice.

'Gabe, open your eyes, man. You're good now.'

A quick glance at Gabe's feed confirmed that the surface under him was unharmed except for some scattered missile debris. As Gabe finally managed to get his legs under him, his optic feed scanned across the massive crater.

Pia gasped as she processed the scene. Crystal spires had pierced a hundred times up into Tycho City, blue flashes strobed the surroundings buildings, and then there was Gabe, out on the outskirts with the face of someone tired of being so regularly almost dead.

But more important was what wasn't there: no explosions, no buildings decompressed, and very little debris dotted the landscape. Lunaia appeared to have deliberately missed everywhere it struck. No more missiles were fired, but the spires stayed put.

'That's an official 'I told you so', sweetheart,' Pia chided.

'Never been happier to be wrong.' Zee laughed. *'Now what?'*

'Have I taught you nothing, holoboy? We negotiate.'

Gabe joined in. *'Missiles. That's their opening offer. Not a lot of wiggle room.'*

'Except now they've met our counter offer up close,' Pia said. *'Nothing demands respect like a knife at your throat.'* Painful memories creeped in at the corners of her mind.

After a moment, Zee responded, *'And is that the type of people we are? Killers like them?'*

Pia regained her composure, shaking off the worry that had smeared across her face. She knew who she was. And now others were counting on her to protect them

'Of course not. Lunaia won't hurt them, at least not on purpose.' She leaned back in her seat and smirked. *'But the rest of Luna doesn't need to know that yet.'*

'So what's our next move?' Zee asked.

'Contact Tycho, Farside, and the Meerkats. Safe to say we have their attention. It's time for hearts and minds now.'

'So good cop?'

'Exactly. Time to flip some corporate cronies to our side. Set up a meeting with Tycho immediately. I'll go to them if necessary,' Pia said.

'Like hell you will. Holovid works perfectly fine for meetings.'

'Awwwww, he's jealous,' Pia teased on the main comm.

'He's smarter than I thought,' Theo piled on.

'Alright, let's get to work, people,' Zee said, then cut off his feed.

Chapter 23

Thankfully, Lunaia held its ground around Tycho City, and the scouts confirmed similar nonlethal crystal strikes at Farside and the Meerkat colony. Tycho was immediately hailing them on the open LunaComm network.

'Unknown intruder, please stand down. Our defenses are controlled by Globalcorps AI, but we've disabled the connection temporarily. We apologize for the hostile welcome. Please respond.'

Back on Cerex, Pia winked at Zee who sat beside her in the command hub. "Two pleases, you heard that?"

"Yeah, I heard. You got lucky, move on."

"They just apologized!" Pia laughed breathlessly.

"And what if Lunaia starts defending a bit more destructively? We can't possibly control it."

"She hasn't destroyed anything unnecessarily. Tycho could be shredded right now, but it's not. I can't imagine that's by accident."

"Exactly, we can't imagine much of anything Lunaia might do. I just worry you're putting too much faith in this creature."

"This *creature* is more advanced biologically than anything we've ever seen. It didn't ask for humans to come barging in destroying everything in sight." Pia's voice shook, and her balled up fists waved with emotion. "All I ask is you take a chance on her, like you did with me."

Zee grabbed her waist and pressed her forehead against his chest. "Ok," he told her simply. He took a slow breath before pulling away to look her in the eyes.

"So...what's the plan, boss?"

Pia glanced around the command hub for a few seconds, then seemed to come to an idea. "Time for a peace summit. Get the three bases within Lunaia's reach on comm. Invite them to Cerex. A single diplomat each. We'll meet them at a neutral location so we can be sure they're not armed."

"And what are we going to say when they get here?" Zee raised a questioning eyebrow.

"Don't rush me. I haven't figured that part out yet."

The three representatives all came to the assigned crater six hours later, with Theo standing as escort. After a few tense moments, they each introduced themselves.

Meerkat sent its third in command, a iron rod of a man with a deeply creased Globalcorps uniform on under his exosuit. "Granson Thekkold, Defense Minister of Meerkat." At this point he checked himself and pointed at the rank on his sleeve. "Lieutenant Thekkold, Globalcorps."

"Ouch," Theo patted him on the arm.

The next man was younger, but wilder looking, and Theo could see right away the kid was Luna born. Natives had a way about them that was unmistakable, a casual grace in their microgravity movements that took years for transplants to develop. Even then, the true Luna born stood out, and this one was no different.

"Moni Haven. Farside Security Chief. Had to come see for myself the Earth thieves who threatened my home."

Theo waved at him, then gestured for the last representative, a woman from Tycho, to break the tension.

"Jenty Ravort, COO of Globalcorps Lunar Division, and the only person here you really need to be talking to."

Theo went last, shaking each of their hands in turn before adding, "Theo Koeniger, I blow shit up. Mostly rocks, but I've been known to make exceptions."

'Theo, let's try to avoid interplanetary warfare if we can, shall we?' Pia scolded him, only half joking.

The group piled into a drone transport which carried them back to Cerex in the most awkward five minute trip of Theo's entire career. When they arrived and were all inside the Cerex cargo bay, Theo volunteered to stow their exosuits, then took the opportunity to make himself scarce.

Pia welcomed them all with a warm smile and a deep bow. Her hair was pulled back into a tight bun, and her Cerex uniform was spotless, a truly remarkable achievement for her. No one spoke for a minute while the diplomats and Pia sized each other up.

Pia exhaled loudly, with nervous energy pouring out of every movement. She took two hesitant strides towards her guests before addressing them.

"Who's hungry?" she asked as casually as she could manage. The diplomats exchanged confused glances before all nodding to play along. Pia backed up a step, and shrugged one shoulder up to her ear. "Follow me." She turned and led them into a nearby maintenance room that had been retrofitted into something resembling a board room.

The entire procession had to be a bit underwhelming for the diplomats, who represented some of the wealthiest Lunar colonies. They all brightened considerably once they saw the spread laid out along the entire center of the round table. Pia laughed at herself for coming up with the idea. Seeing the assortment of freshly printed fruit, cheese, and crackers, she wondered if she should have forgotten the whole stunt.

Her doubts were soon eliminated when she saw how hard the diplomats were working to keep their eyes off the feast. The Cerex crew had long gotten used to filet mignon and lobster, the perks of molecular level 3D printing and bored techs on a long return flight.

Pia addressed each in turn. "Granson, Moni, Jenty, I'm Pia. I'm going to try to keep this as simple as possible...which as I say out loud I realize is insane, because the presence of Lunaia around your homes makes everything complicated."

Jenty rolled her eyes, then sighed in frustration when Moni jumped up out of his seat. "Here we go..."

Moni leaned his whole skinny torso over the table, locking eyes with Pia the entire time. He whispered almost reverently, "You think it really might be Lunaia?"

Pia laughed, a cheerful noise which unfortunately did not produce a cheerful response. "Yes, of course it's Lunaia. But I mean, that's just what I began calling her."

Moni's eyes bulged normally, a common feature among Luna born, but now they seemed ready to fall out of his head. "As in Lunaia, from the Prophecy?"

Pia stood stunned for a moment, mortified that no one in the Cerex crew remembered that the Luna fringe had a whole mythology based upon the coming of a Lunar goddess.

Jenty stood up, shaking her head. "Can we please move on already. I didn't come here for stale bread and sermons. What the hell are you doing with that crystal weapon?"

Granson stood up too, but more in an attempt to command calm for everyone. "Let's at least hear her out." His pointed glance at Jenty drew a nod, and Moni still waited for an answer.

Pia's cheeks grew redder by the second as her welcome got off to such a poor start. She took a deep breath in through her mouth, brushed off Zee's private link message to reassure her, then let the air seep back out her nostrils.

"I don't know anything about a prophecy, but we have found something infinitely better. A planet sized intelligent being, comprising nearly the entire mass of what we call Ceres. This 'crystal weapon' as you call it," Pia cast an offended look towards Jenty, "is an offshoot of the original."

Nobody moved as the diplomats attempted to process this new information, all except for Jenty. Her calculating eyes studied her fellow diplomats instead of Pia.

"We have developed a connection with this creature, who has the ability to use collective energy to manipulate and transport vast resources. In conjunction with the food printers already available, we will have a virtually unlimited capacity to provide universal care for our citizens. This is not about winning you over with some cheese and crackers; it's about showing you that the Age of Scarcity is over. It's time to embrace a future that acknowledges this shift."

Moni blew out hard, an old Luna gesture, and not a flattering one by the expression on his craggy face. Granson shushed him, embarrassed by the rude display.

"Nice try, but I've heard Earthers promising us riches my whole life. If the printer tech is that good, then we wouldn't need your alien mining pet. Earth may be hurting, but there would still be plenty of raw materials available. How do we know this is even printed?"

Pia's face sagged as her big moment fell flat. "I mean, do you think we have fresh grapes on hand from our vineyard or something?"

"Could be brought up fresh from an ally on Earth," Jenty pretended to whisper to her colleagues.

"As we've been informed, Globalcorps runs the entire human race now. You think any orbital craft could make it to us? Through that blockade?" Pia gestured towards a holowindow projection where Earth hung in the Luna sky.

Moni glanced aside at Jenty, seeming to draw confidence from her icy glares at Pia. "Smugglers likely."

Pia threw up her arms and stood from the table. "This is ridiculous," she began, then changed course and beelined it for Granson. "What'll you have, Minister?"

The grizzled man perked an eyebrow up. He was old enough to remember seeing 2D holos of people taking food orders instead of printer walls. His cheeks raised despite his best efforts to stifle a smile. "I'll have sirloin steak, with a baked potato and salad, please."

Pia could've kissed the Minister for playing along, but toned it down to a wink, for Zee's sake. "Moni, what about you?"

"I want an orange...and a cake."

Pia laughed before checking herself once more. "Ok, any particular type of cake?"

"Good cake."

"Fair enough, we'll do our best," Pia chirped.

Jenty just waved her hands in front of her when Pia looked her way at last. "This doesn't prove anything. Let's go."

But Moni and Granson were not so easily ordered around now. Both waited and ping-ponged their eyes between Jenty and the already active wall printer.

"Your crystal attack will be treated as an act of war against Globalcorp. Stand down now or prepare for immediate destruction."

"Go ahead and try if you want, but Lunaia is already deep underground, most likely utilizing heat from the core by now. Only way you can destroy her is to obliterate Luna in the process."

Jenty practically snarled. "My thoughts exactly."

"You would destroy millions of your people and your entire mining operation just to spite us?"

"Who's *my* people? Our company won the Corps Wars by cutting off anything and anyone too weak to keep up."

Before Pia could respond, Moni climbed with uncanny speed up over the table and grabbed Jenty by the throat. Granson bounded his way over to the scuffle, but keeping up with a Lunar native was damn near impossible.

Thankfully, Theo hadn't wandered far, and he was there to assist before Pia even got to them. The massive Norwegian simply threw himself at the fight, grabbed Jenty and Moni, and held them apart at his considerable wingspan.

Moni flailed desperately to get at the arrogant COO. "You threaten Luna, you die."

Jenty shook Theo off her after she stood still for a few seconds. "Quite the opposite, actually." She looked on at her attacker like he was a stray dog. "We're done digging for scraps."

The woman turned abruptly towards Pia, while keeping one eye on Moni who was practically foaming at the mouth. "I should thank you, Ms. Lamotte."

"For what?" Pia tried to calm herself in case the situation could still be salvaged.

"It would have taken us years to set up a functionally significant mining supply chain from Ceres. Fortunately, you've brought it here to us. We can finally stop relying on the local population." At this she gave an exaggerated side nod towards her fellow diplomats.

Moni tried rushing Jenty once more, but Theo had a firm grip on his shoulders and barely budged from the effort of holding the skinny hothead.

Jenty laughed at the scene, angering Pia, before continuing, "The orders had already been sent to begin downsizing our human contingent. This meeting was merely a formality to buy time."

"Downsizing?" Pia asked.

Jenty just grinned and shrugged. "Obviously the machinery is worth salvaging, but the attack will spare most essential-"

Granson interrupted her before Pia could, "what attack? What have you done, Ravort?"

The COO sighed, as if disappointed that her words came as such a surprise. "Save your breath, please. You know I have no say in this..." She paused, considering her next words before deciding on, "not exactly a tough call though. The sooner we transition away from Loonies, the better."

Theo took a struggling Moni and tossed him backwards a couple paces. In the time it took the enraged Lunar to leap back to his feet, Theo had turned and grabbed Jenty by the collar of her Globalcorps uniform. She spit at him as he carried her out of the room.

Pia ran after them, followed by Moni and a wide eyed Granson. Jenty barely put up a fight, and actually managed to smirk as she was dropped down into an airlock.

"And what do you think you're-" the rest of her snide comeback was cut off by the closing hatch and its accompanying hiss of pressurization.

Pia collided into Theo and grabbed his arm to stop him from pulling the outer lock release handle. Theo backed off, leaving Pia at the door hatch.

With Zee's voice trying to grab her attention, Pia stared hard at the stubborn woman. After a few seconds she undid the lock, and pulled the heavy door open just enough to be able to be heard. "When's the attack coming, Ravort?"

"It's already been launched, of course. As soon as your crystal pet showed itself, Globalcorps launched a planet wide strike. You can do whatever-"

"Leave," Pia flicked her hand to the side, motioning for Theo to get her exosuit. "You can use the transport and find your own way back.

Theo hustled over with the suit, which Pia shoved through the door, which was still only open wide enough to see through.

"You need me to call off the attack," Jenty sneered.

Pia's face showed hesitation, but she finished tossing the suit into the airlock. "There's no way you'll stop. Don't bother with your lies."

"We will, if you agree to hand over control of that monster. The missiles can be diverted, but time is running out for you."

"You people are the monsters. You're the ones who are out of control," Pia came back at her. "And I'd be putting on that suit if I were you."

Jenty began to respond, but was cut off as Pia slammed the airlock shut on her. Jenty kept screaming at the window, right up until the air began getting sucked out of the chamber. Pia watched the woman panic as she struggled with the suit, getting all but the helmet on before Pia hit the button to open the outer door.

Jenty lost her grip on the helmet as the extreme cold surged through her body. With one last failed attempt at locking her helmet into place, she finally exhaled her last breath which she had been holding. Her body crumpled into the fetal position as her lungs collapsed, letting the helmet rattle off her head and tap the airlock door.

Chapter 24

Pia stared for one last second, then broke the silence with orders barked out rapidly both in person and through comm. She could feel Zee's presence, but he didn't say anything as time was short.

'Zee, scan for incoming from Earth. We need to know who's getting hit, when, and how hard. Coburn, try to get all Lunar communities on comm to warn them." She went and retrieved her own exosuit from the next room, pointing at the stunned diplomats as she went.

"Moni, Granson, I'm sorry for bringing this fight to your homes, but we need to work together now. Do your communities have any defensive capabilities that could intercept this attack?

Moni cleared his nose hard and swung his arms wide. "We don't have anything Globalcorps felt would be a threat to their control."

Granson added, "but we have plenty of transports from the mining operations. Could help get some people out of harm's way if we hurry."

"Then let's hurry."

Zee came through over the Cerex main comm. "We have less than an hour, Pia."

Pia scanned the panicked faces around the makeshift conference room as she finished getting into her exosuit. Theo latched her helmet and secured her airlock before hurrying to guide the diplomats up to the command deck.

"Pia, where are you going?" Theo asked before leaving her.

"There's no time for evacuations. Alert everyone possible to shelter in place, then order our crew to get egged. I have to try warning Lunaia."

Before anyone could protest, Pia had entered the airlock and closed it behind her. As the air was sucked out of the tiny space, Pia's breath sped from her lips, fogging her faceplate momentarily. When the final buzzer signaled the outer door was opening, she steadied herself as best she could.

The vacuum of Luna surrounded her, and she shoved Jenty's huddled body out the hatch, letting it drift down to the gray regolith outside. Pia bounded off the lip of the opening, over the frozen body, and towards the nearby crater where she had first placed the crystal shard.

Every fiber of her being screamed at her to go find Zee and try to flee in Cerex, but somehow she forced herself forward. During the trek across the crater, she rapidly scanned through the Datanet.

Across Luna, news of the impending attack spread. Luckily, Moni and Granson agreed to personally verify the news Cerex was broadcasting, speeding the process of getting people to exosuits and underground shelters. Only Tycho failed to respond to their broadcasts, although they too appeared to be aware of the attack and were sheltering in place.

The Cerex crew all assembled into the command hub, prepped in their respective egg webbing stations and awaiting word of when the attack would come. Theo's thundering voice complained bitterly at having to cower instead of fighting back, but there was little that could be done.

Zee had the fleet of drones set up a circular dragnet for a bare minimum of protection against incoming missiles. The speed differences meant the little drones' defense would be like gnats trying to intercept bullets. Theo's potato gun setup on Ceres might have given them a chance, but there had been no time since landing on Luna for anything like that.

With barely any fuel left, Cerex couldn't make it anywhere but Earth, which would be a slow trip towards a death sentence. Besides, the scale of this strike was meant to be less an assassination, and more an extermination. Globalcorps was looking to hit the reset button on Lunar colonization, with all settlements appearing to be targeted. There simply was no place to run.

Zee prayed they could avoid any direct hits, maybe buy themselves enough time to fuel up and make another run for it. But mainly his focus strayed to the dot slowly marching across the nearby landscape. He diverted a drone to keep an eye on Pia's progress. She was already approaching the edge of the crater by the time the drone arrived.

Pia shooed the drone back with a wave of her hand. *'Hang back, Zee. I don't want to scare her.'*

The tiny drone zipped up and backwards, but stayed in sight. Pia smiled, still unaccustomed to having someone who cared enough to look after her. She didn't have much experience with relationships, but already got the feeling Zee was more of a worrier than most. Then again, she was outside in zero G about to talk to a planet sized alien before an imminent attack, so maybe he should get a pass this time.

She was less than a hundred meters from the brightly glowing crater. Her breath was beginning to fog her visor as the air recycler struggled to keep up with her adrenaline stoked panting. All around her the blue surface pulsed in rivulets of energy, with the streaks all converging on the far lip of the crater.

As Pia slowed to a steady walking pace, each bootstep caused an electric blue bloom of light to erupt through the ground. She spotted what appeared to be the original crystal location, with lines converging and interacting in a riot of colors, when she noticed a force slightly repulsing her steps. It was as if she had to push her foot down through mud, although the ground was still rigid and cold.

This repulsing pressure built in strength until Pia took a step which never touched the ground. She stood there balancing, while her leading boot wobbled on invisible field lines, until her back foot came up too, and she stood on unsteady legs in mid-air. There was no mistaking the source of the fields now; each burst streamed back from a central translucent spike, a greatly enlarged version of Pia's original seed crystal. Standing nearly to head height (if she had been on the ground that is), the spike vibrated with dozens of shifting colors, nearly a dozen meters away.

Pia climbed the increasing cushion of power until she stood atop a shimmering dome of lights, with just the tip of the spike remaining above the level of her feet. She dropped to her knees, hair spilling across the inside of her visor as her head stared down into the rhythmic pulses beneath her. The spike was vibrating so fast that its edges became blurs.

'Ten minutes or less, Cerex. Now would be a great time to get the hell back here, Pia,' Zee pleaded.

Hearing Zee's voice focused her thoughts, which had been swirling chaotically between life back on Earth, the incident with Miller, and Joni's lifeless body floating out the airlock. Now she grasped the spike and covered it with both gloves, willing herself to transmit radar and other data showing the approaching missiles.

No response.

Pia pulled up geology schematics for Luna, then highlighted the deeper layers, hoping Lunaia would follow her hints.

Nothing.

There were less than five minutes left before first impacts, and panic was seeping into Pia's movements. She began pushing downward on the spike, pushing so hard she was afraid her suit might tear, but still she pushed.

The crystal neither retreated from the surface nor showed any signs of understanding. With no hope of making it back to Cerex in time, Pia slumped down and sat on the invisible platform.

With two minutes left, Pia collapsed onto her back, turning to see if she could catch any glimpses of her impending doom. The glow from underneath her suit was warm with vibrations, drowning out the starfield as she squinted into the void.

It was funny. The closer death was to her, the calmer Pia became. Instead of panicking, Pia stretched her arms out on both sides, feeling the energy flowing around her like water. She held her hands out in front, imagining herself stopping the missiles with her hands.

The energy came in waves, gaining in strength only to melt away in an instant. Then the dips in energy stopped happening. Each high water mark crested with more power than the last, until Pia began to get jostled around.

She held her arms out to protect herself, and through the gaps between her gloved fingers she began seeing flashes. She stared at the blinking beacons as her peripheral filled with bright haze. All around her the landscape trembled, and suddenly there were pillars of light skewering the landscape.

Pia cringed and awaited an explosion that never happened. Instead, these pillars grew up from the surrounding area and solidified into wavy ribbons across the sky. Each ribbon streaked up more than a kilometer before spreading out from all edges simultaneously. Within twenty seconds, the starfield was completely blocked by a gauzy blue ceiling, and for a moment Pia was back home on Earth, feeling the breeze as she surveyed a cloudless day.

Suddenly the static in Pia's comm dissipated, and thousands of voices fought for her attention. All across Luna, stunned voices verified what they saw with other communities, rival and friend alike. Zee came through loudest of all, but clearly had stopped thinking she could hear him.

'She's fighting for all of us.'

Pia snapped out of her trance and glanced around. She was now floating down near the surface, grazing the crater's rim, and close enough to the crystal spike to touch it. Voices she didn't recognize were pleading for help to anyone who could listen, their messages echoing inside the crystalline dome above them all. The last thing she could hear from this crowd was panic and screams just before all communication got drowned out by overwhelming static again.

Returning her gaze upwards was extremely disorienting. Where moments ago there was a glowing shield spanning the horizons, now there were billions and billions of glittering blue sparks, dancing in silent riot like dust in a sunbeam when a door opens. Only this time the breeze was from countless explosions blooming in place of the former shield. Mixed into the blue were real stars, noticeable now as ghostly white observers to the coming massacre.

Pia sat upright, bracing one hand back on the ground, and felt the electric buzz saw of power transmitting through the spike. She could begin seeing the jet exhausts of incoming missiles, which either survived colliding with the shield or had been held back in second or third waves. Either way there appeared to be hundreds still streaking down from the sky. With her free hand, Pia reached out in shock for one of the closest, wishing she could snatch it right out of the sky.

And she did.

Crystal tendrils a kilometer away raced out of the ground, then spread out in a latticework of rapidly changing colors. The missile Pia had been focused on crashed into this defense and exploded harmlessly up in the sky. The crystal at the site of impact glowed brighter in response to the energy, absorbing much of it.

Instinctively she pressed into the ground, through the river of energy hovering beneath her exosuit, digging her heels into the regolith for a sense of connection. Her one hand closed carefully around the central spike, and she felt a torrent of power coursing through her mind even as her body arched backwards in protest.

There were no words to it, no accompanying charts, no explanation, but there was pattern, and undeniable purpose. It came in overwhelming amounts, similar to direct data transfer, but this was two-way, and on all frequencies. It was as if the entire world was alive with thought. Pia surveyed the landscape with new eyes.

From over a nearby crater's edge, lines of energy gathered and fell, holding vast amounts of information, but never isolating it in one location. Pia thought of Pando, how her ancient forest was all connected through a network of roots and mycelium, spreading the necessary nutrients where they were needed most. All of that coordination and balance, but all most people saw were the trees.

The trees. Pia looked back up at the streaks of lights spreading out across the sky as they neared their targets, and she saw branches of a forest canopy. Her fingers groped into the ground, wriggling in deeply, while her other hand remained gripped around the vibrating central core. The blazing trails of the incoming missiles were lit up by the rising sun, when Pia suddenly felt each of them.

The trails of heat, the massive explosions pressing against her skin, she could sense it all disjointedly. Only bits and pieces came into focus. The entire Earth side of Luna was wrapped in a lattice of streaming crystal threads. All the missiles were stopped, their jet trails lost in the cacophony of light and noise, but again their energy remained somehow.

For a kilometer up into the emptiness of vacuum, she could feel an overwhelming pressure crushing her from all directions. The explosions reverberated through her, making Pia's actual body convulse back down near the source. She was in a waking trance, green eyes gleaming with a combination of terror, suffering, and rage.

Tattered pieces of her consciousness flailed about looking for relief, until finally she looked down towards the blue streaks in the soil where her boots had dug furrows. Underneath her lay incomprehensible depths of crystal, all waiting for a purpose.

Pia took all her focus and reached down into the regolith, tracing the routes of power into the center of Luna. The explosions towering high overhead were quickly extinguished by the lack of oxygen, and their combined force spread through the network, each vein of crystal absorbing a portion of the powerful attack.

The silence was total as energy sank beneath the surface and left the crystal webbing to slowly recede back. Spires a kilometer tall melted within minutes of the attack's completion. They dissolved into the surrounding landscape, leaving Pia to collapse in peace.

Inside the artificial dome of her helmet, her breath returned ragged and coughing, then much easier as she mentally upped the oxygen concentration in her air supply. She sat up when she felt able.

Directly in front of Pia hovered one of Zee's drones. Then another drone she didn't recognize joined it, followed by another, until over a dozen camera feeds were trained on her. The little contraptions reminded her of large beetles, varied in size and shape but all keeping identical spacing with one another through AI autopilots.

She abruptly stood up and dusted herself off, but her mind lagged behind her movements. The sky was clear, with stars sparkling due to the recent blast waves, as she began walking back towards Cerex. The drones followed her at a distance, silently fanning out for a full panorama.

Pia reached out to Zee in alarm, fearing another attack, but there was nothing. No datanet at all. Her mind was neither in Lunaia nor able to connect with Cerex. It was then that she looked down at her boots.

She was standing on raised pillars of glimmering liquid crystal which glided along with her every move. As panic flooded her thoughts, the pillars dipped slightly, but were restored along with her focus. Her lip shivering, Pia closed her eyes tight and let out a prolonged exhale before opening them again.

A series of tiny craters stretched out beneath her view, confirming her rapid ascent up nearly fifty meters. Pia scanned until she spotted Cerex nestled into a slope on the horizon, then willed herself towards it. Later on in drone footage, Pia would watch as her body sped off at incredible speeds, cradled in a cocoon of energy which protected her. As it was happening however, Pia felt like she flew.

Wherever she wished to go, she needed only to think of the movement and off she went. Asking Lunaia for assistance didn't feel forced, or even intentional, but rather an extension of her own mind. The fleet of drones barely caught up with her by the time her boots set down gently onto the Cerex main entryway.

One last look down to her translucent blue transport and it too melted away into the regolith. Pia turned and walked on unsteady legs back up the ladder and into the main hatch, fully unprepared to answer a single question about what just happened.

The crew had assembled on their own in the inner airlock area, and stared in silence as Zee ran and wrapped his arms around an equally stunned Pia.

"Think Globalcorps wishes they could get a do over on today?" Moni quipped.

Chapter 25

A week later, Moni bounded up through the forest hab in Cerex, moving effortlessly up the massive tube. Zee followed behind, occasionally ricocheting off ledges after he had misjudged a jump.

When she returned from Lunaia, Pia had reestablished her chip connection and given a brief statement over the LunaComm, courtesy of Granson's access codes.

'We're all on the same team now, and I promise no more violence will come to you. Live your lives as you wish, and build a home for yourselves. Lunaia will protect us from any attacks, and I can request whatever resources that Luna contains within her. This can be a new beginning for humanity, so let's not waste our chance.'

In the days since then, Pia had mostly kept to herself, trying to process what had happened during the attack. Besides a few trips to the common areas, she had returned to her pre-Ceres lifestyle. High up in the overgrown canopy of her forest hab, she lay on mossy ledges letting her bare feet dangle, or else she would run off to dig up plants for her latest garden project. During one such dig, she stopped and stared at the root ball exposed under the soil; the tiny mycelium threads interwoven through them all, processing nutrients from the soil, and borrowing energy from the plants.

Pia barely noticed when Moni and an out of breath Zee began talking less than a meter from where she was working.

"Hey princess," Zee panted, "can we have a minute?"

She turned away from her plants and sat cross legged there in the dirt, a gentle smile blowing across her face at her visitors. Zee had given her space, but he clearly missed her. She held a hand out and cupped the side of his head in a caress, then motioned for them both to join her on the ground.

"Moni and I have something important to discuss with you," Zee continued, "if you feel up to it."

Pia brushed the stray hairs off her face, better showing the bright green of her tired eyes. "I'm ok. What's up guys?"

Moni shifted uneasily, struggling hard to hold back a torrent of questions, and also looking ready to bow down at Pia's feet. His eyes darted to Zee, signaling him to take the lead.

"Ever since the...the attack," Zee charged ahead, "all the former Lunar colonies have pledged themselves to our cause. This has allowed us access to the main Luna/Earth satellite array."

"Not that we expect much worth listening to coming from Earth." Pia gave a half-hearted smile, but it was not returned by the two men.

"That's just it," Zee put a hand on her shoulder. "We don't expect anything pleasant from Globalcorps, although Lunaia's defense will certainly disable most of their capability to retaliate for their humiliation."

"So what's the issue?"

"Globalcorps is not the only one broadcasting...or did you forget my little broken arm magic act already?"

"Free Earthers...how many of you are there? I never thought they would have access to such powerful antennas."

Zee cleared his throat before responding. "There are small communities, living on the outskirts of civilization, perhaps a few thousand in all. But that's not who I'm talking about." This time Zee looked over to Moni before continuing.

"As you may have guessed by my presence on the Cerex mission, there are people like me in positions of power or access all across Earth."

"And Luna," Moni added.

Zee breathed a sigh of relief to finally stop hiding this part of his life from Pia. "Hackers mostly," he blushed, genuinely embarrassed by his specialty despite his genius. "But we hear things, about how Globalcorps is reacting to the loss of Luna. There'll be more attacks, Pia. And if they can't destroy the settlements or Lunaia, they will most definitely be coming after you. And we cannot let that happen."

Moni took an actual knee in front of her as he barked out a rehearsed pledge, "My life belongs to Lunaia, and you as her Conduit."

Pia rested her tired head in her hands while Moni finished, then waved him off like a mosquito. "I have no time for all that, Moni."

She began pacing, her bare feet covered in dried dirt. "I think I had convinced myself that this could be the end of it. They would keep Earth, and Lunaia would protect Luna and its people."

Zee came up and stopped her mid-turnaround. "They want you dead, Pia. If you're gone, maybe Lunaia won't come to our aid."

Pia began to protest, but the words got caught in her throat. "I didn't ask for any of this," she cried, but quickly recovered her composure just in time for Zee's next bombshell.

"They're not waiting patiently, either. Warrants are out for all the Cerex crew, with a million credit bounty. Fifty million credits for you, princess."

"Fifty million..." Pia stammered.

"There's more. Globalcorps has cut rations to all citizens to compensate for their huge predicted quarterly loss report. They have the key to cure all hunger, and still they hold it back in order to keep control."

Pia squatted down on her ankles, tending to a young sapling while Zee filled her in. When she finally spoke, it was with her back facing him.

"I'm not our leader. I didn't want any of this."

"No, you didn't. And it's not fair. But still, all of this happened because of you. And now that they've seen Lunaia, they will never stop coming for you."

"But what can I do? I barely understand how I was able to control Lunaia. About all I can do is program some decent food-"

"Exactly." Zee made sure Pia paid special attention to the next part by placing a hand on her shoulder and squeezing. "You need to set them all free."

Moni jumped to his feet in enthusiasm. "Fuck yes," he blurted out, immediately stepping back and bowing in apology. "Luna has been missing its soul for too long. Now we can be free to live where we want, how we want, in want of nothing, as was prophesied."

"Yeaaaaahhhhh, except I'm no prophet. But I do think it's time someone leveled the playing field for all of humanity." She took Zee's hand as he pulled her up to join them. "What were you thinking, handsome?"

"I was hoping you'd ask that," Zee grinned. "We already attempted to contact our people back on Earth using the Lunar Satellite Array, but surprise, surprise..."

"They locked us out entirely?" Pia assumed.

"Yes, and no." Zee smirked. "On a hunch...I decided to try out one last user and password."

Pia was lost in thought for a moment, then her eyes snapped back into focus. "No...why would it still be active?"

Zee slid in close, "Seems like the kind of thing a competent CTO would have fixed right after the accident was reported."

Pia's smile broke out wide when the full realization hit her. "Except for when the CTO is on a top secret mission...in deep space...and hates Miller's guts. So have you tried it?"

"Of course, nearly an hour ago. We're in, and managed to get a message through to my main contact in Globalcorps."

"Send the printer info, all of it." Pia didn't hesitate. "But first, send our mission log and evidence of Lunaia in action."

Pia took Moni by the arm and led him out of the forest hab. Zee followed behind, already hard at work in the Datanet.

It didn't take long before Zee slumped his way into a chair next to her back on the tech deck. "We got through, but our numbers are miniscule compared to Globalcorps. There's no way Free Earth members can do much with the information except spread it."

Theo and Sara happened to be nearby and overheard their problem.

"We need to hire them to work for us," Theo grunted, causing Sara to reach over and flick his ear.

"Don't be an idiot, dear."

Theo shrugged at Pia and Zee. "We could have Lunaia whip up another diamond mountain like Ahuna Mons."

"Or we could be like zombie ant fungi," Pia said plainly, as if it was a perfectly normal sentence to utter.

Zee spoke up first. "Clearly, zombie ant fungi, yeah. But for Theo's sake, explain some more, he's a bit slow."

Zee dodged a quick swing of Theo's massive hand and bounded out of reach.

"There's a species of parasitic fungi which sinks its tendrils into the brains of ants, completely controlling them," Pia explained.

"Creepy," Sara decided.

"So we use their own infrastructure against them?" Zee guessed.

Pia shook her head. "Not against them. But for the people in need. If there's one thing I know you do well, it's drones."

"Only one thing?" Theo grimaced, quickly joined by Sara, who tugged his beard.

"Give him time, you big slab, he's a shy one."

Pia began to get sidetracked in defense of Zee, but thankfully he was off to the races with Pia's suggestion.

Over the next week, their plan began taking effect, while on Luna things were changing rapidly in their own way. Drone feeds showing Pia silhouetted against the blinding crystal spike, gesturing to the skies and shredding hundreds of incoming ballistic missiles, were on every holowall on Luna.

She went to visit the major settlements, and crowds formed wherever she went. There was even a growing contingent of Luna-born camping outside Cerex, who only left to take necessary trips back to swap exosuit air tanks. Moni did his best not to bow when he came updating her on their progress getting water and 3-D food out to the various cities and outposts.

Moni and Granson represented polar opposites as far as their temperaments were concerned, but both instantly fell in step following Pia's lead. Granson was especially helpful in getting the first trade routes established to Lunaia.

Pia went out to the crystal spike and held it tightly while mentally projecting lists of chemicals, which were soon found concentrated into nearby underground pools for easy extraction. Meerkat and Far Side were especially grateful for the resources, making Pia both a busy prophet and short order cook.

Meanwhile reports started coming in about events down on Earth. Zee had been busy; he had scrambled to coordinate with other Free Earthers who had infiltrated various major corporations. When the time came to strike, they made it all happen simultaneously.

Forgotten by most of the world, too insignificant to warrant much attention, it was actually packaging and delivery drones which made the world economy work. In homes, at offices, throughout stores and factories and warehouses, everywhere was kept supplied by drones. And now each and every last one of these fully integrated Globalcorps machines stopped working, at the same instant, all across the globe.

But just for a moment. Then they were back diligently performing their tasks. Only now their instructions had changed. Across the globe, food and supply depots were ordered to be emptied. By the metric ton, it was being dropped off in town squares and street corners. All alerts of missed shipments were purged before management caught on to what was happening. The hack that took them down was a beautiful thing, and Zee watched it all through his holofeeds.

After nearly a day of futile attempts to regain control of their drone fleet, Globalcorps took the unprecedented step of shutting down their entire network. It was the only way for them to reset commands.

Unfortunately, whatever respite the food gave to people was short lived. Once they were back in control, Globalcorps drastically cut back on all regular food deliveries, claiming shortages made the measures necessary. On top of that, Miller's access codes were finally revoked, leaving Cerex with limited ability to communicate with Earth.

Two agonizing days passed after that, until Cerex convened a Lunar Council of sorts. In addition to the Cerex crew itself, Pia invited representatives from any settlement who wished to work together. Nearly thirty people were seated in the command hub by the time Pia and Zee strode into the room.

The room fell dark, and a holoprojection filled the room of Earth and Luna hovering together in space, prompting Pia to let out a tired laugh.

"I was in this room not too very long ago," Pia began. "And I was sitting where you sit now, listening to someone lay out an insane plan that could cost me my life." She wore her favorite knit sweater, and burrowed her arms into the bulky tan sleeves while she paced slowly in front of their guests.

She turned to them and stood tall before continuing. "So the first question I have to ask you is...do we need the Earth?"

Murmurs filled the air as the question hung there, deceptively easy to dismiss, but more appealing by the second. Of course, Luna had always been reliant on Earth for many essential supplies. But even before the arrival of Cerex and Lunaia, things had changed. Lunar settlements now could grow or trade for almost anything they needed. No longer trapped as colonies of competing businesses, they found themselves in a genuine Lunar-wide economy.

"And if we don't need them, then we need you, is that our choice?" A proud Luna-born named Rego was standing out of his chair, but respectfully.

Pia saw herself in him, connected to the land here and scared of what others have planned for it. Pando forest seemed a distant memory now, but Miller's threat of its destruction is what got her into this whole mess in the first place.

"What we offer is technology so you never need anyone else, ever again. It will always be your choice."

Even Rego smiled at that idea. "We've been promised many things..."

"We have nothing to hide. Our tech and our link with Lunaia, we share freely."

"Perhaps too freely." This was Reid, another small industrial community leader, small and sharp and convinced of his own intelligence.

Zee stepped in front of Pia. "If there is ANY doubt as to Pia's intentions, then we're more distrustful than I thought possible, and perhaps this meeting is over."

Pia waved back her over eager protector. "No. He's right." She walked closer to look Reid in the eyes. "I'm sorry, it's true I set loose Lunaia without consulting any of you."

Now she turned and spread her arms wide to include everyone. "Lunaia has changed your lives forever, and you never chose any of this."

Silence reigned for a few seconds as her point was digested, then Pia pressed on. "But I would never have done what I did if I had any fear of Lunaia. And neither should you. Globalcorps was ready to obliterate all life on Luna just for a tactical advantage. Lunaia saved you. And now she produces lakes of useful resources on request."

Guilty glances passed among some of those present who had put in such requests for chemicals. "For the first time in your history, in anyone's history, we don't need Mother Earth to survive. We'll have protection, resources, and peace, if I have any say in it."

More than a few people in the back muttered, "No Earth?" and, "Hell with them."

Granson took it upon himself to keep the crowd from getting carried away. "We may not need them, but they most definitely need us. Pia, with respect, you haven't had to live under their control like most of us. They were desperate for Luna's resources to keep them profitable before all this. And now, Lunaia threatens all of that. This won't end until we take them out of power on Earth."

A chorus of voices all fought for control of the conversation. Above them all, Theo's booming bass cut through the din. "Send them Lunaia!"

The idea was so simple it stunned the crowd; Theo even surprised himself. "Why not shoot some seed crystals their way? They can't detect something that small, and it would end their power over people."

Pia was the one to pour cold water on the popular new idea. "No, we absolutely cannot do that."

"You did it here on Luna," Rego protested.

"No, on Luna it was different. Yes, it's your home, but it was a dead world. Earth already has a biosphere, Gaia, which is hurting right now. Sending Lunaia there would destroy everything and start new."

Theo sighed along with the rest of the crowd. "So what did you have in mind, Pia?"

Pia walked back to the center of the room, glad the formalities were over. "So here's what we're left with, as I see it. We can either let Zee's network harass Globalcorps, spreading 3D printer tech wherever possible, or we can try to take on Globalcorps head on, and end this now."

Theo nodded to Zee with a flourish. "You know I say take the fight to them." Sara nodded silently beside him.

Others seemed more hesitant. "With what? How do we fight a global corporation?"

Pia grew the biggest grin as a revelation came to her on the spot. "Hostile takeover."

Chapter 26

The Cerex crew gathered quickly once the plan was set, all except for Coburn, who was already off with Moni and Granson carrying out phase one of the plan. Pia and Zee were heading back down to Earth using the private spaceship of a wealthy Tycho City resident.

Santos, Hixley, and Vineland each gave quick hugs, not wanting to cause too much of a scene.

When Lara came close, she whispered, "you're a sweetheart, but try not to take it too easy on Globalcorps. I expect to see proper groveling at your feet."

Gabe and Vineland were over next, having already finished talking with Zee. "You're sure about this, Pia?" the Colonel asked.

"Not at all, but I'm never sure, and that hasn't stopped me yet."

"Just be careful, and follow the plan," Gabe added.

"Yeah, I'm more of an improvisation type, but I'll try."

As Gabe walked away, he turned and mouthed the words again, *'follow the plan.'*

Theo and Sara came over last, each wrapping a friend up in enormous bear hugs. Zee laughed awkwardly as Theo wouldn't let go of him, pinning Zee's head to his chest.

"What are we going to do without our good luck charms?" The booming Norwegian was getting choked up, but fought against it.

"Let it out big guy," Sara chided him, then turned back to Pia. "We still have some work to do toughening them up."

"Agreed," Pia raised an eyebrow towards the huggers, "but we love them."

"Hey, don't start mentioning the L word. Some of us are a bit sensitive on that subject."

Theo finally broke off his massive hug of the helpless Zee, turning to the women in protest. "I told you I love you a hundred times already, let it go, my radiant goddess!"

"But you didn't say it back the first time I said it."

"I didn't hear you right, I thought you said *my glove too*,' so I handed you your glove."

Sara panned her face in slow motion until she met Pia's playful grimace. "So that's who you're leaving me stuck with."

Theo exhaled loudly in defeat, until Sara leaned over and squeezed his butt. "Take it easy, Romeo, just having fun. You know I love you."

"Boys," Pia chimed in, laughing along with Sara. Then her face suddenly tightened. "I'm gonna miss you."

"Oh stop, you turning soft on me now too? You're finally chipped and out of the Stone Age, just reach out to us anytime."

The preparations on their ship were ready, and Zee gently placed his hand on Pia's shoulder, "It's time." With that, the couple gave their last goodbyes, then turned and disappeared through the main entry hatch.

A crew of Lunar spaceport workers finalized the launch pad and removed the fuel hoses. These private ships were often more stylish than they were powerful, but this appeared to achieve both goals, likely a perk for some corporate bigwig. It stood nearly thirty meters tall and had huge retractable wings that were tucked into the main fuselage now, but would allow it to transition to regular flight once they entered Earth's atmosphere.

A lot of things had to go perfectly if they were even going to make it that far.

Pia sat in the copilot station, mentally doing a checklist to make sure they hadn't forgotten anything. Moni had been a great help, leading a group of devotees in learning to interact with Lunaia. While none seemed to have the same level of connection with the entity, they were making progress daily, and Moni had managed to succeed in requesting all the basic resources.

Since Cerex still had the only cutting edge 3D printers, it was decided to leave the ship on Luna to support the people there. Santos accepted the role of main technician for them, doing his best to work with Lunar chemists to tweak the output.

As Pia began the launch sequence, she couldn't help pulling up the internal Cerex video feeds. It had come quite a long way since she first saw it emerge from hiding in the orbital depot. The forest hab had since stretched throughout every corner of the ship, bringing life and beauty along with it. As sad as Pia was to leave her home of the last couple years, this was one item that wouldn't keep her up at night. After everything settled down on Luna following the Globalcorps attack, she had a message pop up on her Datanet that made her smile.

Traxler had been stationed at the underground Meerkat city, along with his partner Fulton. Pia invited them both to live on Cerex, promising to come back and give him hell if Traxler didn't treat her flower babies well.

A low rumble signalled that it was time to focus again. She settled back into her station, an obnoxiously ornate throne of a G seat, and prepared for yet another harrowing launch. Even after all this time, she still got anxious before a flight, but Zee's cool demeanor helped soothe her nerves.

Zee triggered the engines, and their panoramic holo of the surrounding landscape receded in a blink, pinning her forcefully into the foam harnesses. Formerly an endless gray expanse of craters and volcanic basins, hints of blue now broke up the monotony, as Lunaia spread throughout the formerly barren moon.

Once they made it back into zero gravity and the engines ceased, Pia slumped in momentary relief. It would take two days for the trip back to Earth, and they needed to use their time wisely in preparation for the final approach.

Their ship, the Eos, lacked the sheer power and technical capability of Cerex, but made up for this with stealth and maneuverability. They had found it abandoned at the Tycho spaceport, left behind by someone in a hurry. Clearly first meant for a spoiled executive, there was a relatively spacious sleeping area with actual linen sheets and a wildly expensive bathroom with gold trimmed furnishings. But after getting used to eating steak and eggs for breakfast on Cerex, the Eos food printers were torture.

Zee had his hands full trying to coordinate with various Earth factions and operatives, while Pia rehearsed her part in the upcoming plan.

Being such a small ship compared to Cerex had its advantages strategically too, allowing them to cross more than three quarters of the distance to Earth before being picked up by long distance radar. Pia and Zee were in the cockpit when the dreaded *ping* sounded out on their passive sensors, alerting them to the detection. 'We made it ten thousand kilometers closer than we anticipated," she said, trying to soothe her nerves.

The lighting system changed to a dull red glow as it flashed in warning. Pia chipped into the main console and dismissed the alert, instead opting for bright white which better highlighted the surroundings.

"Who the hell wants to have low red lighting in an emergency?" Pia asked in annoyance, looking over to Zee for support.

"Rich assholes who watched too many antique submarine holos?"

"Exact-" she began before getting cut off by the ship's comm.

"Two H Class Space Guard interceptors approaching, five hundred kilometers. Radio transmission is pending."

Zee flicked open the comm feed and turned to Pia. "We're all set on my end. You ready to do this?"

Without hesitation, Pia authorized the feed, turning with a shrug to Zee. "Maybe they just wanna talk?" she joked half heartedly.

'Unauthorized Lunar vessel, identify yourself immediately.'

Pia sighed inwardly, hoping their gamble would pay off. She forced one last deep breath into her lungs and blew it out through the hair floating across her face, hoping to keep her voice steady.

'We are refugees from the uprising on Luna. Requesting protection and safe landing rights on Earth.'

The interceptors continued to close the distance between them as a long pause ensued.

Zee leaned over towards Pia, grasping her thigh to calm her as he grinned. "I think it's above their pay grade. Probably running it through the corporate command chain."

Pia nodded and let out a soft laugh, trying to put on a brave face despite the fear clawing its way up her throat.

'Halt your ship immediately and wait for authentication of your credentials. Refuse and you will be destroyed.'

Panic crept into Pia's face despite having run through these possible scenarios countless times back on Luna.

'Low on fuel. We don't have enough to make our entry window on Earth if we slow down. We'd burn up. Please advise.'

Another pregnant pause ensued while the message was passed along. "Maintain speed and match trajectory being sent to you now. We will escort you until further notice. Deviate from this flight path and you-"

"-will be destroyed, we get it," Pia sighed after muting her mic.

The intercepts were military space fighters, which they anticipated, making any attempt to escape nearly impossible.

'How long?' Pia chipped, but Zee was absorbed in thought. There was no need to be silent of course, but she couldn't help herself. It just felt more personal, more real.

Zee had his holo pendant linked directly into the ship console, allowing him to direct it with his chip instead of the standard controls.

Pia held her chin in her hands, trying to imagine what was happening down on Earth. Since the first global hack of the food infrastructure, Globalcorps had begun isolating their vital systems, making it harder for anyone to access them again. Globalcorps had finally deleted all of Miller's access codes, leaving them in need of another way in through their cybersecurity.

Microjets fired from across the outer hull, nudging the Eos a few meters at a time. Zee altered course as directed, with one intercept falling in behind them while the other led the way.

'Step 1 complete. Still a thousand kilometers before we hit atmosphere. Four minutes, maybe less.'

They shared a lengthy look, broken finally by Zee, who shook his head slightly after monitoring something in his feeds. He sighed before chipping, *'you need to stall for us.'*

'How long,' she chipped back again.

'Not long, I'm almost done.' He took a second to break from his holofeeds to look at Pia, a mischievous grin on his face despite nearly dripping with perspiration. *'You can't rush art,'* he offered sincerely.

With her feet tapping a nervous symphony on the metal floor, she pulled up the main comm. "You can try," she said out loud, before switching her attention back to the pair of cutting edge killing machines flanking their ship.

'Escort ships. This is Commander Pia Lamotte of Free Luna, former Specialist on Mission Cerex. Commander Xander McKinnon of Free Earth is also onboard.'

'Commanders, huh?' Zee poked her.

'Perks of the assignment. If Theo wants to be a Commander, he'll have to come on the next mission to save the world,' she poked back.

This time the escorts were much quicker in issuing a response.

'Eos, you will remain in your current trajectory and follow us through reentry and landing, upon which time you will both be arrested for treason.'

When Zee let out a deep sigh of relief and signaled that his work was done, Pia snapped her vision back to the wall holo showing their would be captors, then bared her teeth in a primal show of anger.

As quickly as her lust for revenge flashed through her, it vanished just as fast. Pia no longer held onto the anger. Her time connected to Lunaia had reinforced a peace in her she hadn't known in years.

Finally, all of the greed could stop. The cycle of destruction that had torn Gaia apart at the seams and threatened the very survival of the human race was now a relic. And as with all relics, they lose power only when they're shown to be unnecessary.

'While we appreciate the offer of an escort, the whole 'treason' charges are a non-starter. Please relay our counteroffer. Oh wait, we can do that for you.'

She allowed herself a quick glance over to Zee, who was giving a supportive nod, so she pressed on, this time speaking to the entire Globalcorps network.

"We are ready to discuss the terms...of YOUR surrender to the Free Earth Directive!"

Pia had gone over their plan back in her forest on Cerex countless times, but it was still beyond exhilarating hearing herself say the words out loud. Her body tightened all the way to her toes as she somehow forced herself to keep her voice steady and confident.

'As your intercept ships can attest, we are now in full control of your internal communications network.' At this she paused, waiting for the inevitable scramble as they first discovered the attack, then attempted to recover control.

Coburn had actually come up with the breakthrough. The satellite network of any country is usually impenetrable, and a megacorps' network was no exception. Except that is, when the corporation in question managed to merge to become the sole global owner of all satellite networks.

While it certainly made it more convenient to only have one impossible network to hack into, it still left them with the unenviable task of hacking a hostile encrypted network on the fly.

'It was our thruster jets, in case you were wondering.' Pia decided to save everyone some time and move on.

'Mixed into the exhausts were thousands of nanosats...which I've recently discovered are fairly badass pieces of tech. They actually squeeze their way into ships through the seams in the metalwork, then hijack the onboard computer. I'll have to defer to Commander McKinnon for the details.'

Zee stifled a laugh, picking up the pace of his work.

'Anyway, long story short, we took over your ship's computer. Your weapons have been disabled. Flight controls can be overridden as we wish. Zee, wiggle their wings for them when you get a moment.'

Both escort ships wagged their wings left and right, nearly spinning over, before returning to normal flight.

"Shit, those things are beasts! Can we demand one for me to play with once we're done?" Zee was bouncing around in his seat like a kid.

Pia disabled the transmission while she laughed at him. "If this actually works, I'll buy you one myself." She smiled warmly, glad that she had Zee by her side.

'With the computer we secured authentic credentials to the Globalcorps Datanet, which is currently being repurposed as the Free Earth Datanet. Of course we couldn't do this using just one measly ship computer, so Commander McKinnon went ahead and open sourced your entire mainframe. Much more efficient this way I'm told.'

Pia felt like she could reach out and pick up whole cities, moving them about like toy blocks. They were literally reshaping the lives of billions of people with each passing minute.

The reentry window was approaching, when communications would be impossible for approximately three minutes, so she needed to drive home her point now while she had them on their heels.

'You have lost. Globalcorps, if we allow it to continue, will use its global infrastructure to benefit humanity. What comes next is up to you.' Pia checked the straps on her harness as friction built up on the leading wing edges, beginning to trail liquid fire as they cut deeply into the atmosphere.

'Oh, and gentlemen,' she added through the increasing static. *'If you can still hear me, we took the liberty of zeroing out all of your bank accounts and holdings. I figured that would speed up negotiations. Looking forward to your surrender. Signing off for reentry.'*

Chapter 27

A formal invitation to meet at a location of their choosing awaited the Eos once they emerged into regular atmospheric flight. Pia didn't hesitate, and soon they were descending to a familiar launch pad outside of Paris.

The landscape had changed even in the short while they'd been away. Despite the countryside around Paris being designated as preserved parklands, from the sky the truth was clear; large swaths of it had been excavated down to bedrock, leaving deep gashes and punctures all throughout the view. The only parts left untouched were cultural sites or strategic Globalcorps infrastructure. As they had descended, what was once northern Europe looked more like the threadbare remnants of a professor's jacket.

Pia and Zee were brought by driverless car from the airport, taking the opportunity to stretch their muscles and begin adjusting to Earth gravity once again. By the time they were being waved through checkpoints at the old Natocorps headquarters where it all started, Pia was feeling much more stable on her feet.

Her dull grey boots made sharp jabs through the silence which permeated the massive building. Zee shuffle stepped along in his retro sneakers, content to drink this moment in.

Where once Pia had struggled to discern the fiber optic bundles running under the hallways, now her chip easily swept across the digital realm like a second sight. The various parts of the electromagnetic spectrum were all at her fingertips.

Her hair was quite enjoying proper gravity again, making springy curls at the ends dance along behind her. Without stopping for a second, Pia burst through the enormous brass double doors.

"Let's get this over with, shall we?" she declared as she took a seat at the head of the table. Everyone paused, cut off in the middle of their attempts to flatter her.

"Lamotte, before we can begin any negotiations we must insist that you unfreeze our personal accounts, as a sign of good faith."

Tense faces all turned towards Pia, then relaxed when her smile reached its full size. Their relief was short-lived.

"Good faith?" She laughed, "I think that we're quite a few years past good faith."

"If there is to be no restoration of funds, then we have nothing more to discuss." The excitable younger exec began scuffing his chair back to storm out, but had no one following him, so he awkwardly paused for a moment. This was no Miller.

"You are correct, we have nothing to discuss. You have stripped and drilled your way through every opportunity on Earth. You are hereby formally relieved of your responsibility. If you choose to assist us in our new mission of global reconciliation, then we can talk salary. In the meantime, sit down, shut up, and give me some papers to sign."

Despite no further outbursts, it took nearly all morning to sign the paperwork. Pia and a council of Free Earth leaders were to assume operational control over Globalcorps' distribution networks, only it was anyone's guess how the new global economy might work. Most of humanity was still existing in VR fantasy worlds, and what was left on the fringes led vastly different lives than what she ever thought possible.

The existence of the established Free Earth communities was stunning at first, and she longed to visit each of them in time. But first, there was one important stop.

Zee empowered a half dozen Free Earth leaders to start hammering out more details with Globalcorps, leaving him and Pia time for a quick and well deserved getaway. They flew Eos west across the Atlantic, both of them mesmerized by the endless expanse of dark blue. The wreckage of North America landscape passed beneath them next, until Pando finally stood out on the horizon.

Usually nothing more than a hillside of trees, it now towered as an unintended plateau amid the strip mines across what used to be called Utah. She was pressed against the window, straining to see the first familiar contours as Zee continued explaining the new Free Earth communities.

"So there's seapunk, icepunk, skypunk, geopunk, trashpunk, and a dozen new ones being created every month, but generally speaking they break down into Naturals and Nanos. Nats have been sneaking away for years, choosing to live off the land again. Groups formed at landfills using recycled trash and geothermal. Some spend months at a time living airborne. Others constructed 3D floating habs and joined up into massive flotillas drifting the oceans.

"The Nanos have pushed the boundaries in every corner of Earth. Biohackers transform people into whatever version of themselves they choose. A popular hackshop special is iceskin, which opened up vast arctic territories to exploration. Weaponry is unfortunately also being added, making for some especially problematic criminals. Hell, I've even heard of full mermaid enhancements."

"And they all belong to Free Earth?" Pia asked, unsure of how she was supposed to lead such a hugely varied base.

"All of humanity is technically Free Earth now, but how much they choose to interact is up to them. Most of them won their independence years ago in the VR wars, and are in no rush to have a Queen, no offense. Meanwhile, vast amounts of people will have to be kept in full immersion if they refuse to live in the new real world."

Pando rose like a crown on the horizon as their helicopter brought them nearer.

"Can't say I blame them, either," Zee added.

"The VR people? Why?"

"So much easier to simulate a life than actually fight for one. It's pretty bleak out here."

"I still need to teach you a few things about unplugging, don't I?" Pia joked, pretending to search for his power cord.

Once they unloaded their meager gear and made it to Pia's old work hut, the scene made Zee stop in his tracks. "Holy shit, it really does look like this," thinking back to the holo replica Natocorps had him throw together back when Pia was being recruited. He turned to her sadly, "I was kind of hoping they'd have torn this down too."

"Shut up, holoboy."

She went and walked the creaky floorboards, eventually settling onto the side of her old field cot, dusty from neglect but otherwise as comforting as the day the Natocorps official first came. She was finally free of their pull, no longer dependent on anyone for survival.

Zee came over to join her, but tripped on a vine that had grown up out of the dirt floor in Pia's absence, diving headlong into a support beam and taking down one whole section of the canvas roof. Flaps whipped around in the early summer breezes, and she pulled him in close as she split herself laughing. He grabbed hold of her waist and made her stop with a passionate kiss.

Pia blinked twice, and her eyes danced with green. She blew some hair out of her face. *'We just saved three whole worlds together, you realize that? How long until everyone finds out?'* she chipped, afraid to ask out loud.

'Finds out what?'

'That I'm just a scientist and have no business running anything.'

'At least a few weeks, month maybe.' Zee teased, causing her cheeks to flush with feigned outrage. She went to give him a slap, but he

intercepted it and held her closer before continuing. *'You've done the impossible more times than I can count, princess. Without you, none of this could ever have happened. And I'm lucky to have you by my side.'*

Pia pretended to be considering something, then shot back in perfect deadpan, *'You are lucky. I really should consider upgrading boyfriends now that I'm the Queen of the Universe.'*

To that he took both her wrists above her head as he leaned her back down onto her cot. She almost fell off the far end before shooting a foot out to that side. Her toes pressed into the soft soil, squeezing it tightly as they made the most of their newfound privacy. With the chip link, the intensity was overwhelming for them both, Pia feeling Zee interwoven in her very thoughts.

As they slumped off onto the hand woven mats, fingers still tangled and heads empty of the nonsense of everyday life, Pia's focus drifted up to the twilight sky shining in through the new hole Zee had torn in the roof. What she saw made her sigh, then a hopeful smile followed, as they were both being bathed in the distinctly blue light of Luna.

About The Author

David Colello[1] is an ecopunk prophet, making badass lemonade out of apocalyptic lemons, and squinting hard to see the good. Following his time at Boston University earning degrees in English and Philosophy, he owned a personal training studio, worked in freelance copywriting, became a stay home father to three little future punks, and now publishes science fiction for a world where wonder is in short supply.

---

1. http://www.davidcolello.com

If you enjoyed Mission Cerex, please consider giving it a rating and review.

For sneak peeks and a chance to receive the next books *FREE* before they get released, sign up to the newsletter on my website, www.davidcolello.com[2].

---

2. http://www.davidcolello.com

Author's Note

This is the end of a very long journey for Pia and Zee, but there are more stories set in the Mission Cerex universe. For all of you curious to learn more about the Free Earth communities, and about what happened to humanity after this revolution, there are many books in the works, including two that are out already.

Here's a sample of the first book in the Skypunk Princess series:

Skypunk Princess

Sneak Peek

Chapter 1

Eliana Skybound, among the first Sky Rangers, lived in the network of floating platforms her people had launched since the collapse of the Globalcorps Hegemony, and now she floated down calm ocean breezes holding a gleaming metallic dandelion.

Her feet stretched out to test gravity as she came to a stop on a floating spit of a raft scoured clean of debris. She flicked a button, retracting all of the strands of her transport back into a two foot long stem that had a viciously sharp edge to its top half.

Her nanoenhanced secondskin deflected the sunlight, making her appear almost like a moving mirage. Attached to the corner of the driftwood was a paddle of sorts, which Eliana promptly began smashing loudly against the nearby wave crests.

After several seconds of splashing, she placed the paddle down and kneeled. From her wrist slid out a narrow chrome and blue tube, which she brought to her lips before drinking from the middle Atlantic. Such nanofilter straws were now commonplace, even among the scattered tribes.

The sea was calm, with ripples of foam drizzled between the slowly rolling waves. As Eliana was almost finished slaking her thirst, she focused in on the human face swimming up at her rapidly from the depths.

The humanoid sliced through the water like an eel, stopping ten feet from the surface to assess the situation. Each of his legs was flattened into a thick oar, kept separated for increased agility, and ended in wide fanned out feet. This was an outdated biohack, crude by current standards, raising her suspicions.

While she watched, a series of massive bubbles began spewing from the sea merchant, floating up to where Eliana crouched.

'*Damn bubble talk,*' she thought, '*even their words are wet.*'

As the bubbles popped, a garbled message emerged. "Friend of Mer?"

Eliana rolled her eyes. If she had wanted to kill the wet noodle of a creature, she could have already. In an exaggerated display of condescending slowness, she wiggled her dandelion stem blade and put it into a thigh sheath.

The Mer was unconvinced, flicking his legs to back down deeper while keeping his eyes locked on the surface.

Eliana reached into her pockets and pulled out a small stack of gold coins, letting one drop into the water and drift down to its target. She tapped a foot impatiently, eager to get on her way, but grinned as the Mer snatched the sunken coin and swam up to meet.

The Mer's close cropped dark hair broke the surface first, lifted with infinite control up from the water by expert and effortless leg kicks.

"Trade?" the Mer got down to business.

She nodded, saving time by showing him a small piece of paper with a few items listed. He grabbed the paper from her hands, to her dismay, reading through the list before his wet hands made a mess of the ink. Most of it was standard resupply, except for the last item, which made the merchant smile.

She wanted to wrap things up already, so she asked his price in sign language. The merman was shocked, but recovered and named a price. Not many Sky People still spoke the Mer's preferred language, which may have inspired him, since the given price seemed fair. The merchant held two fingers up, then disappeared into the darkness.

The clouds stretched out to the horizon, beckoning her home. Trips down to the Soup always made her feel tired.

Hollow clacking of boards perked her ears up, coming from the far end of the platform. It was a new Mer, this one a child, and she had gathered Eliana's list into a small cavity in the gnarled driftwood. The child stared at her, clearly never having seen a Sky Ranger before.

Eliana held up her mesh coin pouch in question, not wishing to scare the child by advancing closer. Suddenly the child sunk down below without warning, leaving the items behind. In the next breath, the original merchant returned, taking the place of the child who was likely his daughter.

These open sea traders were a hardy group, but very isolated, so she dared not let her guard down. The trader appeared to be doing the same, and they did nothing but stare at each other for a minute. Eventually he pushed the requested items forward with a shove: nanofilament refills, vitamin packs, and a bundle of soil grown vegetables.

Eliana held her breath as the merchant produced a weathered box with a latch, no larger than a child's hand. In the time it took the merchant's dripping arm to place it down the deck, the sky ranger had pushed into a front flip and landed beside the box like a whisper.

The mer dove into the waves and disappeared without another word. Eliana pried open the lid slowly, then clamped it back and put it away in her black leather hip satchel.

Her oversized blue eyes danced frequently to her forearm radar display, which drew signals from their nearest Sky Grid outposts. With an expert flick of her wrist, the small purse of gold coins landed in the same small hollowed out knot of driftwood the tiny Mer had used.

A quick refig of her central comp later, she erupted into the humid air like a wasp.

Her cape split into a series of billowing ribbons which sliced up through the air currents, nanoparticles adjusting to the micropressure differences to provide optimal thrust. In under a minute she was over a mile high and her ribbons phase shifted into a locked wing formation. Her suit attached all along the glider extensions, letting her body carve spirals along the massive updrafts. In an hour she was approaching the lower limit of a cumulus cloud bank nearly five miles up.

Eliana missed the land. Not walking on it, but merely the sight of it. She was a rugged creature, weathered but still striking, her features grown in fast forward due to her lifestyle. Now she just saw endless waves, a terrible monotony that went on to the horizon.

She was a respected veteran of countless skirmishes, and confused the Elders greatly with her choice of assignment. The Burning Third, what her people called the tropics, was barren of most surface life, the climate making all Cyber evacuate over time. Because of the harsh landscape, and since the Sky People could thrive anywhere, much of their communication array lay stationed in this barren zone.

Eliana's outpost was stationed nearly at the Equator, and was beneath her stature in every way. In fact, the Sky Council only allowed her request due to her lengthy service and the recent relative peace. There was nothing visible letting Eliana know she had finally reached her goal. Her forearm radar showed an intermittent blip appearing up at thirty thousand feet.

Instead of angling towards the signal however, more material billowed up out of her suit, taking Eliana higher than all the clouds, then higher still. Not until black began mixing with blue on the horizon did she relent, her face stolid against the extreme cold thanks to her nanoskin and bioenhancements. At a certain altitude, all at once, she retracted her suit back together.

Eliana paused, licking her lips as she turned down into a somersault at the edge of space. Up here there were not many signals coming from half the sky, so she could pinpoint the weak signature of Leva's outpost. Now it appeared impossibly low beneath her, but it was there, clear as could be.

Out shot _her_ blade, then her sprouts, gleaming metal filaments which absorbed the sunlight and powered an ion propulsion engine. Down she went, stem cradled beside her chest as she floated down out of the heavens to the woman who had stolen her heart.

Chapter 2

As Eliana approached the last hundred feet, the floating outpost finally took shape in her normal vision. It resembled a boat, with simple wooden rigging cantilevered up from the bottom half of the outpost. These beams had three large turbines lashed between them using leather rope.

The hull of the ship was covered in solar morph paneling, capable of adapting to muffle any incoming signals. It was out of a flap in the paneling near the base of the rigging that Leva's blond bob appeared, then rotated until her angled face shone up with delight at seeing her. Eliana drifted down, using the gentle breeze through her dandelion to guide herself through the wood.

Before she could even land, Leva had leapt up and grabbed hold of both floating ankles. Eliana retracted her "daggerlion" and slid down through the waiting arms.

Unlike Eliana's warrior ancestry, Leva had never fought with anyone, not even as a child. She was technically a Drifter, those Mer who hadn't chosen a fully enhanced form yet. Her skin was sealed at birth, glowing an ever so slight green, but still she walked on slender legs.

Eliana grabbed hold of Leva's waist, lowering her the last few feet into a sheltered living area covered in luminescent sheets. As they sank down into a large net hammock, the warrior's gloved hands slid up along crystalline legs until she reached a baggy silk dress tied with a sash.

The nanobots in Eliana's suit rippled with every touch, forming and reforming to fit into each corner. In response to her command, her fingers webbed for a moment, then separated into thin razors, just as it reached the synthrope sash. To say that Eliana's reflexes were expert somehow understated it, as she stripped off the severed sash in two blinding fast finger flicks.

The crystalline scales covered Leva's entire body, which shined in iridescencent lamplight, and Eliana drank in every second.

"Miss me, fish? she asked the tiny Mer.

Links to the Skypunk Princess, and the rest of my books, are found on my writer's site, www.davidcolello.com[1]